C60024680

KT-403-966

SOUTH LANARKSHIRE LIBRARIES

**This book is to be returned on or before
the last date stamped below or may be
renewed by telephoning the Library.**

A Bewilderment
of Crooks

A Bewilderment of Crooks

John Paxton Sheriff

**HALE
CRIME**

ROBERT HALE · LONDON

© John Paxton Sheriff 2006
First published in Great Britain 2006

ISBN-10: 0-7090-7947-8
ISBN-13: 978-0-7090-7947-7

Robert Hale Limited
Clerkenwell House
Clerkenwell Green
London EC1R 0HT

2 4 6 8 10 9 7 5 3 1

Typeset in 11/13½pt Plantin
Printed in Great Britain by St Edmundsbury Press
Bury St Edmunds, Suffolk.
Bound by Woolnough Bookbinding Ltd.

chapter one

Saturday

In the rugged mountain regions of North Wales there's a choice of so many pubs in spectacular locations it's possible to stick a pin in a map of the Snowdonia National Park, travel anything from five to fifty miles, and always be guaranteed a view of lakes and peaks and limitless skies with your ice-cold lager and salted nuts.

That late September day when DI Alun Morgan of Bethesda telephoned asking me to meet him to talk crime over a drink, I suggested the Pen-y-Gwryd Hotel without hesitation. I was about to hear a grim tale. Murder creates its own atmosphere, and what I needed was ambience that would smother the chill with cloaks of glory.

Ten minutes after his call I was pushing the Audi Quatro that had replaced my written-off Vectra along the narrow track from my house and toy-soldier workshop tucked in the valley beneath the high peaks of the Glyders, crossing the Afon Ogwen and doubling back onto the main road in time to tuck in behind Morgan's ancient Volvo Estate as he roared smokily up the A5. We sped along the rocky banks of Llyn Ogwen, swooped down to cut sharp right through the village of Capel Curig, negotiated the chicane under the tree-shaded stone walls of the Plas y Brenin Mountain Centre where Range Rover Discoveries were hooked to trailers loaded with blue, red and yellow canoes, raced in dazzling sunshine alongside the flat waters of the Llynau Mymbyr and, at the foot of Snowdon, drew into the car-park of the hotel that's seen famous visitors travel just a little bit further than we had to be reunited with friends.

Hillary and Hunt came here often. And the ever-smiling Tensing. Ageing mountaineers from across the world have trekked to the hotel that was the base for a mountaineering team training on the nearby cliffs and crags for the 1953 expedition to Everest, reuniting annually, then less frequently and now rarely – for when the fiftieth anniversary of any event comes and goes the participants in reunions will be fewer, those who do arrive white of hair and ever more frail.

In the hotel's main room the walls display memorabilia, the ceiling the autographs of famous men in an atmosphere haunting with memories that prickle a sensitive man's scalp. When ordering a drink I always felt as if I were jostling for elbow-room at the bar with illustrious phantoms whose climbing-boots I was not fit to polish. I managed it under the amused gaze of the girl at the bar, carried my ice-cold Holsten Pils and Alun's usual half of mild into the log-lined room where he sat waiting near the crackling fire and, when I joined him, we took one refreshing swallow and got down to business.

'You'll have heard of the Liverpool murder,' the lean Welshman said.

'Only what was on Radio Wales. Something about a businessman playing hero, a knife, and a lot of his blood diluted by the pouring rain.'

Morgan nodded, his slate-grey eyes guarded.

'And now the widow's telephoned DI Haggard at Admiral Street, asked for your help. It seems the sheer unexpectedness and ferocity of the attack has left her with a bad case of the jitters.'

'To pass any police work on to me,' I said, 'Haggard must be a desperate man.' I waited for a response, none came, and I said: 'Anything more you can tell me?'

'It was a random killing, no suspects, no leads. That's the gist, and I'd be surprised if it can be expanded.'

'Then the police have another impossible task, the widow nothing to fear. Lightning doesn't strike twice in the same place.'

Morgan downed half his half, and grinned cynically.

'Nevertheless, she's desperate for you. You're Jack Scott, the toy-soldier maker with PI inclinations. Six weeks ago you found Gerry Gault, missing twelve months, and all you did to close the case was act like Quixote and tilt at bloody windmills.'

'Three of us, a week fraught with danger, and most of the time us chasing shadows.'

'That's it, yes, Sian Laidlaw the survival expert, and Calum Wick – and with him having a foot in both camps there's nothing can stop you now.'

'Both camps?'

The detective inspector was fiddling with his beer-mat like a man with problems.

'Wick paints for you, and shares the snooping, but the last I heard he was being had up for shifting stolen cars. Having a man like that on your side,' he said, 'must come in handy.'

'You're thrashing about in the gorse, Alun. It's not me hoping to benefit from Calum's shady dealings, and I'm wondering why they interest you.'

He sighed. 'Maybe I'm waffling, throwing insults hither and yon because I'm a baffled man. There's been a murder in Conwy with remarkable similarities to the one you're about to look into.'

'When?'

'Wednesday. No obvious connection, none likely, in my view. But there's a murder weapon with untraceable fingerprints, blood soaking into the deck of a luxury yacht registered in Gibraltar, an owner hiding behind the name of a fancy business with an offshore account.'

'And those aspects,' I said, 'make your Welsh murder similar to a random killing in Liverpool about which you admit to knowing nothing?'

Alun Morgan was a man who could elude a hook like the

wiliest of brown trout, pass the buck like a politician, or take refuge in his native Welsh when conversation with an Englishman was not going his way.

'Yes, well,' he said, draining his glass, 'I'm leaving those details for Detective Inspector Haggard. My guess is his arm's being twisted. Why else would he use the services of a man who plays with toy soldiers and blows in from the hills only when a scruffy layabout from Scotland needs pocket-money?'

chapter two

The next day a dozen Royal North British Dragoons mounted on their grey horses took me swiftly from North Wales to Liverpool, partly because a few middle-aged men in Gibraltar were rapidly losing patience, but most definitely because Alun Morgan's story had me intrigued.

My going to Liverpool at that time was followed by coincidences I would look back on with wonder, but when I parked the Quatro on the edge of the Mersey in Grassendale and breathed deeply of the salt-laden air before climbing the stairs to a flat that always smelled of paint and coffee, hindsight was a long way down a twisted road of treachery and murder, prescience coyly hiding everything but the work to be done with brushes of fine Kolynsky sable.

I heard Sammy Quade's door creak open behind me as I climbed, caught an odour from Calum Wick's neighbour's room that was not clean nor dirty but merely unidentifiable, reached the top and found Wick's door already open and the lanky Scot stroking his beard as he peered at me through wire spectacles spattered with enamel paint.

I followed him into the big room that boasted a settee and leather easy chairs, Pioneer stereo system, wide-screen television with a Sky box and video over and under, a wall on which the Scot pinned his pictorial history of Liverpool, and a work-table laden with soldiers of tin alloy standing in massed ranks under an Anglepoise lamp so heavily daubed it made Calum's spectacles look like polished Caithness glass.

'These are for those frustrated Gibraltarians hoping to enter them in an exhibition?' Calum said, unpacking the box and bending to inspect the troops.

'Frustrated justifiably,' I said. 'Metal was delayed, I was late casting, now you'll have your work cut out to meet the deadline.'

I'd left the door to Wick's flat ajar. Both of us heard the street door open, slam shut. Door hinges creaked. A voice snapped a command. Quade whined and a door banged. Footsteps, so leaden it seemed that the whole building shook, hit the stairs hard and began climbing.

I looked at Calum, still bent over the table examining my twelve Scots Greys.

'Could it be?'

'With feet like that,' he said, 'could it be anyone else?'

And the question was still hanging in the air like a forlorn cry of protest when a waft of cigarette smoke and Aramis after-shave announced the unexpected presence of DI Mike Haggard and DS Willie Vine.

Haggard was a glowering man in a crumpled dark suit with a king-size cigarette smoking in a big fist. He dropped heavily onto the settee and stared broodily at the bottle of Macallan whisky on the coffee table. Vine joined Calum at the work table and they formed a huddle around the Scots Greys. A tug hooted out on the river. Gulls wailed plaintively. Satan, Calum's black cat, came padding in from the kitchen.

The Admiral Street DI reached down, scratched the moggy's mangled ear and it flopped down and went to sleep with its head on his foot.

'Midnight, pissin' with rain,' Haggard said. 'A middle-aged businessman runs into the street to tackle someone he believes is a burglar, nothin' on but his boxer shorts – the tackler, not the tacklee. He gets a knife in the ribcage, dies in a pool of blood.'

'Woolton Park,' Calum said from the table. 'Couple of days ago, desirable residences in a posh cul-de-sac close to Woolton Hill Road – Dunbar Close.'

'Random killing,' Vine said.

'An impossible task,' Haggard said.

'Hence your visit to the dream team.' I grinned at Calum. 'Can this be happening? Are the police asking for our help?'

'Do constables have flat feet?' he said. 'Does Willie Vine have literary aspirations?'

Haggard looked as if he was drinking raw lemon juice from a broken glass.

'You're bullshittin', Scott. You met Morgan out there where the eagles crap, an' he told you all about your reputation sky-rocketin' because you got lucky with the Gault case.'

'Ergo,' Vine said, 'the widow in the Woolton murder has intimated that the presence of the celebrated private eye at her house would be conducive to a speedy resolution—'

'She wants to see you,' Haggard said. 'I'm against it.'

'And she's not deterred?'

He shrugged. 'She wants you. The dead man was rich, had contacts in high places who pulled strings. So you see her, you listen, you come away and it's like it never happened.' His dark eyes blazed a warning.

'This story reminds me of one of Alun Morgan's,' I said. 'He told me about a murder on a Gibraltar-registered yacht moored in Conwy harbour, said the knife was left behind.'

'No he didn't.' Haggard sneered. 'We've spoken. *After* your talk, hence this visit. And what Morgan told you was "murder weapon".'

'Used in a killing which he suggests has similarities – like lots of blood. So *I'm* suggesting a knife's one of them.'

'Point taken.' He grinned. 'I don't know about Conwy but, yeah, this Liverpool killer left his knife behind,' Haggard said. 'Stuck in the bloke's chest. Fingerprints, but too smeared to be lifted. An' of bugger-all use anyway if he was a yob, a scally, a driftin' layabout with no form.'

'And if he wasn't?'

'Leave it,' Haggard said. 'Leave it now, and when you've talked to her just walk away.' He climbed off the settee like a man weighted with disillusion, dug in his pocket, came out with a slip of paper and handed it to me.

'Name, address. You go there, you listen, you forget – got it?'

'But as time passes,' I said, 'surely she'll ask for the celebrated PI's progress reports.'

'Obfuscate,' Vine said.

'If that means he leaves town,' Haggard said, 'I'm all for it.'

The old house in Dunbar Close which now belonged to the widowed Jemima Laing was set well back behind tall sycamores, oaks and a high hedge. I drove in between high stone pillars from which iron hinge-pins jutted gateless, parked on gravel in bright sunlight alongside a lawn for which the word ragged had been coined and walked across a wide, tree-shaded drive slippery with moss to knock on a door that had been painted red a long time ago.

I waited for a while, letting my gaze drift around borders shaded by more privet hedges and overgrown with shrubs and weeds and wondering how a man watching from anywhere inside this house could have seen a thief running along the road and been fast enough to catch him. Or be caught.

Then the door was opened by a woman in bare feet wearing a colourful caftan like something seen stirring in the warm breeze of a tropical isle. She invited me inside with a smile that was instantly hidden by a convenient sweep of long chestnut hair.

'Straight on, Mr Scott, the room on the right.'

If ragged had been coined for the lawn, filthy rich aptly described the house's interior. The contrast between outside and inside delivered the same sense of shock as that experienced by visitors to the plain terraced house known as 10 Downing Street. It was as if Silvester Laing had deterred burglars by modelling his house on a long-term squat, then filled it with riches beyond my wildest dreams. From the wide, carpeted hall where the heaviest of footsteps would never be heard, I entered a room where timber panelling glowed, marble gleamed, oil-paintings under brass lights announced their value in suitably muted tones and a log fire – on a warm September afternoon – crackled and spat with surprising disrespect.

Smart remarks went unuttered partly because I remembered her recent loss, partly because her style and elegance took my breath away. Instead I smiled, sank almost to my ears in a settee that was too soft for comfort and watched as she poured drinks from a cut-glass decanter. She placed one before me on an occasional table with enough brass and timber for a coffin-lid, and sat down with the grace of a recently retired ballerina.

I drank from the tiny glass, savoured a fiery liqueur like acacia honey laced with poteen. Then, aware of her cool demeanour and chancing my arm, I said, 'I was led to believe you were distraught.'

'And I was assured you were remarkably astute.'

'So let me try again: murder has its compensations?'

She chuckled. 'Millions of them.'

I hesitated. 'But if you're not exactly strapped for cash, and the man who killed your husband really was a petty thief who'd robbed somebody else's house, then why am I here?'

She pursed her lips, crossed slim legs, let me listen to my own question and reach the obvious conclusion. Amusement hadn't reached her ice-blue eyes. They were cool and calculating. A premature death meant a bottomless cash register had stopped jingling and she was left twiddling her thumbs. She was not just miffed, she was vindictive – and again I was asking myself why.

'He died too soon, didn't he,' I said, positing at least part of an answer. 'A year later he'd have been worth double. A chance killing froze your assets.'

'My assets are fine,' she said with a provocative smile. 'But you're right. It's the goose that couldn't stop laying golden eggs that's snuffed it, Jack, and I want you to find out why.'

'We know why he died. He went running out on a rainy night, in his underwear, to tackle someone he thought was a common thief. What we don't know is why he did that.'

She shrugged. 'Anger? Sense of duty? Arrogance – because he was bloody arrogant. Or simply that he couldn't bear to see anyone getting away with something for nothing, something valuable that hadn't been earned?' She spread her hands in a 'you-tell-me' gesture. I couldn't, and I wasn't convinced by her suggestions. Silvester Laing had been rich. I couldn't see righteous indignation pushing him half-naked down that moss-coated drive and out into the road to tackle another man's burglar.

'You say valuable?'

'That's the irony of it,' she said, pulling a face. 'My courageous husband went chasing after a thief who'd stolen a car stereo system. From a Mercedes, yes, but it's not like it was the bloody car.'

'How do you know?'

'What he'd stolen? Because I phoned the next day. Saturday. Mr and Mrs Bone. I know them by sight. Their number's in the book.'

Her accent was Liverpool with a touch of snobbery, the vocabulary devoid of street slang, and the man who'd made that possible had left her marooned. She would have friends, of course, but in the circles where she and her husband had floated on a sea of money there would be bitchiness galore, and Silvester Laing's death would bring lots of gloating.

'What was Silvester doing when he saw the thief?'

She thought for a moment, smiled cruelly. 'He'd taken off his shirt and dropped his trousers, flexed in front of the full-length mirror, tuned in to Jazz FM on his radio alarm, answered his mobile, gone to the window to look out at the rain. Still looking out, he leaned forward and said something like, "Fuckin' hell, I don't believe it". Then he ran out of the room. And I never spoke to him again. When I reached him

there was blood on his chest and his hands and he was dead.'
She smiled sweetly, but her eyes were moist.

'And the Bones's house is where?'

'Across the road, you turn left and it's a short way up the
hill.'

'So the thief was making a fast getaway, Silvester ran
downstairs – the front door was locked, alarms on ...'

'He was strolling,' Jemima said.

'Silvester?'

'The thief. Fiddling with the stereo, making it easier to
carry by winding the speaker wires around the main unit as
he crossed the road.'

'You're very observant.'

She shrugged. 'That's with hindsight. It's not something I
told the police. All I had in my mind when I spoke to them
was this vague figure. But I told you I phoned the Bones,
asked what was missing. Now when I replay the scene in my
mind, the movements I saw make sense.' She bit her lip. 'And
this bloke was actually coming this way, was certain to pass
the house.' She saw my sceptical look and shrugged. 'There
was no panic, so obviously he hadn't set off any alarms.
There were no lights inside the house he'd broken into—'

'Garage.'

'Yes, well, perhaps that's why. The Bones's house would
have an alarm system, but it's not likely they'd have wired up
the garage.'

'Come on, they had a Mercedes.'

'That really was news to me. It must have been a new
acquisition. From what I'd seen in passing, the double garage
housed a tiny Clio.'

'But surely there would be security lights?'

'There are. I've seen them.' She frowned, obviously
reliving the tragic moments. 'But I don't think they came
on.' She thought again, then said: 'No, I'm positive, they
didn't, because I remember actually looking for activity and
a blaze of lights.'

Now it was my turn to frown. I sipped my sweetened

poteen, fiddled thoughtfully with the glass and said, 'It was a wet night, there were no alarms ringing, no lights blazing, no police sirens wailing. So why would you – or anyone else – see a man walking without haste down the road and jump to the conclusion that a house had been broken into?'

'Silvester has – had – built-in antennae,' she said, and lifted one offended eyebrow as I grinned.

'What, like a little green Martian?'

She'd read my write-up in the *Echo*, and knew how to score points.

'If you live in a cave in the Welsh mountains, you worry about bat-shit and dead sheep.' Her crossed leg was jiggling. 'Here we are beset by crime.'

'Beset?'

'Silvester was a constant worrier. His antennae detected villains. He sensed something was wrong.'

'All right, and the thief made it easy for him,' I said. 'While Silvester was struggling to break out of your house, the thief was strolling towards him without a care in the world.'

'And they collided,' Jemima said. 'When the thief crossed the road he was hidden by the hedge. Silvester went tearing out of the drive just as he reached the opening.'

'Did you see what happened next?'

The drink trembled in her fingers. She nodded, her mouth set. 'They came together, wrestling I suppose. The stereo fell to the ground and I saw the glitter of steel … and then Silvester was flat on his back on the wet ground and the man had recovered his loot and fled.'

'What was he like?'

Her laugh was scornful, her composure regained. 'He was a young man in jeans and some sort of waterproof jacket with one of those woolly hats pulled down over his ears. He was thirty yards away, nowhere near a streetlight, it was pissing down and I was having hysterics.'

'Young?'

'He moved well.'

In the sudden silence I nodded, stood up, walked

pensively across thick white carpet to the big windows and listened to glasses clink behind me, a door open and close with a sound like a wistful sigh. I could see the drive, the tatty lawn, the overgrown borders, the tall hedge blocking my view of the road, my car hugging gravel with its windscreen reflecting dazzling sunlight into my eyes. I could see little of importance, and understood less. In response to a widow's summons Haggard had sent me out with orders to listen, then forget, but from a woman economical with words I had heard nothing worth retaining. Jemima Laing wanted me to investigate her husband's death, and I still didn't know why.

I sensed warmth close to me, smelt musk perfume and knew that the door had opened again, this time without a breath of sound, her bare feet crossing the carpet towards me with the stealth of a homecoming philanderer.

'If you're worried ...' she said softly.

I shook my head, turned to face the woman who was standing close to me and almost as tall, her eyes amused but telling me nothing.

'I make toy soldiers for a living and do investigations for fun. But expenses mount up, and this kind of fun can be costly as well as dangerous....' I waited until she ducked her head in acceptance of those vague terms, then said, 'What was the name of this person who was robbed?'

'Sam Bone.'

'And the house?'

She placed a hand on my shoulder to guide me and half-turned away to point elegantly. Across the road and up the hill from her own unkempt wilderness I saw mock-Tudor gables, leaded windows, the tips of those exotic conifers that can be green or blue depending on the light but are always ornamental.

'What did your husband do for a living?'

'He played with money.'

'Meaning?'

'If you look into his death I'm sure you'll find out.'

'I might find out too much. Doesn't that worry you?'

'It would if I had something to hide.'

'Or a lot to lose.'

Did that final barb strike home? At the time I was short of
information and unable to judge, but to say that I was deeply
suspicious would have been an understatement. As I was
shown out of the house by Jemima Laing I was convinced
that the garden path she was leading me up was not only
twisted, it would prove to be even more slippery than the one
I crossed on the way to my car.

I slid into the stifling car, left the door open and pulled down
both visors to cut off the dazzling sunlight then called Calum
Wick on the mobile.

'Where are you?'

'Lurking.'

'For want of something better to do?'

'For want of a nail …'

'So you're smelling a rat?'

'All is not what it seems. You knocked off for lunch?'

'Aye, the Scots Greys are primed and ready for their
uniforms so I'm off up to George Kingman's place. I'll probably see Willie Vine there.'

'Now that's interesting,' I said. 'Ask him if they've got
anywhere with this murder case. Haggard said a random
killing; could be true but it doesn't gel with Jemima Laing's
determination to dig deeper. I'm off to see a feller called Sam
Bone. It was his house that was burgled.'

'Then he'll know nothing.'

'Yeah, but you're forgetting our motto.'

'No stone unturned.'

'Right. So talk to Willie. And I'll see you when?'

'If we've got a case on our hands I might as well go on to
the American Bar. Manny Yates usually has a liquid lunch
there. I can see if he's heard anything, meet you there when
you're done.'

'Right, but don't hurry, I could be a while.'

He rang off and I reversed in a tight arc and pulled out

onto the road to drive a hundred yards up the hill and cut sharp right across the cul-de-sac into the curved drive of the house that had recently lost a car stereo. I drove up close to the up-and-over doors of the big double garage, switched off and climbed out onto gravel that was as thick as Jemima Laing's carpets but a lot more noisy.

And at once noticed the powerful security lights with one-hundred-and-eighty-degree sensors mounted on the garage wall.

The loud crunch of the car's tyres and my feet brought results. A curtain in the big bay window twitched, and as I walked up steps flanked by stone pots of bright red and pink geraniums and overhung by an enormous basket of petunias and more geraniums of the trailing kind the heavy glazed door clicked open and a young woman in jeans and a loose white shirt knotted at the waist looked at me with speculation.

'What's goin' on, I didn't call the police.'

Mistaken identity. I put on an officious look. 'You reported a theft.'

She shook her head. 'No. Nothing's been stolen.' And again that look. 'So if you're not police, what d'you want?'

'Is Sam in?'

She cocked her head. 'Sam who?'

'Bone.'

This time her look would have split granite. 'You're lookin' at him.'

I grinned to cover my surprise. 'Pleased to meet you, sir.'

'Christ, listen to you.' A smile twitched. 'What *do* you want?'

'I represent JC Car Audio Systems—'

'No you don't.'

'I might.'

She shook her head. 'You're a private dick. Your picture was in the *Echo*.'

'Damn.'

'You been to that dead feller's house?'

'Yes. And now I'm here because this is where it started – isn't it?'

'Well, yeah, that yob broke in, stole Jason's stereo. Jason's, not mine. But like I said, it wasn't reported. All the police know from her down the road is there was a random killing.'

'Jason's your husband?'

'My absent husband. She's not the only one—' she jerked her head towards the Laing house '— who's got a man missin'.'

'She's the only one,' I said, 'whose husband was stabbed by the man who broke into your garage.'

'How do you know?'

She watched me struggle to find an answer to that one, then relented and invited me in. Her offer of coffee was accepted, and while she was in the kitchen rattling jars and cups and spoons I stood in the front room and soaked up the atmosphere of a house that was like a mirror image of Silvester Laing's.

Laing hid his wealth behind a façade of poverty. The Bones presented an exterior that screamed of the tastefully well-heeled while – apparently – struggling to pay the bills. The curtains were expensive because the windows were part of the show. But the shafts of sunlight slanting through elegant nets lit flat-pack mahogany furniture, carpets that were end-of-roll off-cuts in 100% nylon, home-made shelves holding paperback books from Oxfam or Barnardos and emulsioned walls hung with large framed prints: a photograph of what looked like a Mediterranean scene, others by famous artists depicting action from famous battles – which struck an immediate chord – but most of them faded by age to a pallid blue.

She came through from the kitchen with two steaming mugs and caught me staring. She was small and pert, I guessed about twenty-eight, and intelligence shone from dark eyes that for some reason were distant with thought as she handed me my coffee.

'I know what you're wonderin',' she said. 'You can't understand what a couple of paupers're doin' with a brand-new Merc. Because she told you it was new, didn't she? An' it was her phoned me the day after the murder, which is how you know about the stereo.' She grinned without humour. 'A proper little know-all.'

She swung away to sit down on the settee covered with a throw as old and coarse as the Turin shroud. When she faced me again it was clear that those eyes were missing nothing.

'What I'm wondering,' I said, 'is what exactly happened on that night.'

'Me,' she said, 'I'm wonderin' what the hell you're doin' here.'

'Looking for a burglar who turned into a killer.'

'I can't help you. He was a kid, a yob. He's probably been watchin' all these houses. If he has he'd know there's no man livin' here, an' he'll've seen the Merc delivered a couple of days ago. So it was take a chance, in and out sharpish.'

'When?'

'Friday.'

'And the Merc came when?'

'Thursday.'

'Your husband was here that recently?'

'No.'

'Then the Merc's yours?'

She glared. 'I told you, no, it's not. I haven't got a clue whose it is. Or where he is. I suppose he ordered it before he left.'

I eased into a chair on the other side of the mock-Indian coffee table, sipped coffee, thought about the missing husband who bought cheap furniture but an expensive car, decided it was none of my business, then found myself unable to leave it alone.

'But that doesn't sound like a man planning on walking out on you – if that's what he did.'

'Jason didn't plan. He was impulsive.'

'He gave you no warning?'

She shook her head irritably. 'Some – but I thought you were looking for a killer, not my husband.'

'All right.' I took the hint. 'So your garage was broken into on Friday, the thief walked across the road, Silvester Laing tackled him and was stabbed to death.'

And suddenly she was angry, her eyes furious and her lips tight as she gripped the coffee-mug.

'Why the hell did he do it? What in God's name possessed the bloody man. I just don't understand it, I really don't—'

'Some people are like that,' I said, and she looked at me sharply. 'They see something wrong, they have to put it right. It's the way they're made.'

She took a deep breath, let it out slowly. 'An' it's the way they die, isn't it.'

'Sometimes.'

There was a silence. She finished her coffee, put the mug on the table, sat back. Her eyes were restless, moving around the room, frequently glancing towards the window. Suddenly I saw her as a frightened young woman. She was alone. Her privacy had been invaded. A man had died.

'Were you here when the scally broke into the garage?'

'I was in bed.'

'Did you hear him?'

'Yeah. Breakin' glass. He went in through the side window. An' I got out of bed, looked out …'

'But it was too dark to see, wasn't it.' Again she looked at me sharply, and I raised placating hands. 'I was told the security lights didn't come on.'

'Miss Know-all again.' She allowed herself a rueful smile. 'Big moths were settin' them off every fifteen minutes on Friday night. I switched them off.'

'Then Saturday it rained, you forgot about them and figured you'd be safe enough for one night.'

'And I was, wasn't I?'

'You were, but you lost an expensive stereo.'

'No, he did. Jason. Probably. And he's not here, is he, so who cares?'

On the way out I gave her a card bearing my name, business motto and home and mobile phone numbers, not expecting to hear from her but because it's something I do. Then I drove down town, parked in the Mount Pleasant multi-storey and walked down the hill to the American Bar on Lime Street.

Calum Wick was at a table on the long wall with Manny Yates. I lifted a hand, waved Calum back into his seat and went to the bar.

Yates was a short fat licensed investigator who wore waist-coats without a jacket and smoked slim Schimmelpennick cigars. I suppose that was where Calum got the habit. Many years ago Yates had given me a job when the imported car scam I worked with Calum after a long spell in the army drove me ever more frequently to the bottle. From Manny I learned how to poke my nose into other people's business, got restless again, discovered a talent for toy-soldier making, found an empty farmhouse called Bryn Aur in a valley beneath the high peaks of the Glyders in Snowdonia, estab-lished a reputation for modelling excellence then moved back into investigating part-time because it was something I knew, something I missed. By then Calum had also moved on. We both knew he was still involved in the shady side of life – as did Haggard and Vine, to their eternal frustration – but he now painted toy soldiers for me and was an invaluable partner in my war against crime.

Is that what it was? Sian, the survival expert, would giggle at my pretentiousness.

I carried my Holsten Pils over to the table, sat down, winked at Manny.

'Word is Calum drinks in here because there's enough lead on the roof to block that Global Positioning Satellite.'

'I wish,' Manny said. 'He drinks 'ere because you pay sweat-shop wages an' he knows I take my wallet for a walk every fuckin' day at this time.'

'I will have you know that I am not bloody tagged,' Calum said, and adopted a superior pose. 'All charges were dropped for lack of evidence, and because the polis realized a man with integrity' – he grinned – 'wouldn't be seen dead ferrying stolen cars across the border into Wales.'

'What I 'eard,'Yates said, 'is that 'im and Jones theVan got off that charge 'cause all the documentation was in Welsh and no one 'ere could understand a fuckin' word.'

He collapsed into a shaking mess of smoke, cigar ash and oily flesh. Over the wet sound of Yates's laughter and the rumble of the traffic on Lime Street I eyed Calum and said, 'Anything fromWillie?'

He watched Yates suck in a wheezy breath, wipe his brow with a filthy handkerchief and waddle to the bar.

'Nothing additional. They're looking at a random killing, by a scally off his head on crack who probably stole to finance his next hit. No info on where he'd been, what he was doing.'

Fresh from my conversation with Jemima Laing, I digested that interesting bit of news and said, 'Then why warn me off?'

'Sheer habit, perhaps – and maybe the company you keep?'

'And the premises we both frequent,' I said, remembering that he had met Willie Vine in George Kingman's club off Lark Lane. I sipped ice-cold beer, ran a finger down the condensation. 'Talking of which, I have today visited a rich house masquerading as poor, and a poor house doing its damnedest to appear rich.'

Manny was back with his podgy fingers wrapped around two glasses of Scotch and a bottle of Holsten. He sat down puffing and said, 'He always figured he was foolin' the human scavengers, Silvester Laing. Actually, 'e was foolin' no one.'

'He fooled the sneak thief; he went elsewhere.'

'If that's what he was.'

'You think not?'

'I'm puttin' it to you. It's you's been talkin' to the Queen of Sheba—'

'And Little Orphan Annie across the road.'

'Who's that, the bird who was robbed?'

'Sam Bone.'

'Right, and you bein' trained by me, you should now have it all sussed.'

'I believe,' Calum said, 'that Jack fears there is dirty work afoot.'

'Justifiably,' I said. 'First, there's a rich woman who wants me to find the random killer who stabbed her husband.' I looked from Wick to Yates. 'Why would she do that?'

'Because her husband,' Yates said, 'started as a loan-shark and worked his way down to where he could make real money. He's bound to have been holdin' out on 'er.'

'Well,' I said, busy thinking, 'Jemima did say he played with cash....'

'What he did was partner a devious bastard who washes other people's dirty money.'

'Partner as in personal life, or business?'

'As in take fifty per cent of massive fuckin' profits. Ed Carney's the feller he teamed up with, a flash bastard who pulls rich plums out of more pies in dirty corners than little Jack Horner even dreamed of.'

'Mmm.' I poured the second Holsten and said, Confucius-style: 'Murky business makes random killing appear less likely.' Calum rolled his eyes. 'And if I'm going to start digging, where do I take my spade?'

'Link Associates,' Yates said. 'On a dark night when you're really depressed and feel like endin' it all.'

'All right, put that to one side and answer me this one: how would a man who can't afford furniture find enough cash for a new Mercedes?'

'Without asking who this enigmatic chappie is, I suggest you think John Lennon airport,' Calum said.

I watched Manny look across at him and nod approvingly, and said, 'You're referring to the practice of stealing cars when the owners're looking the other way.'

'Right. And this car was undoubtedly stolen to order,' Calum said. 'If we're talking new Merc, then your man was either hiding his true income from wee Orphan Annie, or he went down that road and bought a hot car.'

'Which suggests he isn't squeaky clean. Not many people would know how to take the first step.'

'Yeah, right,' Yates said, 'but there's been no one complainin' about a stolen Merc, so doesn't that also tell us about the owner?'

'Something to hide, so he writes off the stolen car, puts it down to experience.' I looked at him questioningly, saw something in his moist, hooded eyes, and said: 'You *do* know something.'

Manny grinned. 'There was a carjackin', a couple of weeks ago. Black Merc stopped at the kerb, a bloke opened the door, tossed the driver on his arse in the road and buggered off with the car.'

Outside a horn blasted, tyres squealed and someone yelled abuse in a hoarse smoker's voice.

'Quite a way from here, actually,' Yates said, 'but there were witnesses – and 'ere's the man who saw everything.'

chapter three

The first time I'd seen Jones the Van he'd had a cigarette dangling from his lips as he was picked up and bounced on the bonnet of his own rusty white vehicle. We were in the middle of the Gerry Gault case, Calum had been doing the muscular bouncing.

Now, as the squeal of tyres faded to be replaced by the muted rumble of traffic, Stan trotted jauntily in from Lime Street like a bookie's runner. One hand was rubbing the tatty white whiskers he called designer stubble. Sharp blue eyes were doing their best to identify everybody in the place in one sweeping glance. He was on course for the bar when he saw us, exchanged glances with Manny Yates, and changed tack to bear down on the table.

'I'm leavin', Stan,' Manny Yates said. 'Sit down an' tell Jack about that Merc.'

The fat PI threw a crumpled twenty-pound note on the table and was gone in a haze of stale sweat. Stan Jones scooped up the cash, veered away without breaking stride and made for the bar.

Calum had been watching the activity like a casual observer losing touch with reality. Now he shook his head.

'I know we're pretty shrewd guys, but the fact is on a wet night a man was stabbed by a passing scally. So why the hell are you wasting time on this Merc?'

'You said it yourself: I smell a rat.'

'Explain.'

'A man murdered in what looks like a random killing

turns out to be a loan-shark gone bad. The private houses involved are both presenting a false face to the world. You have two women, one's husband's just walked out on her, the other's dies. There's a minor theft and, hey, it's from a stolen Merc that's not been reported.'

'Let me guess: the stereo system?'

'Right.'

'From a woman called Sam Bone, who now – if you're right – suddenly finds herself in possession of a stolen car.'

'Her husband's stolen car.'

'A sublime example of Scott's wild flights of conjecture.'

'PI instinct. Never fails.'

'Is that what it's called? So what colour's the car from which this stereo was randomly plucked?'

'Black.'

'You've seen it, then?'

'No.'

'Hah!'

'Hah your fuckin' self,' Stan Jones said, sitting down with a pint of Guinness. 'What's goin' on?'

'You're about to tell us about this carjacking.' I watched him drop his roll-up in the ashtray, take a deep swallow of dark stout while his devious mind skipped around looking for pitfalls.

'I was comin' out of Peel Street, turnin' down Park Road towards the Dingle. Traffic was held up, this black Merc was in the line. Then a bloke jumped out of the car behind it, ran around an' opened the Merc's door an' dragged the driver into the road. While this was goin' on a second bloke was gunnin' the engine of the car behind. Then the first bloke gorrin the Merc, wheeled out of the traffic an' both cars pissed off down the middle of the road.'

'Two blokes,' I said, and looked at Calum. 'Manny said one.'

'Manny was in 'ere,' Jones said. 'I was there, watchin' it all happen.'

'So who were they?'

His eyes narrowed. 'What,' he said, 'you mean those two big bastards?' He shook his head. 'Never seen 'em before.'

'But you could find them,' I said. 'Find out where the car was taken, what happened to it.'

He glared. 'Why me?'

'Inside knowledge.'

'Go 'way, will yer!'

He half-turned in his chair, showed me a back as bony as a greyhound's while drinking his Guinness and staring moodily through at the black-and-white photographs of boxers from the fifties and sixties hung in the back room.

'Intervening on behalf of my colleague,' Calum said, 'but with loads more tact, we'd appreciate it if you'd nose around for a wee while, sniff the air, test the wind.'

'I'll tell you who is sniffin' around like he's smellin' a load of truffles,' Jones said, and he twisted towards the table, dragged out his tobacco and began rolling a cigarette.

'Haggard?'

Jones nodded. 'Him and Vine're tryin' to pin this one on you an' me—'

'Ah, now hold on a minute,' Calum said. 'If you've been coming clean there must be a dozen people who saw what went on at the Dingle.'

'Yeah,' Jones said, licking the paper and sealing his misshapen cigarette. 'But I don't work alone, do I.'

He struck a match, lit up, blew smoke and flashed a fiendish yellow-toothed grin at Calum. 'The way they see it, maybe I was out there, you know, like, directin' the traffic and divertin' attention, and the feller who jumped in the car could've been anyone – couldn' it.'

'Meaning me?'

Jones shrugged.

'For Christ's sake,' Calum said, 'that's bloody ridiculous.'

'All I know,' Jones said, spitting a shred of tobacco, 'is them two're actively followin' their dicks, and Christ only knows where they're pointin'.'

He stood up, drained the Guinness in half a dozen gulps

that set his Adam's apple bobbing and was gone into Lime Street like a whippet with a mission.

'He'll do some digging,' Calum said. 'Don't let his scally image fool you.' He toyed with his drink for a moment, then looked up with some amusement and said, 'Isn't it remarkable the way all of a sudden you and I are again involved with expensive German cars?'

'Mmm. Yet I'm not even sure the Merc I'm involved with is stolen.'

'Or even,' Calum said, 'if it has anything to with the crime you're investigating – assuming you know which one that is.'

'Good point,' I said. 'Haggard sends me to look into a murder I'm supposed to forget, and I end up making up stories about a car I haven't even seen.'

'So which is it you're looking into?'

'There are two crimes, both committed by the same scally. And as there's nothing at the scene of the second crime—'

'Murder?'

'Right, then I'm forced to cross the road and investigate the first crime—'

'Theft. And do what? Sit in the corner of the garage and hope that wee laddie who stole the radio comes back for the car?'

'You're joking?'

'I'm joking.'

'But your joke is better than my plan?'

'No,' Calum said. 'Your plan is an excellent joke. It can't be bettered.'

Like two pavement chess players appreciating a zugzwang we clinked empty glasses across the table, but as always beneath our banter there was more than a grain of truth. Unlike that chess position, the move I was about to make might not be to my disadvantage, but as Calum and I left the American bar to go our separate ways it was difficult to see how working from Sam Bone's end could lead me to a killer. After all, hadn't I told Alun Morgan that lightning doesn't strike twice in the same place?

A BEWILDERMENT OF CROOKS

I was still firmly of that belief as I collected my car and headed towards Aigburth.

As it happened, I was proved right – but it was a near miss.

The first Liverpool policeman I'd spoken to six months ago when I was looking into the disappearance of Gerry Gault had been a woman: Meg Morgan, a valuable contact and friend, sister of dour Welshman Alun Morgan and a delightful character who'd been promoted to DS, moved out of the city centre to Admiral Street nick and got personally involved with Joe Leary.

Joe was a detective inspector who'd seen his fiancée killed by a stage knife-thrower and worked his way down a rank by poking his nose in when he'd been told to keep it out – rather like I was doing. Fine, me being freelance made it acceptable (in my eyes), but when last I'd spoken to Joe he'd been treading the thin line that divides the bolshie but tolerated from those openly insubordinate and back walking the beat.

I thought of Meg when I was driving up Booker Avenue. My last meal had been breakfast in North Wales, fried eggs on grilled pork chops washed down with my usual brandy-laced coffee. I tell Sian the Rémy Martin and caffeine cancel each other out. She's not convinced. Anyway, that was more than nine hours ago, and now I was being drawn to my mother's cosy flat overlooking Calderstones Park by a subliminal food fantasy so strong I was dizzy.

But I slowed as I reached the corner because Stan Jones had interested me. If Haggard was threatening him with the Mercedes carjacking, it suggested the wily DI had nothing to go on and with all his detectives tied up on more pressing matters he was letting Stan off the leash. Using him, again rather like I was doing. If Haggard *did* have something to go on, then Joe Leary probably knew about it, he'd have discussed it with Meg – if she wasn't already involved – and with luck I'd catch her on her own.

And then I suddenly remembered something that had slipped my mind but meant that a meal at my mother's was not an option: Eleanor – as she insisted everyone call her – was not at home. Three weeks ago she had answered the call of Reg, a retired British diplomat, and gone to stay with him in his luxurious house situated near the governor's residence on Europa Road, Gibraltar.

My plans changed, I drove on, but not too far.

Meg had the ground-floor flat in a house set back off Yew Tree Road, just a hundred yards from my mother's place. I slowed, blinked right, crossed the narrow road and drove through the open gate under drooping laburnums that trailed bright yellow blossom across the windscreen only to find found further progress blocked by a dusty Mitsubishi Shogun parked in front of the black wooden doors of the garage.

Meg had company. And suddenly the case of the murdered moneylender was suffused with warmth and colour, my snide remarks to Jemima Laing were consigned to history and it was as if I stepped out of the Quatro a changed man and floated towards the front door to the accompaniment of a thousand soaring violins.

Or, to put it more simply, Sian was home, and I was quite pleased.

I had first met Sian Laidlaw, my Soldier Blue, in Norway – she taking a break from military duty, me on holiday and stepping gingerly onto skis for the first time since my own stint in uniform – and from then on it was a sometimes turbulent but always fascinating relationship with a woman who had talent, courage and ambition and, incomprehensibly, a goodly measure of fondness for a bumbling amateur private eye.

This was a woman who had seen her Scottish seafaring father lost overboard in an Arctic gale when she'd been ten years old and illegally aboard his ship, had returned to nurse her dying mother in the Cardiff slums and, years later, with a university degree under her Shotokan karate black belt, move north to become something of a legend among the high peaks of the Cairngorms.

She was worldly wise and caring with it and used to dealing with fractious executives on the survival courses where she sometimes assisted, often led. But that was a little way in the past. A radio phone-in after a Cape Wrath episode in which she had saved a man's life had brought the prospect of a short series for Granada Television which we'd both welcomed, because it meant we would spend time together in my Welsh retreat. But studio work was still in progress, those mouth-watering benefits were as yet unrealized. Until now. Could this be the start?

Meg answered my knock, fluttered her eyelids, left the door open and melted away.

Sian was in the front room.

She'd been away from me for seven days and I'd known her more years than I could count using the fingers of one hand yet I walked towards her feeling as if my joints were stiff leather hinges, my limbs operated by a puppeteer determined to make me look like Quixote's lame donkey. I looked into flashing blue eyes that danced with suppressed glee, saw thick blonde hair snatched back and gathered into the usual rough ponytail by a plain elastic band, saw firm breasts thrusting against a faded denim shirt and businesslike jeans stretched over hips that were ripe enough to cause the usual ache in my throat.

She searched my face hungrily, the sparkling delight turning to amusement that softened as her eyes darkened and welled with an emotion she revealed only rarely and, I liked to believe, only to me.

'I missed you, Soldier Blue.'

'A week,' she said. 'That's all.'

'Imagine if it had been a month.'

'Well, we're not exactly falling into each other's arms.'

I shrugged, smiled crookedly. 'We're not in Wales, this is not Bryn Aur, we are not alone.'

She nodded understanding. 'I phoned there to let you know I was coming.'

'My answering machine gets all the luck.'

'And now you're here,' she said, 'and you thought I was in Manchester so you're visiting Meg, not me, and if you're not chatting her up then it has to be crime.'

'Still as sharp as ever.'

'And with studio work finished, relaxed and at a loose end.'

'Mike Haggard, on the other hand,' Meg said, coming in from the kitchen, 'is as short tempered as a clog-dancer with gout.'

'Because?'

She grimaced at Sian. 'He was outranked, forced to let him-from-the-hills in on a murder, did so with reluctance and a warning to listen to a certain Jemima Laing's story then walk away – and he knows there's no bloody chance.'

'Things,' I said, 'have a way of ramifying.'

'Bloody hell,' Meg said, 'you need a drink.'

What we got in the large dining-kitchen during the course of the next hour was the grub I'd been fantasizing about: home-made beefburgers garnished with fried Spanish onions and English mustard and served with a side salad, cherry tomatoes, white baps and a red wine called Château Condom that was the last of the six bottles Sian had brought back with her from a trip to France.

And we were flushed, sated and sublimely happy when we returned to the lounge and sat down with the evening sunlight slanting through the trees and glinting on the facets of lead-crystal wine-glasses we held with all the limp-wristed, nonchalant insouciance of those mellow enough to care little for possible ugly red stains on expensive Axminster carpets. Which, if I knew Meg's landlord, these were not.

'That reminds me,' I said, 'are you and Joe now cohab-iting?'

'Me and Joe,' Meg said as Sian tutted, 'are together but apart – if you see what I mean.'

'He's digging,' Sian said. 'He wants to be sure Joe's not going to walk in while he's grilling you.'

'Joe still might,' Meg said, looking smug.

I chuckled. 'Fine by me. Then you can both tell me what you know about a Mercedes carjacked near the Dingle.'

'I thought you were looking into the Silvester Laing murder – and that not too deeply, because Mike's warned you off.' Meg was innocently wide-eyed.

'Laing?' Sian said. The name had registered, and she was frowning. 'Hang on a minute, I'm sure I know something interesting about him.'

'Good,' I said, feeling the first faint stirrings of excitement as I sensed the case warming up. 'You can tell me later – but no, it's definitely the Merc I'm interested in.'

'What you'll get from me is mostly negative,' Meg said. 'Stan Jones is the only witness to come forward. He can't remember the Merc's licence number. Didn't recognize the thieves. Nobody reported the car missing. The driver – who, according to Stan, was dragged out fiercely enough to crack his head on the road – hasn't been seen since.'

'Ah yes,' I said. 'The driver. I asked Stan to name names. He reacted nervously.' I looked at Sian, leaning back in an easy chair, the sunlight touching the wine in her glass and reflecting redly on the soft underside of her chin. 'You know, I think he might have recognized all three people involved.'

She pursed her lips thoughtfully. 'Is that helpful?'

'Well, the man driving the Merc was either the owner, or he knows the owner. And the owner's lying low. Manny Yates reckons that means he's bent. As in crooked.'

Sian shook her head. 'Again, so what? The car's gone. The owner's bent. Big deal.'

'All right,' I said. 'So why is Haggard putting pressure on Jones the Van?'

'All theft is police business,' Meg said. 'We're short of bodies, and Stan's like a bloody ferret. More to the point, why the hell are you so interested?' She tried to read my blank look, grimaced and said, 'This morning Haggard tells you about the Laing killing. I know for a fact the dead man drove a BMW. You spend half an hour talking to Jemima, and suddenly you're making all kinds of connections and looking into the Park Road carjacking of a Mercedes.'

I hesitated. 'If pressed, which I'm not, I could probably come up with the name of someone who might recently have become the owner, if I'm right – though I might not be.'

Suddenly Meg was confused, but interested. 'Go on. Pretend I'm pressing.'

'Er … no, better not.'

'Damn it!' She plonked her glass on the table, looked around for the bottle, didn't see it, stood up and started for the kitchen and said over her shoulder, 'Why the hell not? Didn't I press hard enough?'

'Client confidentiality,' I said.

She came back in, stood glowering, holding the bottle by its neck.

'If you've got a client – and you shouldn't have – it's Jemima Laing. But her husband was too rich to be bothered with carjacking, and anyway he's dead. So who's this confidentiality crap relate to?'

She leaned towards me. Wine splashed aggressively into my glass. She was bent over, her eyes close to mine and blazing with curiosity.

'Sorry,' I said, 'I can't say.'

She swung away, topped up Sian's drink, sat down, stared moodily out of the window. But Meg was never one to brood for long. After a few minutes she sighed, looked at me with a baffled shake of the head, and went over to switch on the television. She and Sian sat sipping wine and watching a soap in companionable silence. I drifted off into something that began as deep thinking but fizzled off into shallow dozing. In time the daylight on the other side of my eyelids faded, dusk turned into night, then a table-lamp clicked on and a shadow came between me and the warm yellow light as someone drifted across the room and into the kitchen. I heard running water, the rattle of cups and, after a while, the burble of a percolator and the rich smell of coffee.

Cushions sank voluptuously as Sian sat by me on the

settee, put her head on my shoulder. Blonde hair tickled my cheek, I opened my eyes, smiled, yawned – and my mobile phone beeped.

No caller ID.

When I switched to receive, it was Sam Bone.

'I'd like you to come now,' she said. 'My house has been broken into, and whoever did it was lookin' for something special.'

chapter four

Pleasurably tired from a long day in the studio and the drive
back from Manchester, Sian was content to stay and enjoy
the freshly percolated coffee I hadn't got time for, then go to
bed early in Meg's spare room.

I left her to it, but before I pulled out of the drive and
pointed the Quatro towards Woolton I phoned Calum, told
him what had happened and arranged to meet him outside
Sam Bone's house. He had never owned a car. If Jones the
Van wasn't available to give him a lift, he said, he'd be forced
to take a taxi. It had started to rain, and it was that time of
night when Liverpool taxis are in demand.

Calum beat me to it. Huddled under the sycamore that
drooped darkly above the ornamental grey conifers I had
first seen from Jemima Laing's window, he was a tall stooped
figure with his hands stuffed in his pockets and in the open
collar of his faded denim shirt a pepper-and-salt beard
sparkled like rain-beaded cobwebs.

I pulled into the empty drive, climbed out as he jogged
after me and drew level with the car, and nodded to the security lights over the garage.

'Switched off.'

'Or broken.'

'That's not what she told me.'

Then a light did click on, this one inside the hall, and
seconds later the door was pulled open by a kimono-clad
Sam Bone, a vision in lemon-yellow with lustrous dark hair

pinned high in a careless manner and her eyes flashing
angrily as she gnawed her lip.

'Oops,' Calum said softly, and I pushed by him using a
hard elbow and ran up the steps.

'Posse's here,' I said, wiping my feet.

'The bandits're long gone.'

She left me at the door, swept into the front room and I
heard the low murmur of a masculine voice.

Calum and I exchanged glances. I shrugged, spread my
hands, then led the way inside.

A tall man in his thirties wearing a black leather jacket
zipped over a white T-shirt was moving out of the deep bay
window, treading carefully. He was lean and hard, dark-
haired, with eyes that glittered in a long clown's face that
could be lugubrious or jolly but never, ever without expres-
sion. Right now it was showing deep concern, and as he
reached Sam Bone he grasped her hand and I saw their
fingers interlock, her knuckles white.

'This is Tommy,' she said. 'Tommy Mack, my brother.'

'I came as soon as she phoned,' he said. 'Told her to get
changed, act normal, pretend nothing'd happened.' He
looked around the room, shook his head, gestured helplessly.

I grimaced in sympathy. Furniture had been tossed
around like empty orange boxes, settee and chairs
upended, upholstery slashed, drawers dragged out of side-
boards and corner units and their contents scattered and
trodden into the cheap carpet. Even the faded prints on
the walls had been moved, or ripped down and smashed,
as if the intruders hadn't the sense to realize that this was
a house that would not boast anything as sophisticated as
a wall safe.

'How'd they get in?'

'Back door,' Tommy said. He looked at Sam. 'It wasn't
locked.'

'Not locked,' I said, flabbergasted. 'And the security lights
are still off?'

'I went to work, an' I forgot, all right?' She was defensive, glaring at me as she clung to her brother's hand. 'I'm not thinking straight, am I. Jason's gone, I'm here on my own …'

Calum had pulled on his wire glasses and was prowling, picking up this and that, now nudging the upturned settee aside.

Sam was watching him. 'I know you from somewhere, don't I? I mean, I know you were with him in the *Echo*, but …'

'Ah, the price of fame,' Calum said, and charmed her with a crooked smile as he unhooked his glasses and dangled them from a bony finger. 'Is the upstairs the same? So we don't need to look. Things tumbled about like you've been hit by a tornado?'

'Pretty well.'

'And anything missing? As far as you can tell in all this bloody chaos?'

'No, nothing.' Her lip curled. 'Anyway, Jason's too tight, the only thing worth takin's the tele.'

'So whatever it was they were looking for, it wasn't here,' Calum said.

'Or,' I said, 'it was here, and now it's not.'

'Oh God!' Sam said, suddenly looking very young and vulnerable as she turned to bury her face in Tommy's shoulder.

'Let's get something to calm your nerves,' he said, and led her into the kitchen.

Calum was wandering, absently straightening pictures. Still busy with my thoughts I righted the settee, found the voluminous throw, draped it over the back.

Tommy Mack came back in. Behind him in the kitchen a kettle had started to sing. He was carrying a bottle.

'Drink, anyone?'

I shook my head. 'Coffee'll be fine, if you're making one for Sam.'

'Hot and laced,' he said, nodding. 'She likes it with the Rémy.'

'While that's being sorted,' I said, 'is there any chance of looking at this new car.'

'New?' The look on Mack's face was cynical; he hesitated only for an instant. 'Yeah, come through, there's a connectin' door from the kitchen.'

Sam was sitting in a chair by a spindly kitchen-table. Her fingers were drumming a faint tattoo and she watched nervously as we followed Tommy out into a small inner hallway. One glazed door led to the back garden. There was wet mud on the cushion flooring, probably trampled in by the intruders. Tommy opened another door, clicked a light switch, and as I went past him I smelt oil and petrol and unpainted brickwork, felt the damp breeze on my face from the broken window.

Three steps led down into the double garage. I skirted a smart little red Clio, gleaming under the naked overhead bulb, passed a hand over the bonnet and felt the lingering heat.

'I wonder where she works?'

'All-night petrol station in Halewood,' Calum said. 'Stan fills his van up there. I've spoken to her before now, that's why she recognized me. But it was briefly, and she must see hundreds of motorists every night, hence the puzzlement.'

I was only half-listening. Beyond the Clio there was a Mercedes C200. Black. The latest model.

'What was it Pythagoras said?'

'If he had any sense,' Calum said, following my eyes, 'he'd've leaped from his bath knowing there was more than one black chariot in Athens.'

I chuckled. 'Maybe – but my nose tells me something stinks.'

While talking I opened the Mercedes' offside door, leaned in and looked around. Cool. The rich scent of new leather, and another faint smell I couldn't place. A gaping hole in the dash where the stereo had been ripped out. Holes in all four doors and the parcel shelf indicating where speakers had been located. I backed out, then bent lower, reached in beneath the steering-wheel and pulled the bonnet-release catch. Calum had anticipated the move. He was already at the front of the car, and now he hoisted the bonnet and waited for me to join him.

'What are we looking for?'

'Bloody hell,' I said softly, 'hasn't Jones the Van taught you anything?'

But now Calum was caught up in the excitement. He put on his paint-stained glasses, bent in over the engine with his beard scratching cold metal and, as he rubbed shiny bits somewhere on the engine and compartment with a bony finger while trying to keep his long body out of the light from the dangling 100-watt bulb and squint at what he was doing, I wandered restlessly.

The broken window was on the far side wall. Inside the garage shattered glass still glittered on the concrete floor. The Merc had been here a couple of days, didn't belong to Sam. My guess was her concern had been for the Clio. Once she'd checked that and found it unmarked, she'd have glanced at the Merc, seen the missing stereo equipment and gone back into the house leaving that for Jason to worry about – if he ever returned.

And again I wondered why the theft of the stereo had gone unreported, and why after this violent break-in she had telephoned me. What was I missing? What did she know?

Calum came out from under the bonnet.

'Stolen, definitely. Identification marks professionally removed.'

'Which means?'

'Wee Orphan Annie's absent husband was playing devious games.'

'Then with an expensive car illegally but successfully acquired, why's he absent?'

'He went a couple of weeks ago, she said. But we'll ask her.'

'I raised the point. She brushed it aside.'

He unhooked his specs, pulled up the collar of his denim shirt against the chill, damp draught, and reached under his jacket. He carried a tiny Kyocera digital camera in a belt pouch. He took it out, switched on and took a couple of close-up flash photographs inside the bonnet, reviewed them in the LCD monitor, nodded approval.

'More?' I said. 'Plush interior so we can drool. Inside the boot?'

'General view. Forget the boot, it'll be empty.' He backed away and took another three shots, then closed in to take a couple more of the damage inside the car. He reviewed the latest pictures, deleted one and stowed the camera in its pouch. He leaned back against the car's gleaming black body.

'Something quite small,' he said thoughtfully, 'could easily have been stashed inside a car stereo system that was nothing more than a few fancy shells.'

'And if that's the case,' I said, 'and this *is* the Merc Stan Jones saw carjacked on Park Road, then it raises several interesting questions.'

'Like, just what *was* stashed in the stereo and those handy wee speakers?' Calum suggested.

'Right. And maybe that's the easy one. What about, has the scally who broke into this garage discovered what he's got, or already sold the stereo in the nearest pub?' I thought for a moment. 'And was the first available Mercedes stolen to order for Jason Bone, or was this *particular* Mercedes singled out for some reason?'

'In which case,' Calum said, 'if we are now seriously considering the notion that the stealing of the stereo and subsequent murder could both have been planned, we have to wonder what kind of deep game we've stumbled upon, and just who the hell's out there now, watching us.'

Were we being observed?

At the time of our conversation in the garage and with our only view that through the broken window overlooking next door's shrubbery, there was no way of knowing and, when we'd run out of ideas on an investigation that had taken me from one young woman to another and seemed to be drawing us into a morass of intrigue, we went back into the house.

The kitchen was warm. Two mugs steamed on the table, but Tommy and Sam had moved back into the living-room and rearranged enough of the furniture so they could sit in comfort. We tramped through carrying our coffee; in the living room the drinks had already worked their magic. Sam had mellowed, and was sitting curled up on the settee with her eyes closed. Tommy's face had softened and he was perched on the arm next to her, one hand gently kneading the back of her neck. Guitar music of the easy-listening kind purred softly in the background from a boom-box that had somehow escaped the mayhem.

Sam's eyes opened as we walked in. 'What d'you reckon?'

Calum stepped through the wreckage and stood sipping his drink and looking out of the windows. The curtains were still open. I could see fine rain sweeping across sodium street-lighting, ornamental conifers, the big sycamore dripping at the end of the gravel drive.

'It's a stolen car,' I said, and she nodded.

'Yeah, well, that's the way he does things.'

'On the cheap, stuff off the back of lorries?'

'God, no. Cheap's relative, isn' it? A new Merc's expensive wherever it comes from. This place is furnished like second world war utility because Jase struts his stuff elsewhere. I'm his last consideration. He likes to impress the low life in clubs that're all glitter and no class.'

'So where does he get his money?'

'Don't ask me. And don't ask me what he's worth, because I haven't a clue.' Her face turned sour. 'I know he wheels and deals in some poxy insurance firm. Comes in lookin' miserable on a Friday night and hands me fifty measly quid for housekeeping and I don't see him again all weekend.'

'All week,' Tommy said, and she nodded.

'Yeah. Only now I don't see him at all because he's been gone a whole fuckin' *two* weeks and I'm supposed to survive on the pittance I earn.'

Calum had turned away from his study of the wet gardens, and was watching me. I tasted the coffee, then pursed my lips.

'Sam, why don't you talk to the police?'

She shivered. 'Because I'm scared.'

'Scared people ask for help.'

'I am. I'm askin' you.'

She walked over and switched off the music, swung to face me.

'Find out who did this. What they were lookin' for. Then tell them to bugger off because I haven't got it.'

'From what you've told me, I'd say Jason would have some answers.'

'So find him. I mean, he went away, then a couple of weeks later that Merc turns up – and now I'm bein' targeted. Why? What's here? What the fuck's he done?'

'Apart from his habit of impressing people who are not worth the effort,' Calum said, 'is there anything he's done in the past that's making you fearful?'

'I don't know what he's been up to,' Sam said, 'before, during or since,' and again she shivered. 'But *something's* goin' on, and here's me talkin' to an expensive private eye and he's going to help me and I'm flat broke....'

Her eyes were challenging and imploring and at the same time unreadable as she looked across at me. I thought I saw her lower lip quiver, the glint of a tear. She seemed to shake herself, and as she walked towards the door the yellow kimono was that trashed room's only touch of brightness. Tommy stayed where he was. Calum and I left our coffee unfinished and followed her, and in the hall I said, 'Switch those security lights on *now*, and ask Tommy to stay the night.'

'He will.'

She clicked a wall switch, opened the front door.

I let Calum past, said quietly to her, 'Don't worry, I'll see what I can do,' and she smiled suddenly and brightly and stood on tiptoe to kiss my cheek.

When I stepped outside into the fine drizzle, the security lights had clicked on as Calum emerged and he was standing on the top step looking at the Quatro.

All four tyres were flat.

The valves had been sliced off with a sharp knife and lined up on the wet bonnet like a shiny row of ugly black slugs.

We'd held our councils of war in peculiar places, but none more bizarre than at a table in the smoky bar of the KING OF CLUBS as blue and red spotlights made a gaudy circus clown of the drunken singer clinging to the mike on the platform where, what seemed a long time ago, Gerry Gault had plunged a knife into a young girl's throat and a suave taxidermist had for a time been the king of karaoke with his lazy Sinatra impressions. Big George Kingman, glistening with sweat, was watching the performance and us, perched on a stool on the wrong side of his bar with a cigar smouldering in his sovereign-ringed fingers as he drank Vat 69 from a glass I wouldn't have given to Calum for his used paintbrushes.

The singer was Solly, the song 'Crazy', which made some kind of sense because the last time Calum and I had seen his bloated face had been through the windscreen of the clapped-out Land Rover he and greasy Jimmy Beggs were driving full tilt into my Vectra. Both men were employed by Kingman, both had received suspended sentences for the deliberate collision that had written off my car, and it was symptomatic of the mental state induced by a highly unusual day that I was wallowing in memories of a previous case while actively involved in another.

Actively? Now that *was* a laugh.

Sian was watching me with amused eyes over the rim of her glass, as usual reading my thoughts with uncanny accuracy.

'Tommy will look after her,' she said. 'She saw your car with its tyres slashed and still rejected police help. What more could you do?'

She was right, of course. I'd stood on the gravel drive in soaking drizzle to get a mobile signal, phoned her at Meg Morgan's, filled her in with some sparse details, then asked her to get out of bed and pick us up in the Shogun. Then I'd called Stan Jones and arranged for the Quatro to be collected by a garage he used to keep his rusty white van on the road. And all the while Calum had been snug and dry sheltering under the hanging basket of petunias and Sam had been watching from the front window, her face grim, the yellow kimono a splash of bright colour.

'What we've stumbled upon,' I said, dropping words into a pause that had grown too long for comfort, 'is a chain with a missing link, and the only thing I know for sure about anything is what I've been asked to do.'

'Let those requests be our starting point,' Calum said. 'Jemima Laing's asked you to look for a random killer. Sam Bone wants you to find the men who trashed her home, and her missing husband.'

'And the vague connection,' Sian said, 'is that Silvester Laing's killer happened to have stolen a stereo system from Sam Bone's garage.'

'So for now,' I said, 'let's concentrate on what we know has happened, what we know about the people directly involved.'

'According to Manny Yates,' Calum said, 'Silvester Laing was a loan-shark who worked his way into the big time. Partner in ... what was it, Link Associates, some kind of legit business involved in illegal activities.'

I nodded. 'And in that line of work it's not hard to see him treading on the wrong toes, thereby attracting the wrath of someone very nasty and more than capable of sticking a sharp knife in his ribs.'

'But that person,' Sian said, 'is unlikely to take the form of a scally lugging a stolen car stereo in the rain.'

'All right, so we know we've got a shady character – now dead – but we seem to be lumbered with a random killer.'

I looked from one to the other, saw reluctant nods of agreement, and leaned back in my chair as Jimmy Beggs arrived with our drinks, plonked them down sloppily and left us with the lingering smell of stale sweat.

'What about the Bones?'

'A crafty scally saw a Merc delivered,' Calum said, 'came back in the dead of night and stole the stereo. Easily carried. Easily sold. Made off with it. Turned violent when tackled.'

'And tonight's break-in?'

'For some reason, wheeler-dealer Jason Bone walked out a couple of weeks ago. I'm thinking it's possible he left something important behind, but didn't want to return. So he sent some pals to collect it. Only it wasn't there. Or it was, but now it isn't.'

'Possible. Just. But that's not the way we read it when we'd gone down to Sam's garage and looked at the Merc.' I reached across, plucked the slice of lemon from the rim of Sian's gin and tonic and sucked it down to the pith as I poured ice-cold Holsten and mused on possibilities.

'How *did* you see it?' Sian said.

'As a much more complicated scenario.'

'Let me guess,' she said, eyes sparkling with interest. 'Jason Bone scarpered because he'd fallen foul of some baddies. He left something behind, but it was valuable and it belonged to them. They went looking for it in his house, and either found it or didn't. So they'll come back, or they won't.'

'We certainly think this involves something of value, and it's pretty obvious we've been tossing around the idea that it was hidden in the Merc's stereo system,' Calum said. 'But we hadn't linked that particular line of thought to Jason Bone.'

'Then try this for some plot thickening, you two,' Sian said. 'You're packing your brains with thoughts on random killings, theft, housebreaking, secret stashes, layabouts and dodgy finance companies. Instead,' she said softly, 'why don't you ask yourselves what in the name of God one or both of those two young ladies is playing at?'

In the sudden silence there was a distant click and over the empty board stage the lurid red and blue spotlights blinked out. Solly had long gone, his lonely wailing outlaw solo finished when his sozzled brain ran out of words, his thick legs out of strength. Now all around us lights were doused until we were illuminated only by the weak glimmer from behind the bar which itself was dimmed by big George Kingman's long shadow.

Then footsteps pattered along the passageway from the frayed, grubby curtain covering the Pelham Grove entrance, and Stan Jones strutted in.

Sian was already up from the table and halfway to the wide doorway leading into the passage. Calum was paying Kingman. I was last, and in deep shadow, but it was me Stan was after.

'Guess what?'

'Tell me,' I said, pulse quickening. 'The Quatro's four wheels are fixed, it's outside now and I don't owe you a cent.'

He sneered. 'As if. It's still at that bird's house waitin' to be picked up. It'll cost four hundred minimum, an' then there's my cut, but what you owe me now is a double Jameson's – Christ, no, make it a fuckin' bottle.'

'For that, this had better be good.'

'It is. You asked me to find out things.'

'And?'

'I didn't pick just any old garage.'

'You don't mean,' I said, 'that the garage that's about to fix my car has recently worked on a certain unusual Mercedes?'

'Yeah. I do. It's in Old Swan. The garage. Yer flashy Quatro'll be ready before twelve. An' here's the owner's card. Ronnie Maguire. Only when you go there tomorrow, you'll have to tread careful. Ask the right questions. Of the right people. An' I don't think it should be Ronnie.'

Calum had sharp ears. He came across with a bottle of Jameson's, I handed it to Stan as payment and we all walked out into the chill of a wet night.

Stan had come in his van and was first away, roaring into Lark Lane in a cloud of blue smoke. Sian was going to drop Calum and me at his flat in Grassendale before making her way in the Shogun back to Meg's spare room. That should have meant the long night was almost over, but there was one, final twist.

As the lurid red-neon crown on the wall above George's KING OF CLUBS winked out, my mobile rang. It was Alun Morgan calling from his Bethesda home.

'More information on the murder on board that dodgy businessman's luxury yacht.' he said. 'I wouldn't be bothering you, but I reckon it'll be of especial interest because there's a link that's quite astonishing.'

'After the day I've spent here, Alun, nothing will surprise me.'

'Don't be too sure of that. Remember I told you the fingerprints we had on the knife were untraceable? That was because without a criminal record to go on the police computer was acting bloody stupid, as likely as not to link vicars and cabinet ministers to unsolved atrocities. But new information's being input all the time, isn't it – and now we've got a match.'

I frowned. 'With what?'

'What the hell d'you think?'

'Not the stabbing in Liverpool?'

'And why not?'

Sian was watching me from the Shogun, anxious for me to get a move on. I quickly waved acknowledgement, then turned away to concentrate on the call.

'Because it's not possible,' I said. 'There's got to be a mistake. A scally stole a stereo, stabbed the man who tried to stop him. I know from Mike Haggard his prints were too smeared to be of any use.'

'Ah,' Morgan said, 'but I'm not talking about those prints, am I.'

There was a silence and I could picture Alun with his feet up in his office in the dark lee of brooding Carnedd Dafydd, a glass of Islay or something similar in his hand and a crafty glint in his dark eyes as I stood in the drizzle with rainwater trickling down my neck and my mind racing to a conclusion that defied logic.

'When I spoke to Jemima Laing,' I said carefully, 'she told me there was blood on her husband's hands.'

'There would be, wouldn't there,' Alun said, 'if in his dying agony he clutched the knife and tried desperately to draw it from his body?'

'So you're telling me,' I said, 'that Laing's dying grip on the knife that killed him smeared his killer's fingerprints, but left his own perfectly identifiable?'

'There's clever,' Alun Morgan said. 'And it didn't take you too long, did it?' He chuckled darkly. 'Well now, unless you're right and there *has* been a monumental cock up, matching Laing's prints with those found at the Conwy killing means he was on that yacht. And if that's the case then at some time around midnight on Thursday he went down to the galley, got himself a bloody big carving-knife, and used it to stab a man to death.'

chapter five

The tin alloy, gloss-painted toy soldiers I design and manu-
facture are recognized by connoisseurs as some of the finest
in the world. I concentrate on a period in history when
uniforms were at their most colourful, and in particular I'm
known for British grenadiers of around 1751 when they wore
scarlet tunics with cuffs and turnbacks, a variety of belts
carrying swords, grenade- and cartridge-pouches, and tall
mitre-caps bearing elaborate regimental designs.

I do the designing, moulding and centrifugal casting in my
mountain workshop. In the painting I'm always helped by
the skill of Calum Wick, the enigmatic Scotsman I first
encountered many years ago outside a pub in Brixton when
he was about to be beaten to a pulp by three huge Yardies.
Together we prevailed, washed the blood off faces and split
knuckles in the ice-cold water of a cracked basin in an evil-
smelling underground gents' toilet, and went on to become
partners in a scam that involved bringing expensive cars of
dubious provenance over from Germany and selling them on
through a bent Liverpool detective-sergeant who had
contacts with fat wallets.

If either of these activities can be called careers, then they
would seem to leave me ill-equipped to investigate violent
crime. But before meeting Calum I was a regular soldier, and
over fifteen or so years my tours with the Royal Engineers
and SAS were complemented by a lengthy spell with the SIB
– the army's Special Investigation Branch. When, disillu-
sioned and conscience-smitten, I left Calum and his lucrative

scam and began hitting the bottle, I was rescued and taken on by Manny Yates in his Lime Street firm of private investigators – a five-year apprenticeship in investigation techniques that sort of brings us in a roundabout manner back to the conversation in the American bar.

All of this and much more was rattling around in my head some while after three shattered musketeers had climbed into Sian's Shogun, motored through wet, silent streets to Grassendale and I'd bid farewell to my Soldier Blue as she turned around and headed for Meg's to resume her interrupted sleep. Calum and I had banged with childish cruelty on Sammy Quade's door, scampered up the stairs, breathlessly dumped coats on leather chairs and enjoyed a nightcap – it was hot drinking-chocolate, I promise you – in the silent room where freshly primed Scots Greys looking like the ghosts of soldiers past stood in patient vigil beneath the dark, cold Anglepoise. Fifteen minutes later I was lying back on the pillow with my hands laced behind my head in the dark of Calum's spare room, staring like one of Franz Mesmer's patients at the lights from across the Mersey twinkling like lazy fireflies on the other side of the net curtains.

And I think what I was trying to do in a muddled and blurred sort of way was convince myself that I was competent to conduct an investigation that seemed to be spiralling out of control, and before going to sleep settle on a plan of action.

The problem was, where to begin.

Well, a stolen Merc's stereo had itself been stolen by an unknown scally who then murdered Laing. Two thefts, two slender leads. So, the first step was to try and trace the stereo, and the scally, by talking to regulars in the local pubs. That would be Calum's job. And he could paint Scots Greys for disgruntled Gibraltarian collectors all morning, because he couldn't start that particular line of investigation until the pubs opened.

However, not only did we know the Merc had been stolen, we also suspected that something of value had been hidden in the stereo. I was picking up the Quatro – before twelve, according to Stan Jones – so my job was to talk to someone at Ronnie Maguire's garage. But not Ronnie, Stan said. So Ronnie Maguire must be up to his greasy elbows in something very dodgy, something he wouldn't want to discuss with me or anyone else for fear of getting a bloody big spanner thrown in his highly lucrative works. I believed. From experience. Which thoughts immediately sent me winging on wild flights of fancy.

And at some point very soon afterwards, there being no further matters to cogitate upon, I must have fallen asleep.

Monday

When I slapped barefoot from the spare room at half past seven the next morning – that same morning, to be precise – and dropped two thick slices of wholemeal bread into the toaster, Calum was already there at the table with elbows either side of a greasy plate containing nothing but sticky egg-yolk and soggy crusts, a stained coffee-mug at his elbow and most of his gaunt, unkempt presence hidden behind a crumpled *Daily Telegraph*. With his shaggy grey beard he looked like a homeless derelict caught folding his bedding at last night's park bench.

My toast popped up. Calum folded the paper. I joined him at the table and made a lot of crumbs and scraping noises as I applied Lurpak butter and Tiptree orange marmalade while he stretched an arm out to the stove for the percolator and poured two coffees. When he leaned back in his chair again his eyes were speculative.

'You know,' he said, 'that's it's likely we were followed from Bone's last night?'

'And then from Kingman's club? And they tailed Sian after she'd dropped us off?'

'If they were persistent.'

I bit into crisp toast, watched more crumbs fall to dance

like summer flies on the surface of my coffee, and shook my head.

'Slashing the tyres was a warning. Their only interest in me is making sure I stay away from Sam Bone.'

'Unless,' Calum said, 'it was your first visit that caught their attention.'

'Ah.' I sipped coffee, reflecting. 'If they knew the stereo had gone from the Merc before my first visit, then the tyre slashing was a mild warning. If they didn't discover the stereo had gone until they broke in last night – and how else could they know about it? – then they think I've got it. And whatever it contained.'

'Maybe.'

'And so the warning becomes a serious threat, and I watch my back?'

'Always.'

'But not in daylight.'

'Daylight didn't help the driver of the Merc.'

'Are we connecting him to this?'

'I don't know. But we look at all possibilities. Because if they think you've got the stereo, and what it contained is what I think it contained, you're in trouble.'

'So what *was* in it?'

'We will leave that,' Calum said, 'to be discussed later today if you return from your adventures with the mechanics.'

'If.' I grinned. 'Is a back-street garage in Old Swan more dangerous than Woolton's pubs at lunchtime?'

'There's not much in it. The difference,' he said. 'is in the calibre of the investigator.'

It took another ten minutes to order a taxi to take me to Old Swan. When it arrived I slipped the card Stan had given me from my pocket, leaned forward and held it so the driver could see.

'This is where I want you to take me.'

He glanced sideways at the grubby card, then flicked his eyes back to the road.

'Yeah, right.'

'And?'

'And nothin'.'

'Your tone was ...'

'Noncommittal? Sceptical?'

I grinned. 'You and Willy Vine, wordsmiths both. No, I was thinking scornful, pitying, something like that.'

'Yeah, well. An' who's Vine?'

'A friendly detective-sergeant with Mills and Boon aspirations,' I said. 'Or something. But what about Maguire? My tyres were slashed, he was recommended by a friend.' Not strictly true. Stan had found a bent garage and given them my expensive toy, but I was looking for a reaction. It came in the form of a snort. Definitely derisive.

'What was it when you last saw it?'

We'd reached Allerton Road. At the lights he swung right into Queen's Drive and accelerated up the hill while I chewed on his strange words and tried not to read into them the very worst.

'My car?'

'Yeah, what make was it when it went in?'

I sucked a breath. 'As bad as that, is it?'

'Fuckin' close. Let's just say if there's a Bermuda Triangle where flash cars disappear, Ronnie Maguire's workin' the gate.'

'But if you know all that,' I said, 'so do the police.'

'If I know all what?' the driver said, and I chuckled as he closed the conversation, swung into the roundabout at Childwall Fiveways and settled to his driving.

Five minutes later he dropped me on Prescot Road and I walked along Derby Road and down a side street to the address that was on the card and between ranks of terraced houses, came upon a square that was like a concrete parade ground trampled by boots black with grease, at the back of which Ronnie Maguire had a timber and corrugated-iron workshop with big double doors and a sign telling me to keep out.

A red rag fluttering to enrage the rampant bull.

I took hold of an iron hasp with my white hands, dragged one half of the double doors open a scant foot and wriggled inside.

Is there something intrinsically menacing about the gloomy, deserted interior of a littered motor-vehicle workshop, or is it circumstances that determine the frame of mind?

During my long spell in Queensland I'd pumped petrol on forecourts alongside Golden Fleece service station workshops through which weekend customers in shorts and floppy hats would happily walk barefoot. In Sydney I'd cleaned cars at a British Leyland garage on Pacific Highway where the packed grease of a quarter of a century would need to be removed from the workshop floor to get the first glimpse of concrete. Ronnie Maguire's place fell somewhere between those two extremes, but I knew that on the greasy footing between heavy wooden benches littered with spanners and jack-handles and oxy-acetylene torches and cracked batteries and jars of electrolyte strong enough to burn skin my Rieker casuals would be no match for cleated leather boots with steel toecaps, my grip on that slick surface nowhere near enough to resist the assault of a man used to hoisting cast iron cylinder heads from bench to engine block and applying arm and shoulder muscles to hefty chrome torque-wrenches.

Outside it was a dull day. In here weak light filtered through windows whose cracked glass was draped with grey cobwebs as thick as Welsh wool, to fall on blackened benches and the greasy floor on which yellow water from what must have been a thousand cracked radiators lay in stagnant pools.

I couldn't see my car.

But did I want to see its gleaming paintwork and plush upholstery in that greasy shed where one accidental brush from a mechanic's overalls would be enough to wipe a thousand quid off market value?

No, this might be the workshop from Hell where Nasty

Things Happened, but it was not one where anybody in their right mind would park expensive late model cars. And Maguire – even if Stan Jones and the taxi driver were both entirely wrong about his nefarious practices – was surely a man in this tough game only for the money. So through the ramshackle door I could see at the far end there would be parking and further work areas, at the very least a shed dedicated to bodywork and spray-painting; and I recalled now that as I had crossed the greasy forecourt to approach this building I had noticed rutted tracks with central ridges of coarse grass leading around both its rotting timber sides.

'How the hell'd you get in 'ere?'

I swung around with my skin prickling, hearing my soles hiss on the compacted grease, my hand shooting out to grab hold of a cold metal bench vice for support as I wobbled dangerously.

Standing before me in greasy blue overalls that would be waterproof at ten fathoms was the biggest man I'd ever seen. He was flanked by the second biggest, his meaty hands holding a piece of rusty angle iron as big as a modest RSJ.

The office was probably cleaner and tidier than the workshop but because it was smaller it looked ten times worse. Claustrophobia was a constant threat. Maguire's immense bulk made the condition critical. He was like a rock-fisted colossus behind a brown wooden desk so old it probably bore the carved initials of stiff-collared clerks employed by the London Midland & Scottish Railway at its founding, and I sat sort of diagonally across from him wedged in a corner by the door with my face up against reeking overalls suspended from a massive iron hook like a clutch of hanged men.

The big garage owner was the kind of man to sit with his dirty boots on the desk, and the desk was certainly big enough. Unfortunately it was stacked with so many invoices, vehicle-parts books, cracked mirrors, brake shoes, wiper blades and other bits of junk that an attempt at nonchalance would have caused an avalanche. Which wouldn't have mattered. Walking was difficult, because the floor was as littered as the desk. Where one ended, the other began but, like the sea and sky of a grey November day, it was impossible to see the join.

'Coffee?'

In amongst the clutter, the crusts on three stained mugs attracted families of flies. I shook my head.

'So what 'appened to the Quatro?'

'Vandals. Parked outside for fifteen minutes and it was on its rims.'

'Could've been worse.'

He heaved himself out of the chair, did a half turn with the grace of all men of his bulk and filled one of the mugs with steaming grey liquid from a filter machine standing on a shelf under a hatch leading to the workshop. That dismal area was empty again. Confronted by the two men, I'd shown Maguire his own card, mentioned Stan's name, asked after the Quatro. The man hefting the angle iron had sneered to hide his disappointment, spat close to my feet and turned towards the double doors. Across the back of his overalls as he went out I saw MAGUIRE'S in dirty white lettering.

'Bargin' in unannounced like that,' Maguire said now, 'was a bit risky.' He swung round, sank like ship's ballast into the chair. 'There's usually a big German Shepherd runnin' loose. He'd've slobbered all over your nice shoes.'

'Most aim their ambitions a little higher.'

'An' what about you? What d'you do for a livin' that gets you an Audi Quatro?'

I found a Magna Carta card in my wallet, placed it delicately among the papers on the desk to accentuate the skill in my fingers while masking the strength I would unleash on him if things got rough. But why should they? Maguire was on his own patch, unthreatened, tidying up a favour done for a friend that would net him a few hundred quid.

'Toy soldiers,' he said, and flicked my business card dismissively as his lip curled and his mind slotted me into the pigeon-hole marked "small-time suckers with cash". I watched him drink from the mug and begin scribbling with a chewed pen in a blue duplicate book and wondered how, if I couldn't ask delicate questions of Maguire, I was supposed to get information. From the world's second biggest man? There was not a sound to be heard and I wondered if I was a privileged customer in a workshop that was pure front; if this was a closed shop of two where few employees meant fewer leaks; if these two were the men who had worked the carjacking in Park Road.

'Four hundred,' Maguire said. 'Plus VAT.'

I read the inflated figure upside down, wrote and signed a cheque and handed it to him. He tore out the invoice copy. I folded it, tucked it away. And all the time I was thinking. Walking away left me with nothing. If I pretended to walk away then doubled back and nosed around I might stumble across a workshop where mechanics toiled under bright strip lighting changing identification marks and number plates on stolen cars. More likely – from what I'd seen – I'd end up in another damp and dismal workshop where nothing happened and probably blunder into the second biggest man in the world lurking in wait for me with his angle iron.

'Max is bringin' the car round,' Maguire said, and he came trampling out from behind the desk with a threatening finality that told me it was time to leave.

The Quatro with its lustrous new black tyres was already on the concrete hard standing. Of big Max there was no sign. I climbed in, caught the whiff of Lynx and stale sweat, felt the tackiness of his big paws on the steering-wheel as I started up and drove out. I was frustrated, and at a loss. The circles Stan Jones moved in gave his information about this garage hefty credence, and I knew that driving away from Maguire's set-up with nothing gained left Stan's reputation untarnished but emphasized my shortcomings as a private eye.

I swung away from the decrepit workshops, started up the side street towards Derby Road, managed a hundred yards and saw a short, skinny man in grubby blue overalls being towed towards me like a grounded kite by a long-haired

German Shepherd. The dog must have caught the scent of a cat in a nearby alley. He growled, coughed like a hunting lion and tried to drag the man with him as he leaped for the littered opening. The skinny feller spun, braced his legs, leaned back, hung on. Across the back of his straining over-alls was emblazoned the word MAGUIRE'S.

I nudged the new tyres against the kerb, pulled up, switched off and got out.

'Excuse me, you work for Ronnie Maguire, right?'

He'd dragged the slavering dog back so it was facing the right way, and was deliberately cutting off its air with a short choke chain. His eyes slid to the Quatro, and I knew he recognized it and so had me tagged as one of Ronnie's customers.

'Yeah, why?'

I slipped a twenty-pound note out of my wallet, held it out.

'What's your name?'

'Les.'

'I'm glad I saw you, Les. I was supposed to slip this to Stan Jones, as thanks for getting these tyres done, but he's not here. I might not see him for some time, so can you ...?'

In a piece of brilliant legerdemain the dog was kept effortlessly under control but the money I'd been holding disappeared. Stan wouldn't see it, but that had never been my intention. I'd bought a mate: for as long as it took him to get rid of me, Les was twenty quid's worth of best mucker.

'I didn't mention it to Ronnie,' I said confidingly, 'because I know it's already gone, but that Merc ...'

'What Merc's that?'

I looked around, then back at him, and winked. 'The black one. You know. Park Road, a couple of weeks ago. God, I'd've topped anything Jason'd offered if I'd known sooner.'

'Jason ...?'

I was talking dangerously, and there was a limit to what twenty quid could buy. 'Jason Bone,' I said. 'According to a friend of a friend, that car's been sitting in his garage since Thursday.'

Reluctantly, agreeing in a loose way without implicating himself or Maguire, Les said, 'Yeah, well, I suppose that could be right.' Meaning he knew of a carjacking, the car was a Merc and it had to be somewhere, and if I'd heard something ... It was like a verbal shrug, a noncommittal agreement that left me stranded.

The dog was slowly choking. Les eased back on the chain. He was itching to go but he had my money and the name Jason had grabbed him and he didn't know what I knew so he was willing to spend a couple of minutes letting me dig my own grave. Or bring Ronnie some profit.

'I suppose,' I said, 'Ronnie could always get me one?'

Hostility began to fade as he smelled business, but caginess and cunning were a way of life.

'I suppose he could, if he happened to be in that line of business,' he said. And then, giving me some rope: 'But if he did – an' I'm not sayin' he could, or would – it wouldn't be like the one you're talkin' about.'

'A black Merc's a black Merc.'

'What I'm sayin' is that Justin—'

'Jason.'

'Yeah, well, maybe that Jason feller was very specific.'

'How specific can you get?'

'Let's put it this way,' Les said. 'Supposin' you fancy the Lord Mayor's big limo an' you must have it an' no other car'll do ...'

I grinned sceptically. 'Too recognizable, I'd have to keep it under wraps, you're having me on.'

'Yeah, but I'm tellin' you what could be done by certain people for certain people,' Les said, and with a wistful look down the road he slipped the dog's chain and let it go. 'I mean it doesn' have to be the actual fuckin' mayor's car, does it.'

The German Shepherd barked, took a step backwards. The heavy tail flicked from side to side, then drooped. Rich dark eyes stared out of a tawny face liberally streaked with black.

Acting daft, I said, 'I suppose not.' I thought, then said, 'So what if I don't want a particular car, a *specific* car, just ...?'

'Oh, for Christ's sake,' Les said.

His tone had reached the dog. Its ears flattened. It looked towards me and whined softly. Its lip curled. A snarl rattled deep down in the soft membranes at the back of his throat. White teeth glistened. Stiffly, never taking his eyes from my face, it backed away.

'Listen,' Les said, 'if I'm going to get this cash to Stan ...' He began walking away, and in a sudden flurry of movement the big dog had gone, racing ahead of him. 'An' if you want to discuss cars of any kind,' he called over his shoulder, 'you'll have to talk to Ron, only remember there's three dogs, all of 'em loose....'

I climbed back in the car, feeling smug.

Before driving off I reached Calum at the bar in the first of the pubs he'd got lined up.

'Old Swan was fruitful,' I said. 'Back-street garage, two men who've handled a stolen black Merc. Jason Bone almost certainly the cash buyer. And it wasn't any old Merc; that particular car was selected by Bone.'

'Why?'

'For what was in the stereo. Has to be.'

'Which is now being touted by a scally unaware that he's carrying a time-bomb.'

'Or it's not.'

'What are you suggesting, Jack?'

In the mirror I watched Les turn onto the concrete fronting Maguire's garage. Twenty quid to the good, thinking only of his next drink? Or reporting to Maguire about the nosy feller in the Quatro asking about the black Mercedes? With a soft hiss of breath I turned the ignition key, blipped the engine.

'Two possibilities,' I said. 'The scally accidentally discovered he'd struck gold; or the stereo was stolen deliberately for what it contained. If either one's right it means the stereo won't show up in the pubs.'

'And what it contained,' Calum said, 'is something we'd decided to discuss later.'

'Over dinner tonight sounds a good idea.'

'The steak house?'

'Mm. Can you let Sian know? She's down town with that director, Adrian, talking TV. We could all meet there about seven.'

'I'll do that. It should prove an interesting evening.'

He clicked off.

The phone rang at once. It was Mike Haggard.

'Get down here, Ill Wind.'

'Here being where?'

'Admiral Street nick.'

'Trouble?'

'Developments. You'll be fascinated.'

I let in the clutch, and headed south.

chapter six

Haggard was at his desk in shirt-sleeves, cigarette in one hand, phone in the other. Willie Vine was flicking through creased manila folders on a creaking trestle-table near the window. The two detectives had been together in this same room when, bruised and bloody, Calum and I been taken there from the hospital after the crash that wrote off my Vectra towards the end of the Gault case. I couldn't decide if they deliberately got together when I was expected, or shared the room permanently because of lack of space.

'That's the trouble with mobiles,' Haggard said as he slammed the phone down. 'The person you're talking to could be sunbathin' on the fuckin' moon.' He fixed me with his dark, brooding gaze. 'That's you I'm talkin' about. Where the hell were you?'

'Old Swan.'

'Balls. Woolton Park on Jemima Laing business, more like.'

I shook my head. 'I spoke to her, Laing's dead, the killer's gone. My time's too important to go chasing shadows.'

'An' what about the paint-spattered gay Gordon, what's he pokin' his nose into?'

'Round about now, I'd say a cooling draught of best beer in a hostelry out Woolton way.'

Vine was looking innocently at Haggard. 'So now it is Woolton,' he said.

Haggard was very still. 'If it's not Laing,' he said, 'what wild fuckin' coincidence takes Wick out that way the day after I told both of you to keep your noses out?'

'I've got a nasty feeling,' I said, 'that you're about to tell me something fascinating.'

'Ever heard of Sound Bites?'

'Yes,' I said, 'it's the new crunchy chocolate bar from Cadbury—'

'Try a down-at-heel business flogging in-car audio systems as a cover for something much bigger.'

'Calum Wick has in the past used various businesses during his meanderings in the shady world of stolen cars,' Willie Vine said.

'Ah. And Sound Bites was one of them. But this has got nothing to do with audio systems.'

Haggard lit another cigarette, leaned back, narrowing his eyes against the trickling smoke. He was rocking in the chair, nodding absently, his gaze thoughtful.

'I'll ask you again. Where's Wick?'

'Enjoying a drink. I don't know where. He's a free spirit.'

'So if some of my men raided Sound Bites, they wouldn't find him there?'

'No.'

'He's been seen there, several times.'

'You said it yourself: he works with cars.'

'I also said the audio business was cover for something much bigger.'

'As in?'

He looked at Vine.

'Drugs,' Willie said. 'Like an electric current they go in one end, come out the other. Invisible. And your friend Calum Wick's caught slap-bang in the middle.'

'Aye, they would say that,' Calum said, 'because it seems that when it comes to me and Stan the Van they can see nothing but guilt.'

It was still light outside, but cloudy, and the candles guttering on the tables in our favourite steakhouse set back off Smithdown Road cast a warm glow over now empty platters which had been laden with sizzling peppered sirloin steaks in a rich spicy sauce with chips and mixed veg. Or in Sian's case a side-saddle. Which is how she was wont to describe a salad that arrives in a little curved dish to nestle alongside the main meal.

Sian was watching my deep disquiet at Calum's blasé response to Vine's accusation, blue eyes alert, blonde hair snatched back and looking fairer than usual in contrast to cheeks flushed by a glass or two of excellent Merlot. As we finished our meal she'd listened intently to my recounting of the talk in Haggard's office, raised her eyebrows at the mention of drugs, reached out to cover the bony Scot's hard hand when I got to Calum's supposed involvement. She was loyal and sentimental, but too many paces removed for her judgement to be accurate. I'd worked with Calum Wick on too many scams, condoned – no, that was the wrong word – chosen to *ignore* his excursions on the dark side that I suspected he embarked on when he was not painting my soldiers. But six weeks ago he'd been suspected of car theft. He'd got off on the flimsiest of technicalities. I wasn't prepared to dismiss entirely Mike Haggard's suspicions.

'So there's nothing in it?' I said at last.

The grey eyes looked at me with a cold glint that would have sent an enemy cowering.

I smiled resignedly. 'No matter. By accusing you of that particular crime, Willie Vine's given me a lead. So tell me, what happened in your quest for the missing stereo?'

'I just about got myself sloshed to my bewhiskered gills buying drinks to jog sluggish memories and loosen tongues. And ended up with bad news and a headache that lingers still. It's sold.'

I think my jaw dropped.

Calum's grey eyes were amused.

'Aye, it was a scally all along. And the audio equipment he was flogging was too good to miss. Radio, CD-player, speakers. Extolled as being fresh out of a new Mercedes. Not surprisingly, it sold in the first pub.'

'So why all the drinks?'

'Well now,' he said with a roguish glint in his eye, 'by a wondrous quirk of fate the first pub that wee scally went into happened to be last on my list.'

I looked at him. 'What about the contents? The stuff that makes the stereo valuable. Tell me what you think's in there.'

'Don't need him,' Sian said, eyes dancing. 'I can put two and two together and get truly magical results. Mike Haggard's talking about an audio business suspected of dealing in drugs, so the stereo of which we speak must have been stuffed with heroin, cocaine....' She gave a gallic, *et voilà* sort of smug shrug.

'Rocket science it ain't,' Calum said.

'But fascinating it is,' I said. 'We're looking at a Mercedes on its customary drive to Sound Bites, where the drugs will be taken out of the fake stereo and the car driven away to be made ready for the next trip. Only this time it's carjacked in Park Road, and doesn't make it. But we know the audio shop's owner must have been expecting it. So if we want to know who owned the Mercedes, we go to the audio shop. With which establishment,' I said pointedly, 'you are familiar.'

I hailed a passing waiter who removed the plates and went off to get three coffees. The dining-room was filling up. Dishes clattered, wine glasses tinkled, drinks were quaffed, laughter bubbled, and outside the big windows beneath the now high clouds the light was turning a ruddy gold in the west which increased warmth and intimacy.

I said, 'We're now pretty certain we know what was in the stereo. Thanks to the Admiral Street detectives we've got a lead to the owner of the Mercedes. He wants his drugs back. Once we find him we've got the man who broke into Sam Bone's house.'

I leaned back out of the way as the waiter eventually arrived with the hot drinks. They came on a tray, with *cafetière*, cream-jug and sugar-basin and several foil-wrapped mints. Sian poured. We spooned, stirred and nibbled and, when we were again settled, I went on, 'We're still working on Sam's problems, but the trouble is we're assuming: we're *pretty* certain; we *think* we've got a lead; that *should* tell us; and that way of thinking is not good enough. We could so easily be wrong. As well as hunting down the driver of the Mercedes, I think we've got to keep the investigation wide open; operate on two fronts. We've got that unexplained murder to look into for Jemima Laing, and I really cannot believe a scally *accidentally* stole that particular stereo, then *happened* to be accosted by Silvester Laing and ended up murdering him – then disposed of what has to be a fake bloody stereo in the first pub he walked into.'

I paused, waited for their reaction, saw slow nods of agreement and said, 'Which brings us to the missing husband, Jason Bone; who went to a lot of trouble to order that *particular* car to be stolen; and who then inexplicably walked away.'

Delicately licking froth off his moustache, Calum said, 'If you think about it, this business of a fake makes it possible that the stereo sold in the pub by the scally might not be the same stereo that was stolen from the Merc. And if we admit to that possibility,' he went on, 'it seems logical to go one step further and conclude that the scally who sold the stereo that might not have come from the Merc, *might* not be the scally who stuck a knife in Silvester Laing.'

'Or,' I said, actually feeling my pulse quicken as I warmed to his theories, 'that the person who stuck a knife in Laing might not even have been a scally.'

'Somebody wanted it to look that way, right?' Sian said, and now her face was animated as she got caught up in the chase. 'Somebody stole the stereo, but then they *hired* a scally, gave him a cheap stereo, and sent him off to market.'

'A false trail has been laid,' Calum said, 'as the real perpetrator slinks away into the shadows.'

'So where's the fake stereo, the one containing the drugs?'

He blew smoke and squinted at me. 'Somebody's holding onto it, for any number of reasons, all of them worth a mint.'

'And that, surely,' I said, 'brings us back to the missing husband, the man who ordered a very special car.'

'Jason Bone,' Sian said – and my mobile rang.

Once again, it was Mike Haggard.

'Mike,' I said, putting weariness into my voice, 'it's a pleasant night, I've got company and I'm just finishing dinner—'

'Shut up.'

Sitting closest to me, Sian heard that, and froze.

'I told you to talk, listen, and walk away,' Haggard said, his voice grim. 'So now—'

'I listened, I walked away, I've not been back—'

'Will you shut up? I'll say it again: I asked you to walk away. Maybe I was wrong to do that, maybe not, but it was me brought you into the case so now it's only right you get the news from me.'

There was a heavy silence. I could hear Haggard breathing, something else, voices in the background.

'Jemima Laing's dead,' Haggard said. 'Her body was discovered an hour ago. She'd been beaten to death, Jack, in her own livin'-room; those plush carpets you walked on are soaked with wine and blood.'

chapter seven

'Who found her?'

'A neighbour. The front door was wide open, lights blazin', a mangy moggy sniffin' around. The neighbour kicked its arse, knocked, got no answer; went inside and called 999 on their phone when his hands'd stopped shakin'.' His face was grim. 'Even the fuckin' phone had blood on it, if you want a picture paintin'.'

'The only neighbours I know round here are the Bones.' I risked mentioning the name, half-expecting him to nod or ask me how I knew them – but it went over Haggard's harassed head without touching.

And then he surprised me. He said, 'D'you want to see her?'

I had vivid recollections of a flowing caftan that brought a splash of colour and tropical warmth into this house, but it was the memory of an intriguing woman with ice-blue eyes and the scent of her musk perfume as she moved close to me that lingered, and without speaking I shook my head, saw him shrug and drift away.

Blue lights flashed lazily. The crime scene was taped off. I turned away, wandered back down the road to my car and got in.

Calum had taken Sian back to his flat. I'd see them both there later, bring them up to date. Before that I had to decide whether to call on Sam Bone and her brother, if he was still there at her house. What for? Well, the commotion would surely have attracted their attention, the massive police presence and the killing that happened just a couple of days ago lead them to suspect a second. I wasn't sure if confirmation would ease her mind – this time the killer hadn't come straight from her house – or make her more nervous. And I wasn't sure if I should yet raise the possibility of Jason's being deeply involved. Or if she already suspected him. It must, surely, have crossed her mind.

I glanced at my watch. Close to midnight. What to do? I tapped the steering-wheel, started up, drove the short distance that took me across the road and up the gravelled drive to the house where security lights were a joke and a new Mercedes with gaping holes in its plush interior stood gathering dust in a garage with a shattered window.

I climbed out. Underfoot, gravel crunched. Behind me the flashing blue lights could be seen flickering high in the branches of the tall trees around the Laing house. The street's sodium lighting sent my shadow dancing in front of me as I climbed the steps beneath Sam Bone's petunias and trailing geraniums.

She answered my knock almost at once and I guessed she'd been watching my approach, the presence of police cars making her jumpy, the nightcap changed from Horlicks to something much stronger.

'Hello Sam.'

There was no response. She was asking me to protect her and she couldn't pay my fee and now I'd turned up on her doorstep with the police in force across the road, but even if she hadn't wanted to invite me in her curiosity overcame reluctance. So she stepped back wordlessly to let me by and the lemon-yellow kimono she wore whispered softly against my sleeve as I brushed close and I thought again of a caftan coloured like a tropical sunset, the sad widow who would wear it no more.

Yet even as I went into the warm, subdued lighting of the front room that had been tidied and restored by Sam and her brother I knew that horror and abhorrence were making me elegiac, turning fiction into fact. There had been no evidence of sadness in Jemima Laing. The woman whose husband had been both killer and killed had met the same horrible fate, and her death reinforced what I had suspected when she was alive: when she spoke to me her lips had been telling one story, her cold blue eyes another; for some reason that I was convinced was linked to a random killing, Jemima Laing had been bending the truth.

There was nobody in the living-room.

'He's at the club, Tommy is,' Sam said, anticipating my question as she followed me in. 'D'you want a drink, or what?'

She was holding a whisky glass of lead crystal. She must have been trembling: the ice in it was clinking faintly, like the background sound in a sleeping house when something in the fridge vibrates.

'I'll have some of that,' I said, indicating her glass. 'What's the name of Tommy's club?'

I followed her into the kitchen, watched her pour from the bottle that was on the table; took the drink from her with a smile of thanks.

'Night Owl,' she said, 'in Canning Street. Jason goes there a lot.' She was watching me.' 'D'you know it?'

I tasted the drink, shook my head. 'But Calum's bound to.'

She was already nodding impatiently, edgily.

'What's goin' on?'

Across the road, she meant. Her knuckles were white on the glass.

'Jemima Laing's dead,' I said, and one hand flew to her mouth as if jerked by string. 'She was murdered, Sam. But not stabbed. She was ...' I paused, shook my head. 'Let's say it was different, so it was almost certainly a different killer.'

'Well isn't that nice, now there's two of them out there.'

'Don't let it worry you. The first was random. This was either robbery gone wrong, or—'

'Or linked to her husband's gangland deals, or one of his shady pals decided to move in while the silk sheets were still warm, or—'

'That's enough.'

I went to her, took the glass from her unresisting hand and felt the tremor in her slim body, led her into the other room. Sat her down on the settee with its coarse throw. Switched on the electric fire's second bar. Gave her back her drink and sat down close to her in one of the chairs.

'I came here partly to see if you were all right, with all that kerfuffle over there; partly to let you know what I've been doing.'

'Go on.' She was cautious, but there was a little more light in her eyes as she watched me warily.

'I've found the garage in Old Swan that handled the stolen Merc. Got reasonable confirmation the car was ordered by your husband. He didn't ask for any old Mercedes, it had to be that one. And I think the two men I saw at the garage in Old Swan did the Park Road carjacking.'

She looked puzzled. 'So how's all this supposed to help me?'

'It puts me a step closer to the man the car was stolen from, a step closer to the men who broke into your house.'

She'd gone pale at the news of Jemima's death. Now her colour had improved, and she was sitting up straighter. She frowned, concentrating.

'It's not enough, is it. I mean, the car was delivered to my garage, so who the hell else could have ordered it. An' those fellers in Old Swan aren't goin' to name names, are they, so how does that put you close to the Merc's owner?'

'Yes, all right. Looked at from that angle I'm not closer – but I *am* more sure of where I'm going.' I smiled ruefully. 'What I haven't mentioned is that, because of another, unconnected police investigation, we've stumbled on a business dealing in car audio systems that's actually a pipeline, a filter – well, I don't know what they call it so let's just say it's a place where ordinary cars go to have their extraordinary cargo removed.'

And now I had got her interest – and she was very sharp. 'Like stereo systems,' she said, 'with something hidden inside them?'

I nodded.

'And that's why Jason wanted *this* car – something was hidden in the stereo?' She tilted her head. 'But if that's right, he wouldn't just leave it, would he? And listen, how come a scally just happens to smash my window and steal a stereo containing – what?'

'Drugs.'

'So how?'

'Think about it. Listen to what you've just said.'

'What? *What* did I say?' Her eyes were fastened intently on my face as she hung onto my every word.

'Come on,' I cajoled. 'You know it doesn't make sense for Jason to order that particular car, with what it contained, and then walk away. Yet he did. Leaving behind the valuable cargo he must have schemed to get hold of. And you know what happened next.' I waited, saw her mentally negotiating the logical steps that could lead her to the only possible conclusion, and said, 'Which means …?'

She could see it, now, but it was beyond belief. 'No. Because it still doesn't make sense. I mean, why would Jason do all that schemin' to get the stuff, the car and everything delivered, walk away – then come back and steal it?'

'I don't know.'

'But you think he did?'

I know she saw me nod, but I'd got her started and her eyes were distant because now she was with her husband as he sneaked up the edge of the gravelled drive and along the shadowy side of the garage to smash the window with a brick, undo the latch, climb in and moments later steal away into the wet night with a stereo whose contents might have a street value of a million pounds; cross the road towards the high hedges bordering the Laing house, draw near to the tall, gateless pillars and the mossy drive made slick by the rain and hear the sudden slap of running footsteps....

'He stabbed Silvester Laing, didn't he?' she said, aghast.

'If we're right,' I said, 'he must have done.'

'God!'

'Where is he, Sam?'

'What?' She shook her head. 'How the hell do I know?'

'Where did you go, together? Holidays. Weekends.'

She was dazed. 'I don't know. Anywhere. Nowhere.' She took a deep breath. 'We spent time in North Wales. He liked Bangor, the Lleyn Peninsula … the sea….'

The realization that her husband had probably murdered Jemima Laing had left her stunned. I picked up her empty glass, said firmly, 'Sit there, don't move,' and went into the kitchen. She'd put the whisky-bottle away. I found it in a high cupboard, unscrewed the top, paused to listen as I thought I heard the snarl of a car driving away then *did* hear the front door open and close. I looked at the wall clock; almost twelve; poured Sam's fresh drink, taking my time now, knowing it would be her brother and wanting her to break the news to him while she had him on his own. Listening to the murmur of voices I found a second glass, wondered if Tommy would appreciate a drink after a session at Night Owl, poured one anyway. I spent another three or four minutes wandering round; found some paprika Pringles; nibbled a few and almost choked, wasted more time snatching a hasty drink of water and wiping my eyes.

Then I carried the drinks through into a sudden heavy silence, placed Sam's on the mock-Indian coffee table in front of her.

She was sitting where I'd left her. Tommy Mack was slipping out of his black-leather bomber jacket. He tossed it onto a chair. Under it he again wore a white T-shirt. The front was smeared with blood.

He saw me looking at it, and his eyes crinkled.

'The Owl's like that,' he said. 'You go for a quiet drink and end up separatin' a couple of middleweight contenders.'

I handed him his drink. Finished mine.

'I'll be off, leave Sam to bring you up to date.'

'She's said enough. An' if it *was* that prick, Jason …' His face had hardened. 'So what's the next step?'

78

'For now, forget Jason. He caused your problems, but finding him won't stop them. So we pay Sound Bites a visit.'

'Have you given that any thought?'

'In what way?'

He sat down on the settee next to Sam, absently touched the back of the lemon kimono, rubbed his sister's shoulders as he tasted his drink.

'You're tellin' me this feller's into drugs, that's what this is all about. Fair enough, they've got to be carted around in something, he needs a status symbol and a new Merc beats a pushbike. But then he goes and loses it to a couple of carjackers. And when he does find it again, the best he can do is trash the house.'

'Right, go on.'

'For Christ's sake – what was your name again, Scott was it? Jesus, Scott, he'd traced the car, so when he got here he must've looked in the garage, maybe even climbed in through the broken window. And when he looks in his shiny Merc, the first thing he sees is the stereo's gone. Ripped out. So where does he look for it? In the fuckin' house.' He shook his head, pushed himself up off the settee, paced angrily towards the window, swung around with hands on hips. 'What the hell did he think happened? Somebody stole it, then gave it back? An' why didn't he take his Merc?'

'What would you have done?'

'What I would have done,' he said in a voice as brittle as glass, 'is made myself cosy in the house until she came in from work' – he jerked a thumb at Sam – 'then sat down with her over a cup of tea and asked her very nicely what she'd done with my fuckin' drugs.'

Neatly understated, and all the more chilling – and I knew he was right.

'The point being?'

'The point being,' Tommy Mack said, 'what I think we're dealin' with here is small-time crooks, Mickey Mouse suppliers, traffickers, whatever – and they're chasin' their own tails. They're lost, out of their depth, runnin' round in circles. So you do what you're supposed to do, you find them and then you help them out: you give the poor buggers what they want.'

'They could act first. You've painted the picture. What if they have a second shot at it, come after Sam on one of your poker nights?'

He grinned. 'I like that, second shot. What if Sam gets hers in first? She's well prepared.'

'Prepared how?'

'I know a feller who knows a feller. So now she's got a neat little pistol that'll blow a hole in their big ideas.'

'Illegal – but I'm not knocking it.' I looked at Sam. 'Do you agree with what Tommy suggested?'

She was already nodding. And calmly, coldly, she said, 'Yeah, he's right. When you find them, give them what they want. Give them Jason.'

chapter eight

Tuesday

When I got back to Calum's flat it was almost one in the morning, but if I'd expected dim lights and the soft breathing of two tired people in deep sleep I was mistaken. At his work-table, Calum was a bent figure under the concentrated light of the Anglepoise, smeared wire glasses slipping towards the end of his nose as he held a mounted figure and applied a No 1 brush laden with a colour carefully mixed from several Humbrol enamels to match the precise shade of the grey horses ridden by the Royal North British Dragoons.

Sian was curled up on the settee, on her lap a lever-arch file that I knew contained the scripts for the series of adventure and survival television shows she'd just completed. But completed didn't mean done with, or out of mind. They would be screened nationwide over the coming weeks and, like all perfectionists, she was still going over what she had written and performed when it was way too late for anything to be altered. It was a form of torment, mental torture that wouldn't ease until the series was finished and then only to metamorphose into something even more fiendish as she waited for the flood of letters and e-mails of criticism to come pouring in. That the radio broadcasts leading to her television series had earned nothing but praise was neither here nor there; she would be all aquiver at the possibility of being pilloried and, fighter that she was, she was already girding her loins.

Neither of them had looked up as my key turned in the lock and I walked in. I made my way through the twin sweat shops of silent toil, dropped my coat on my personal leather chair in passing and continued to the kitchen doorway. And waited.

Calum looked up first.

'Aye,' he said, his black eyes twinkling. 'Coffee and toast, my man. Two sugars in one, thick butter on the other. And don't get confused.'

Sian was bleary-eyed. 'Jack,' she said, and yawned. 'Is it that time?'

'What time?'

'Supper.'

'Try breakfast. An early one.'

She smiled, and the room lit up. 'Whatever. But make it two of what Calum just ordered.'

It took me ten enjoyable minutes in the warm kitchen where Satan prowled and purred like a sinuous shadow, the coffee perked with a rich gurgling, and six slices of toast popped up like tanned jack-in-the-boxes leaping from a miniature trampoline and threatened to set the smoke alarm shrieking. In the end the small banquet reached completion neatly and synchronously in a way only achieved by good luck or long experience, so how I managed it was anybody's guess. When I carried through the steaming tray the Anglepoise had been switched off, a weary Scotsman was stretched out in an easy-chair with eyes closed and ankles crossed – I think that's right – and the lever-arch file had been pushed onto the floor to be replaced in Sian's lap by a scarred black moggy who thought he'd gone to a pussy heaven.

'Wow,' Sian said, and wriggled into a position from which she could eat and drink without disturbing the sleeping cat. I put the tray on the coffee-table, slid two small tables from a nest and dished out the goodies, then sat down in the leather chair and started munching on hot buttered toast that coated chin and arteries with shiny fat but gave us all a brief taste of Elysium.

But all things luscious must come to an end.

'I believe you've looked closely upon death,' Calum said. He put down his plate with a sigh that was satisfaction mixed with regret, settled back clutching his coffee and waited expectantly.

'No, I passed on it without reluctance,' I said, pulling a face. 'Jemima Laing died violently, bludgeoned not stabbed, a lot of blood. I left the gruesome details to Haggard and Vine.'

'Poor soul,' Sian said. 'She asked you to look for her husband's killer, but wound up dead.'

'Mm.' I sipped coffee, thought about Tommy Mack. 'I called in on Sam Bone. She was badly shaken, ready for bed but unable to settle while the police were across the road. Her brother came in later. He had a bloodstain on his T-shirt.' I paused for effect. 'He saw me staring at it, put it down to a fracas in Night Owl; said he got it separating a couple of drunken brawlers.'

'Did he now,' Calum said softly. 'Well that doesn't gel with my intimate knowledge of the club. It's a refined and venerable establishment – well, maybe just old. But the bouncer's seven feet tall and the wee fellow really cuts a dash in a tux.'

'So you're saying we should treat Tommy Mack's explanation with some scepticism?'

'Indeed,' Calum said. He thought for a moment, then said, 'Are you suggesting Mack murdered Jemima Laing?'

I shrugged. 'He went out. Jemima Laing was bludgeoned to death. A while later he came home sporting fresh bloodstains.'

'Have you checked the timing?' Sian said.

'What, when Tommy went out, time of death and so on?' I shook my head.

'Gut feeling then,' Calum said. 'If you want to check his alibi, I know someone who can get us signed into the Owl.'

'Tell me it's Manny Yates.'

'It's Manny Yates.'

I rolled my eyes. 'Well, he'll probably be his usual self:

obnoxiously useful.' I paused. 'Who's this bloke you know at
Sound Bites?'

Calum grunted. 'Tony Pope. Army radio op turned civvy
hi-fi whiz-kid.'

'And will he give us customers' names? Come up with the
man who used to have a black Merc?'

'No chance.'

'Why not? It's a genuine business, everything there will be
legal, at least on the surface.'

'And on the books they keep for show, all there for VAT
man or police, if they ask. But why should he tell you?'

'All right, so we break in.'

'Of course.'

'In darkness.'

'How else.'

'Tomorrow night.' I looked at my watch. 'Tonight.'

'Sooner the better.'

'You two,' Sian said, pushing the protesting cat off her lap
and climbing to her feet, 'are like two drunks at the end of a
pub-crawl. For Christ's sake go to bed, both of you.'

'And you?'

'Get me a blanket. The settee's fine.'

'Your legs are too long. You can have Calum's spare bed.'

'That would be kicking you out. I'm happy curled up
here.'

We were all up on our feet, so tired we were swaying like
saplings in a summer breeze. Calum flapped a hand and
headed for his room. He was stopped short by Sian.

'Before you go, here's a couple of points you live wires
may have missed.'

She was standing tall and slim. Several strands of blonde
hair had worked their way loose. Her fingers were tucked in
the back of her jeans. Our attention caught and held, she
said, 'First of all, breaking into Sound Bites is a crime, and
we all know Calum's walking a tightrope. Secondly, if
Sound Bites *is* some form of pipeline, there must be big-
time drug-dealers at the other end. And now that a valuable

consignment's gone missing, I think those dangerous men are going to be very, very annoyed.'

When I did eventually totter from the living-room after draping a blanket snugly over Sian and kissing her a lingering good night, sleep wouldn't come and I eventually found myself lying beneath a rumpled duvet watching a misty yellow dawn break.

We'd shared a bed several times, me and my Soldier Blue, but on more than one occasion the initiative had been hers, the arrangement on her terms. I don't know if that said I was an old-fashioned prude, showed commendable concern for propriety and her feelings, or was just a silly old slowcoach, but over the weeks since the Gault case we'd been apart more than together.

During that case, there had been some friction between us. I remember one late night in a pub out Hale way when the moon rising over the Welsh hills glistened on the Mersey and we'd walked across a gravelled forecourt like strangers, our relationship close to breaking. But isn't it always the case that the serendipitous influence of strangers can intervene to show you the folly of your ways? That night the differences that were driving us apart had been laid bare as childish petulance by the antics of a drunk with a drooping cigarette clinging precariously to a bar-stool, and a marvellous pianist, a huge black woman with hair as fiery as a Vesuvius eruption on a dark night who played jazz classics while sipping delicately from a cocktail-glass.

So we'd come out of that one unscathed. Now, as the darkness of another long night was softened by the approach of a soothing ochre dawn, I came round to the consoling realization that what had been keeping us apart was not the bleak winds of change but the pressure of work. Since Gault I'd been totally immersed in the production of toy soldiers from my stone workshop beneath the high peaks of the Glyders, Sian somewhere halfway between radio and television, Liverpool and Manchester, but rarely where she could be pinned down.

Now the persistence of some distant Gibraltarian collectors and the more relaxed work-schedule of a woman weary of teaching grown men with soft and lily-white hands how to skin rabbits and light fires with damp wood had brought us together, once again working as a team with the unpredictable but irreplaceable Calum Wick.

The last time the three of us had hunted a killer, Sian had been the one to suffer. From the way this case was progressing the dangers could be much greater, our evil opponents more numerous, their deadly underworld skills professionally honed.

If that had been spoken aloud – if Sian had heard it – she would once again have scoffed with gentle good-humour at the spectacle of a grown man playing Knight Templar riding to defend the under classes from the forces of evil. The simple truth was that this time I would be ready. I would make sure that, if Sian Laidlaw was an active part of the investigation, she would use her intelligence, street savvy and plain old common sense without exposing herself to danger.

Well, not too much.

And from this time on – for always, if I had my way; and maybe now it was not Knight Templar I was playing but the soppy romantic lead in something written by Noël Coward – from this time on, we would be together.

What do they say nowadays? In your dreams?

In the morning the togetherness was a threesome of unkempt, baggy-eyed musketeers, two of whom emerged from bedrooms to find the third in an awkward Z-bend under a blanket on the too-short settee with a black cat curled up snugly behind her knees. As doors clicked the cat awoke, rolled, stretched, yawned, hit the floor with a thump and padded towards the kitchen. Calum had already veered sluggishly in that direction like a junk in a heavy swell; I stood waiting for the sounds of tap-water gushing into a battered coffee-percolator and wondering if that, or anything, would wake Sian.

The answer came with the faint, distant bleeping of my mobile. One blue eye opened, a second followed, and with a petulant grumble the intrepid survival expert swung her legs off the cosy makeshift bed to sit tangled in the blanket like a tousle-haired toddler waiting for instructions. I grinned, patted her cheek, twisted away as one bare foot jabbed at my thigh, and headed back to the spare bedroom to take the call.

Not Haggard, this time. Gibraltar. Nine o'clock here, my head still too fuddled to work out whether the time difference put the caller ahead or behind.

'Hey, Jack Scott of bloody Magna Carta,' Gibraltarian lawyer Tony Macedo said. 'I rang your house, got the answer machine, now what the hell took you so long to the mobile, eh?'

'Long story,' I said, 'and I'm too tired to remember most of it.' I braced myself mentally, put the question. 'You're after your Scots Greys, right?'

'Of course. Me, Charlie, Rick; all of us. The exhibition is too damn close now. Raise my spirits, Jack, tell me they're on their way, we'll get them tomorrow, maybe the next day?'

'Maybe next week.'

He groaned. 'This is not Magna Carta I'm talking to, Jack, this is some crap firm peddling inferior figures and trying to stall because they're going bust.'

'No.' I could hear the coffee bubbling; would willingly swear I could smell it. 'I apologize again, Tony, but you know what caused the delay.' I hesitated. 'Calum's hard at work now. And I repeat my promise to you: if it gets too late for parcel post, I'll carry the box onto a Monarch flight and deliver it personally.'

We chatted for a couple of minutes, Tony looking for crumbs of comfort, me racking my brain for ways to speed up delivery by round-the-clock painting done while the two skilled artisans were breaking into car audio businesses in the dead of night and getting sloshed gathering information in up-market night-clubs named after a nocturnal bird of prey.

Was that, I wondered, a harbinger of doom?

Over breakfast Sian listened while I discussed with Calum the work he had still to do to complete the Scots Greys. Bulk painting of horses and uniforms was still not finished. After that came the fine-detail work that was Magna Carta's claim to fame but so time-consuming and labour-intensive that riches down that artistic road would always be beyond my grasp.

But today the lanky Scot could put in a lot of hours. The raid on Sound Bites was planned for around eleven that night, the visit to Night Owl immediately afterwards if we managed to stay clear of the law. That meant if I didn't pick up a brush and work alongside Calum – and I knew damn well he wouldn't let me – I also had a clear day. Sian had figured that out, and was watching me.

'It's Meg's day off. We thought we might have coffee on Allerton Road, do some shopping.'

I thought for a moment then nodded. 'I'll hang around here, later on call on Mike Haggard.'

Calum was dubious. 'For what? With tonight's adventures on your mind you'll walk in on him looking like a guilty schoolboy.'

'Businessman stressed out by bolshie highlander. I'll look harassed, play on his sympathy, pick his brains.'

He still wasn't convinced. 'I thought we had this sussed. Sound Bites to find the Merc's owner. Night Owl for Mack's alibi.'

'A man who murdered in Wales is himself murdered in Liverpool. It was Haggard's lot that found his prints and there could be a development.'

Calum shrugged, already looking towards the lamp poised over the Scots Greys and hooking his wire glasses over his ears.

I took a taxi to Admiral Street police station and caught Haggard on the way out. He told me he could give me five minutes but I sensed a willingness to talk, probably because he wanted to check on my movements, issue more warnings.

The nearest unoccupied space was an empty interview room. The chairs were hard, the air like bad breath, the table between us as stark as a deserted battlefield.

'So what's this about?' Haggard said.

'Catching up. I walked away from Jemima Laing because that's what you wanted. She'd asked me to find out why her husband died. In twenty-four hours I got nowhere, and now she's dead and there's nobody to tell. I'd like to know why.'

He took a deep breath, searched for his cigarettes, lit one.

'There was no break-in. The door was open when the neighbour got there, but it'd been left like that when the killer walked out. Two wine glasses on that fuckin' big coffee table....' He blew a stream of smoke. 'Suggests she knew the killer – right?'

'Man or woman?'

'The murder weapon was a lead-crystal decanter.'

'I saw it, drank of the exotic liqueur with Jemima.'

'Right. So you know it was heavy, easy to hold. A man or woman could strike one hell of a blow with a lazy swing.'

'Fingerprints?'

'Not on record.'

'Wouldn't they tell you the sex?'

His eyes had narrowed, and not from the smoke. 'You're diggin'.'

I hesitated. 'I'm going to Night Owl tonight. Depending on the answers to questions I'm going to ask, I might have something for you.'

He glowered. 'These questions're about a man?'

I nodded.

'Name?'

'If I get the answer I'm expecting, he'll be in the clear and you won't need to know.'

'So why's he a suspect?'

'When I saw him, he had blood on his T-shirt.'

'What time?'

'Soon after I left the Jemima Laing crime scene.'

'Where?'

I shook my head.

His hand on the table was a white-knuckled fist. He wanted to throw his weight around, but knew he'd get nowhere.

'Sound Bites,' I said. 'Definitely crooked? Drugs in one end, out the other?'

'You're diggin' again, and I've had enough.'

He was up on his feet, mashing out the cigarette.

'That's a yes?'

'You're the PI,' he said, 'so go and investigate.'

And, somehow, I got the horrible feeling he knew that's exactly what we were about to do.

I went back to Grassendale with nothing new under my PI hat but an additional worry for the cat burglar I was soon to become. Had Haggard read me like a book? Would he react and ruin our plans?

Time continued to pass slowly. Painting that went on until late in the afternoon was followed by a dinner of three-cheese pizza washed down with stale Merlot followed by coffee and more painting which led to some leisurely lounging that brought with it the dangers of drowsiness.

Sian had returned and agreed that as the male members of the team would be out late, tonight was a good night to return to her bed at Meg Morgan's. Calum and I dressed in dark clothes, soft shoes, debated over masks and coshes and decided against. Awaiting us there was probably a locked metal filing-cabinet. I suggested a tyre lever might make a suitable key. Calum found a Maglite to search for clues. I thought we might need something to carry them in, and put a folded Tesco's plastic bag in my pocket.

All this, as you've probably realized, was us generally pissing about to hide chronic nervousness.

But then, inevitably and soundlessly, night fell.

chapter nine

Sound Bites Audio Systems was located in a side street halfway up Park Road in Liverpool's Dingle, the premises a converted concrete double garage up a wide alley where customers could park their cars. Double timber doors with a big shiny padlock, a pitched slate roof, windows of armoured frosted glass on one side, power and telephone cables drooping like ancient clotheslines from a creosoted pole with enough carvings to qualify as an Indian totem.

Parking was fine for daytime customers, but what about my Audi Quatro when we were about to indulge in some innocent night-time breaking and entering? The best bet, according to Calum, was far enough away not to attract attention, but not too far to be beyond easy scampering distance if we had to make a hurried escape.

I chose the public car-park below High Park Street, reasoning that if a classy motor was going to attract attention it should be in an open space where vandals were less likely to launch an attack. If that was my idea of reasoning, Calum informed me, he'd eat his wee bonnet for breakfast. On that optimistic note I shoved a short tyre lever up my sleeve and we walked back down the hill, sloped gaily into a side street and, like smoke whipped by a gusting wind, we were gone.

We slipped silently into the upper end of the wide alleys, stumbling over the uneven surface, slinking in the shadows along the grotty six-foot brick wall with a rasp of clothing. From an open upper window Robbie Williams was baying at the rising moon. A siren wailed in the distance.

Apprehension causing the skin to prickle. Sound Bites loomed. We were approaching the side with windows, but hadn't yet decided how to get in. Smashing armoured glass with cold steel would be like breaking bottles in a tin shed. The door would be quieter – but what about alarms?

'None that I can see,' Calum said quietly.

'Maybe they rely on insurance.'

'No. If they're baddies they'll be left well alone.'

'Makes it easy for us.'

'Unless,' Calum said, 'there's someone in there,' and I realized that through the nearest window a faint light glimmered.

'Shut that bloody row,' Calum said and, as if he'd reached up and yanked the plug, Robbie was choked off in mid-yodel. We slowed our breathing, listened with ears pressed against the ex-garage's cold concrete walls.

Nothing.

'Security light,' Calum said, and his teeth flashed white. 'Time for the key.'

We opted for the window. Calum whipped off his sweater. He held it as a pad. With several swings of the tyre lever I smashed glass and wire reinforcing. Within thirty seconds we had scrambled over the sill and were inside.

Both of us were nervous, breathing hard. Broken glass crunched underfoot. There was a strong smell of electrical appliances. With the doors closed, it caught at the throat. The security light was a 25-watt bulb in a cheap table lamp on an old desk. It cast a weak pool of light that faded into shadow before it reached the walls.

The double garage had been divided equally into an office and an open area, flanked by banks of metal shelving holding boxed audio equipment. Cars could be driven in when the weather was bad. Or when there was the need for secrecy; you don't merrily remove hard drugs from stereo equipment, out in the open, in broad daylight.

We were interested in the office.

'Basic,' Calum said. He was donning his sweater, picking at glittering shards of glass.

'Mm.' As well as the old desk with the feeble light, index-card boxes and telephone/fax there was another holding a computer, monitor and printer. Tall shelves were stacked with catalogues, instruction manuals, electrical gadgets and miscellaneous radio speakers trailing snipped-off wire. There were two green, four-drawer filing-cabinets.

'Ahah,' I said softly.

Calum was in shadow by the shelves, sniffing at the speakers. He turned.

'Forget those, go the easy way.'

'We need a name—'

'That's right enough,' he said, 'so why don't we spend a few minutes looking through those index cards.'

Cursing my own stupidity, I flipped open one of the two W.H. Smith plastic boxes and held the first card under the desk light. It bore the customer's name and address, telephone number, vehicle make, year, model and colour. I would have to flick through them all, looking for a black Mercedes.

But if there was more than one …

I thought hastily. 'In Sam's garage. You took photographs—'

'Side on.' He was catching on fast. 'No room in there to include number plates.'

'And you don't remember the Merc's registration number?'

'If I did, what use would it be?'

'Without it I can't find the right car. With it, I flip through these cards.…'

The sardonic amusement in his eyes told me my thinking was awry. I backtracked mentally, suddenly saw where I'd gone wrong and shook my head.

'The Merc was stolen. The plates will have been changed.'

Calum tossed one of the speakers aside and came away from the shelves.

'Have you ever met two such incompetents? Find the Merc, you said, that'll give us the man's name. Break in, you said, and I agreed and here we are only we're looking like a right couple of lemons. All we've done is put our reputations at risk breaking into this place. We haven't the foggiest idea how to locate the car, never mind the bloody owner.'

I did some fast thinking. We couldn't find the Merc's owner without the original registration number. It would be printed on a card, staring us in the face – but we wouldn't recognize it. DI Mike Haggard had shown an interest in the Merc, but *he* couldn't come up with the number because the only witness to the carjacking—

'Stan Jones.'

'What about him?'

'He was in Park Road when the Merc was stolen.'

Calum grinned. He pulled out his mobile, checked the signal, and wandered closer to the window to make the call. He got through at once, spoke in a low voice, laughed a couple of times, then hardened his tone. He did some more talking, brittle, laced with menace, listened, looked over at me and shook his head – and suddenly his bearded face was bathed in brilliant white light as a car turned into the top of the alley and came rocking and bouncing towards us.

I thought Haggard, police, cursed the big DI's astuteness as I held a hand up and stared into the blinding lights.

Calum cut the call, slid the mobile into his pocket. Headlights drew near, swept blindingly across the side of the building, the gaping window. The empty frame's edging of jagged glass glittered. I thought I heard someone's muffled yell. The car's horn blasted and it passed in a rush, its slipstream buffeting. Stones peppered the doors like pellets from a shotgun. Tyres squealed as brakes were slammed on at the lower end of the alley and the wheels locked. Then the engine kicked into a roar that rapidly faded into a receding drone as the driver pulled out into the next side-street and accelerated away.

'Get the number?'

'No.'

I stared. 'So what now?'

'Go through the cards. Look for black Mercs.'

'Note the addresses, then knock on doors?' I nodded, seeing no other way.

'But make it fast. I was caught in the headlights – and I'd like to know why that car came down this particular alley.'

'Joy-riders.'

'Maybe. But what if they were coming here, about to pull in when they saw me? Right now they're probably on the phone to Tony Pope. And they'll be back.'

I was listening, feeling danger and crackling tension in my increased heart-rate and shallow breathing. I dropped into one of the tatty swivel-chairs and began working through the first box of index cards.

In addition to names, addresses and make and model of car there were dates and details of what had been fitted or repaired. The cars worked on covered the whole range of popular makes. As I searched I caught myself speculating on how many of the routine tasks masked Tony Pope's dealings in drugs.

Calum had pulled out another chair and was working through the second box. I finished, sat back. Watched him reach the last divider, look at the single card filed under Z.

'Nothing?'

He shook his head. There was something in his eyes. 'One or two Mercs. Old models. Wrong colour. What about you?'

'I didn't find anything,' I said. 'But you know that, just as I know you *have* come across something.'

'Look at the dates. There's nothing more recent than the year 2000.' His eyes drifted lazily towards the other desk.

I sighed.

'Computer?'

'Aye. At a guess I'd say he waited for the millennium, then moved all his records from index cards to disk.'

'And we can't get into the computer without a password.'

'If I know Tony Pope, he'll have nothing on the hard drive, everything on CD-Rs, the CDs locked away in a safe – at home.'

'Why didn't we think of this last night?'

He shrugged. 'We were too tired. All of us. Bad time to make plans.'

'The inability to organize a piss-up in a brewery springs to mind,' I said.

And after that there was a long silence.

Eventually I said, 'What have we been assuming? That the Merc owner's a dealer, he imports drugs then brings them here? I admit to knowing nothing about it, but surely a dealer would be carrying more than a few little bags of the white stuff.'

'Indeed he would,' Calum said. And after a moment's thought he said, 'So the movement must be the other way. The drugs are smuggled into the country in bulk by a big-time dealer. Then they're brought here to be handed out by Pope.'

'To pushers like the owner of the Merc,' I said. I shook my head. 'The Merc that was carjacked. Stan neglected to tell us which way it was travelling on Park Road. It wasn't stolen before it got here, it was on its way *out* with its cargo; it was heading downhill towards the Dingle.'

With a gesture of disgust Calum tossed the useless box of index cards into an oil drum being used as a bin.

It hit with a clatter.

And almost drowned the sound of the car purring into the bottom end of the alley.

I stood up, mouth suddenly dry.

'Time to go.'

But, as usual, Calum had beaten me to it. I couldn't remember blinking, but he'd kicked over his chair and was at the window with a long leg hooked over the sill. And then I was crowding him, urging him on. We tumbled out of the window, hit the ground staggering into a loping run. Then we were sprinting up the alley, our long shadows cast by the car's halogen lights racing ahead of us and behind us nothing but silence.

We hit the side-street still running, slowed to a walk, turned onto an almost deserted Park Road.

'It's best we split up,' I said. 'You head down the hill, I'll get the car and pick you up.'

'They're not coming after us, Jack.'

'Nevertheless.'

He nodded, clapped my arm and set off. I crossed the road, looked back once and saw nobody coming out of the side street and quickly cut across the car park to the Quatro.

Two minutes later I'd picked up Calum opposite South Hill Road and we were taking the long, sweeping bend at the Dingle and accelerating up Belvidere Road.

Wednesday

The arrangement with Manny Yates was that we'd arrive at Night Owl, give his name to the doorman and Manny would come out to sign us in. But our thinking was still up the creek because we strolled up to the door after midnight looking like a couple of footpads who'd walked nonchalantly through the side of a greenhouse. The beefy character with gold earrings, shaven head and ears like chewed pink bubble gum who glared at us through the hatch was not impressed. Standing in a vestibule that smelt of tomcats and mould, I used my mobile to reach Manny who eventually escorted us past a resentful doorman.

Entering Night Owl's main room was like opening an oven door but stepping into a crumbling stately home. A dozen or so drinkers were breathing air that was a fug of hot smoked alcohol. Carpets were red Axminster worn thin. Crystal chandeliers dangled from ornate roses threatening to part company from a nicotine-stained ceiling. Deep-dadoed walls were hung with gloomy Victorian oil-paintings depicting moustached men wearing medals and swords, shaggy Highland cattle hock-deep in misty lochs.

A number of panelled doors led into unseen rooms steeped in mystery. The murmur of conversation was secretive enough for a gathering of spies.

'Over there,' Manny said.

He'd come out to meet us from a table under a wall light fashioned from an old gas-bracket. On the way back to it he stopped at the curved oak bar and grabbed a tray of drinks. He must have ordered when I bleeped his mobile: a bottle of the Macallan, three glasses and an ice bucket. I hoped the wallet he took for its daily walk had started out fat.

'You look like a couple of fuckin' Sicilian bandits,' he said as we settled and he poured. 'What's goin' on?'

I accepted a drink, sipped with relish. 'Alibi checking.'

'Whose?'

'Tommy Mack.'

Manny was puffing on the ubiquitous thin cigar. Waistcoat buttons were threatening to pop and fly into the chandeliers. His fat face was a ball of glistening dough but his eyes were sparkling windows to a brain like Deep Blue.

'Poker player,' he said. 'If it was Monday, he was 'ere, in the back room.'

'Times?'

'Serious stuff. The game would've started in the mornin', players comin' an' goin'. Tommy would've sat in, stayed until he was skint.'

'That's what I need to know. I was in Sam Bone's kitchen pouring her a drink when he arrived home. That was close to midnight. By taxi it would take him, what, fifteen minutes from here to Woolton?'

Manny nodded, then called out to a bald, unshaven man wearing wrap-around aviator shades and sitting on a padded stool with his elbows on the bar.

'Hey, Willie, what time did Tommy pack in on Monday?'

'Half eleven.'

'Certain?'

Around the cigarette dangling from lips like a slit in thin rubber he said, 'We shared a taxi, argued the toss along Princes Road an' then I got out at the park gates.'

'So there we are,' Calum said. 'There's no way he could have killed the woman.'

A BEWILDERMENT OF CROOKS

'You could've asked me about Tommy over the phone,' Manny said knowingly. 'There's somethin' you're workin' your way around to, isn't there?'

My partner in crime leaned back, lit up a cheroot. The smoke drifted towards the pall hanging under the yellowing ceiling.

'You're right, there is more,' I said. 'When we were talking in the American bar on Sunday, I mentioned Sam Bone.'

'Yeah, right.'

'You didn't tell me you knew her husband.'

'Jason?' Manny grinned. 'You never asked.'

'And now I am. He comes in here, doesn't he? What's he like, who does he talk to?'

'Nice feller. Skint most of the time, but if there's hard drinkin' and a kitty on the table he's never shy. Who does he talk to …?' He twisted heavily in his seat, looked around, indicated a table near to one of the closed doors. Three men were drinking shorts and playing a game of cards.

'Vick Valentine's one. He's not in tonight, but that's where he'd be. He's a stocky feller with a neat vandyke beard, always wears a dove-grey suit an' a cravat, got a manner as arrogant as a preenin' peacock.' He grinned. 'Usually loses, and you should see 'im sweat.' He nodded towards the bar. 'Hard to believe but Billie Tobin, that scruffy bastard, he's one of Valentine's mates.'

'So who is he?'

'Vick? He comes in, plays cards, goes home. By profession he's a sawbones or a GP.'

Calum cocked an eyebrow at me.

'On the face of it, a wasted visit.'

I looked at Manny. 'Does that sum it up?'

'I think it depends on how you view Vick, your friendly GP. This is not gospel, but there have been rumours.'

'Like?'

'Well, like certain people go to 'im to get certain kinds of prescription.'

I thought for a moment. 'How often do you come here?'

99

'Two or three nights a week, regular as clockwork.'

'When did you last see Jason Bone?'

'Couple of weeks ago.'

'And when was that black Merc stolen?'

Now his eyes narrowed. 'I already told you that. An' I can't believe where this is goin'.'

'You'd better. In that ordinary, strapped man's unremarkable garage a most remarkable car is gathering dust.'

'And where's Bone?'

'Gone. Hasn't been home for two weeks.'

Manny reached for his glass, tossed back the Macallan in a way no man should treat an aged single malt and swiftly poured another.

'Right,' he said, mashing out his cigar. 'Tell Uncle Manny.'

I told him of a rainy night when a stereo was ripped out of a car, a fatal knifing by the thief when he was tackled. Of an elegant woman living in style who became a widow and wanted to find out why her husband died. Another younger woman, with a stolen Mercedes she knew nothing about standing in a garage with a shattered window, who was also minus a husband but more worried about the strangers who had walked in and wrecked her house. And I told him how the elegant widow had been beaten to death, and hours later the second woman's brother had come home with blood on his T-shirt.

'Tommy Mack?' Manny said. 'I didn't know he was her brother – but we learn something every day.'

I nodded. 'He said he got the bloodstain separating a couple of drunks who came to blows in this room. Calum thinks not.'

'No chance, not in here,' Manny shook his head. 'Go on.'

'The Merc stolen in Park Road went through a process of change in a garage in Old Swan. Sam knows nothing about it, thinks it was probably stolen at the request of Jason – but he's missing so we can't ask him. An unrelated discussion with DI Mike Haggard then suggested a link between the Mercedes, the stolen stereo, an audio business also in Park Road.'

'Sound Bites,' Manny said. 'Involved in drug traffickin'.'

Calum was busy pouring himself another Macallan, safe in the knowledge that I'd drive him home. Manny was leaning back in his chair, ash on his shirt-front, sweat shining like thin snail trails in the folds of his double chins.

I said: 'What do you think?'

'Tell Sam Bone to move,' Manny said. 'If you're talkin' drugs in stereos goin' through Sound Bites an' a loaded stereo's gone missin' an' they've searched her house and found nothin' – they'll be back.'

'Tommy's with her.'

'Big deal. What's he going to do, stay awake day an' night?'

'He's a tough-looking character; he'll do his best. But what he suggested was I find the men hounding them, and toss them a bone.'

Manny chuckled in delight. 'Yeah, right, her missin' husband – and she agrees?'

'All for it.'

'Then do it – if you're dead certain Jason's guilty – but in the meantime tell her to move out. Stay with Tommy, anybody, but well away from that house.'

'I'll phone her first thing—'

'Now.'

He was right, of course. I pulled out my mobile, and as the bald derelict in the shades left the bar and came over to the table to talk to Manny on his way out I got through to a sleepy Sam Bone. Told her of the danger. Told her that a man wiser than me was insisting she go somewhere safe. And when I put the phone down I had her agreement.

'She'll move in with Tommy,' I told Manny as Tobin drifted away and went out.

'An' what's your next move?'

'Find the owner of the Merc before he twigs where Sam's gone.'

'Any clues?'

I shook my head. 'We broke into Sound Bites looking for names, but ...'

'You couldn't get into the computer.'

'My God,' Calum breathed, 'I told you there was someone outside watching us—'

'Piss off,' Yates said, grinning. 'Everyone's got them, common sense isn't it – or did you bust in there expectin' a nice easy rolodex?' He studied our faces, said, 'Christ, you did, didn't you. But didn't you think it through? Like, if there was a card index of some kind, how would you have known the right Merc? Or the right man?'

'You *should* have been with us,' I said gloomily.

'*Before* we set out on that crazy expedition,' Calum said.

Leaving Calum and Manny to work on the Macallan I wandered to the bar, all too aware that I'd be driving back to Grassendale through deserted streets where policemen lurked. I called for a pint of water with ice, turned to look for enlightenment in the club that with its gathering aura of gloom now more than ever resembled a crumbling aristo-cratic pile – and my mobile bleeped.

This time it was a voice from the faraway hills.

I listened keenly, grunted noncommittally to mask my intense interest, agreed with feigned reluctance to a deliber-ately half-hearted suggestion, and switched off.

It was almost two in the morning.

I drank the full pint of water, left the ice to melt, went back to the table wiping my chin and told Calum we were going to Wales.

We left Manny to finish off the whisky and I drove away from Night Owl. I crawled uneasily through Liverpool's brightly lit streets, considered the danger of being stopped by the law greatly reduced when I was beyond Halewood, and from there settled down grimly to a hectic drive that would take little more than an hour. My loyal Highlander was stretched out on the back seat, his snores like an old bagpipe's cracked drone.

In daylight the journey from Liverpool to Alun's office in Bethesda is half misery, half delight as the drab industrial landscape bordering the Mersey changes gradually to the hills and valleys that always sing a welcome. At night-time every mile of it becomes a trip through a changing wonderland, Runcorn bridge's steel arches soaring against the stars, Stanlow oil-refinery an island of jewels in a flat sea of fields, the eventual approach to mountains silver tipped by moonlight like something observed by Alan Quartermain during his trek to King Solomon's Mines.

Half an hour later I was quite thirsty. Thirty minutes after that I would have sold Calum Wick for a single suck on a damp sponge, and when a match flared behind me and cigar smoke curled about my head I could cheerfully have opened the door and kicked him out onto the hard shoulder.

Only by then there wasn't one. I was speeding around the curves of the A5 beyond Llyn Ogwen, below me the lights of Bethesda were twinkling when the road ahead straightened enough for me to see, and before we reached them I had pulled into the driveway of the house that nestled in the lee of Carnedd Dafydd and life-giving liquid was but a few short steps away.

'Coffee,' Alun Morgan said when he opened the door. 'Strong and black, a dessertspoon of sugar in each and at the very least I'll know I'm talking to a couple of sweet-tempered, wide-awake drunks.'

We stumbled into the tidy hall, blinking in the bright light, and were directed to his office as he disappeared into the kitchen to produce the promised treacly brew. Calum had met the detective sergeant, but it was his first time in the Welshman's house. I saw him glance at the shiny wall-board where two languages fought for supremacy, switch his gaze to the fine oak desk that challenged my own for chaos, then sink into a chair against a wall where bookcases held hefty volumes on law that were outnumbered by others on whose covers bearded men in rags clung by their fingernails from impossibly sheer crags.

The coffee came swiftly, was as swiftly tasted. Alun went behind the desk and sank into his chair, swivelled restlessly, grey eyes brooding. I took my usual chair at an angle in front of the desk. Placed my mug against a precarious ledge of manila folders. Looked at Calum.

'The good life,' I said.

'Convince me, not him,' Alun Morgan said bitterly. 'I've been up all bloody night.'

And it was as if realization of the hours he was putting in turned the key that started the engine and set the wheels in motion.

'This business in Liverpool,' he said. 'Tell me where you're up to.'

I filled him in swiftly, taking him from what I knew of the theft of the Mercedes right through the series of events culminating in our Sound Bites disaster.

'I asked you out here,' he said, 'to see if between us we could square a right cow of a circle. It seems there's links everywhere, but figuring out what they all mean is a bugger of a job.' He looked at Calum. 'Has he told you Silvester Laing almost certainly committed murder here in Conwy?'

'Briefly, no details,' Calum said.

'Didn't have any,' I said. 'All I know is his prints were on a knife found on a Gibraltar-registered yacht owned by a company with an offshore account.'

'Link Associates,' Alun Morgan said. 'Drugs, money-laundering ...' He shrugged.

'Manny Yates came up with that name,' I said. 'Laing was a partner in Link. So who owns the yacht?'

'Link's other half,' Morgan said. 'Ed Carney.'

'And who died?'

'Tony Carney. Ed's son.'

I stared. 'That was Wednesday, you said. By midnight Saturday, Laing was dead.'

'A random killing,' Morgan said, and his grey eyes sparkled a challenge at us over his steaming coffee-mug.

There was a pause as we chewed over developments, considered causes and consequences, tried to anticipate what lay ahead. I knew that in major crimes involving drug-trafficking or money-laundering operations I was out of my depth – but that was of no great concern. With Jemima dead my priority was locating Sam Bone's persecutors and getting them off her back; major crime I could safely leave to DI Morgan in Wales, DI Haggard in Liverpool.

But what if major crime and Sam's bogeymen were linked?

'It seems to me,' I said, 'that Link Associates was a smooth-running criminal organization operating under the umbrella of a legal company. Then something went badly wrong. For a reason we don't know the first partner's son was murdered by the second partner. Then there's a bizarre coincidence. At a time when the first partner was almost certainly simmering with hatred and thoughts of getting even with the second partner, a random killer does the job for him.'

'If we can accept that,' Morgan said. 'The word random came from the lips of a woman herself now dead, so I'd say we're temporarily stuffed.'

'Unless,' Calum said, 'we're missing something that's staring us in the face.'

Alun was nodding slowly. 'That Merc's the one common link. It links Laing and his killer. Its stereo packed with drugs creates a link to Sound Bites. And I know damn well that Link Associates use Sound Bites, though until you filled in some details I didn't know why.'

I stood up, stretched.

'Fascinating stuff, but it's police business and all about the hunt for killers. What we're hoping to do is find the owner of the Mercedes before he finds Sam Bone.'

Alun leaned back and yawned, his eyes bright. 'Bloody good luck to you. I got us together to exchange information, but I'm not sure it's helped. I mean, why did Laing kill Tony Carney? Did the scally *really* steal that particular stereo by pure accident? Did he stab Laing because the man *genuinely* got in his way?' He shook his head, climbed wearily out of the swivel-chair and pressed both hands to the small of his back. 'Are we, in fact, looking for all manner of conspiracies when none bloody well exists except in our imaginations?'

'I don't know,' I said, 'but I'm going home.'

And we did.

In fading moonlight and the golden light of a new day's dawning I drove the short distance up the A5 to the turn-off, swooped down across the river and a couple of minutes later was rocking across the stone bridge over the dry gully and under the trees onto my front yard. The spare key was where I'd left it beneath the heavy stone pot and its tangled red azalea, and we tramped through the darkened porch and into the tiled passageway where the early morning light reflecting up the stairs cast its warm glow over my soldiers in their stone niches, loyal sentinels watching over me as I slept in my rural retreat but powerless to defend my Soldier Blue when her travels were so unpredictable.

The door to the living-room was on the right. I opened it and went through, clicked the switch and at once the big, slate-floored room was illuminated, the white stone walls warmed by red-shaded wall lights that cast velvet shadows in the deep inglenook and touched the delicate silver bark on the iron basket of birch logs.

I could hear the monotonous bleeping of the answering machine.

Calum brushed past me, dumped his coat on the Ercol coffee table and sank onto the settee. I dropped my car keys on his coat and went through to the office, pressed the play button.

'It's Meg, Jack. It's two o'clock now, and Joe and I are still up. We were expecting Sian at around ten. She never arrived.'

chapter ten

'You'll kill yourself.'

I shook off Calum's hand, swept my car keys off his jacket. When I turned from the coffee table, he'd moved to the door leading into the passage. Tall, raw-boned, his bearded face was impassive but I thought I could see in his eyes a buccaneering glint: he was lapping it up; the big Scot was daring me to take him on.

'I'll be fine,' I said. 'It's an easy drive, piece of cake.'

'You're still over the limit, too fired-up to think straight and knackered to boot.'

'All right, you can notch up a first, drive a Quatro.'

'Oh aye, and you'd trust me to do that in my bloody state? I was downing the hard stuff at twice your speed in the Owl. I'm not going anywhere – and neither are you.'

In the heavy silence the keys jingled as I tossed them from hand to hand.

'You heard Meg. She's a police-sergeant. If she's worried about Sian, doesn't that tell you something?'

'Meg knows very little about what we're doing. And maybe you misinterpreted her message. She didn't actually say she was concerned. Her tone of voice was neutral, like she was passing on some news.' He came away from the door, still watching me but obviously seeing that common sense was getting through. 'She could have been asking you for reassurance. Maybe she's expecting you to phone, tell her Sian's OK.'

For a moment I hesitated – but only for a moment. He

was right. I was in no fit state to drive. And where would I go? In Liverpool, Sian stayed at Meg's, or Calum's. I'd have no idea where to look. And maybe I had read into Meg's message sinister undertones that perhaps didn't exist. I was probably worrying over nothing – a sure sign of overtiredness.

I sighed, again tossed the keys onto his coat, and headed for the kitchen. Coffee seemed like a good idea – sobering in style, not the brandy-laced caffeine-kick that was a Bryn Aur staple.

Calum had followed me in, and was leaning against the wall by the door. I filled the percolator at the tap, spooned in Columbian ground coffee. As I did so, my mind again began calculating.

Meg had reached my answering machine at two. By then, Sian was three hours late.

It was now after four, and Meg was silent. If she *had* been worried, that was bad – wasn't it?

Where had Sian gone?

'Forget it, Jack,' Calum said softly. 'Coffee, then sleep.' He gave a short little laugh. 'Personally, I think she's OK – so maybe I know your girl better than you do.'

My girl. My Soldier Blue.

'It's always possible,' I said as the coffee began to perk, 'that she's been summoned back to Manchester. A telephone call from flash Nigel at Radio Merseyside or one of the Granada TV producers would do it.'

'And she'd know better than to phone your mobile, because we were either down a dark alley smashing windows, or checking on alibis with the riff-raff at Night Owl.'

I chuckled, watched the liquid bubbling up in the little glass dome, perceptibly darkening. 'There's another much more sinister possibility, isn't there?'

'Aye, I'll admit that.' He came away from the door, got two mugs out of the cupboard, sat down at the table. 'There's always the chance she's been taken by a man hedging his bets, right? The Merc's owner might believe Sam's got his precious stereo, but you were at her house so you always looked like a nice juicy suspect. Snatch two women, use them as bait to reel in the man. Only, thanks to Manny Yates's quick thinking, Sam's still on the loose.'

'As far as we know.'

He flashed me a look. 'Christ, you have got the miseries.'

I poured coffee, passed Calum a mug and we trailed through into the living-room. Calum picked up my keys from his jacket, tossed them to me, and then picked up his jacket.

And we both froze.

'Isn't that,' Calum said, 'a certain survival specialist's mobile phone?'

'And the keys to the Shogun.'

Calum was watching my face with huge delight. 'If you'd only thought to ring her mobile, we'd have known right away where she was.'

'Here. Upstairs in bed. In the spare room.' I grinned, suddenly gloriously happy. 'But I can't wake her now, can I.'

'So unless I want to share a bed with you, I guess it's me for the settee.'

'I'll throw down a duvet.'

Wednesday's breakfast was a cracker of a lunch served by a bright eyed wench to a couple of private investigators not yet recovered from the previous night's formidable wilt. The kitchen was hot, sunny and airy, and a fresh breeze was lifting the curtains at the open window and carrying with it the aromas of oak and sycamore and mountain-ash, fast-running water and sheep, carrion gently ripening in the heat. Thin steaks smeared with English mustard and topped with fried eggs were eaten with crusty white bread and lots of coffee, and we were watched with undisguised contempt by a beautiful cook who had eaten her more meagre fare of muesli and fresh fruit some five hours earlier and since then walked six brisk miles over terrain steep enough to tire a goat.

'What I want to know,' I said through a mouthful of some-thing tasty, 'is why you didn't tell Meg what you were doing, and what brought you here?'

'I didn't tell Meg because by the time I thought of it I guessed she'd be in bed.'

'She wasn't. She was waiting for you,' Calum said, and shrugged when I glared.

'As for what brought me here: when I realized I couldn't phone Meg and didn't have a key for Calum's flat I rang Night Owl. Manny told me you were here.'

'The timing's interesting,' Calum said. 'You rang Manny when we'd already left the club, we drove straight to Alun Morgan's and stayed there not all that long.' He cocked an eyebrow. 'I'd say you couldn't have been here too far ahead of us.'

'I heard you come in.'

'Well,' I said, 'now's the time to come clean: what exactly were you doing between leaving Grassendale and phoning Manny Yates?'

She smiled sweetly. 'I went to Sam's house,' and from her stool near the stove she met my surprised glance with smug-ness. 'I was with her when you phoned from Night Owl and told her to scarper.'

I pushed my plate away and leaned back in my chair. 'So what took you there in the first place?'

'When we left Grassendale you two headed for Sound Bites, I was going to Meg's. But in the car I found myself going over the old Gault case. I remembered that when you first interviewed Sadie Gault, you came away expecting to find missing people without the foggiest idea of what they looked like.'

'Stupid of me, yes; I'd forgotten to ask her for photo-graphs.'

'So how are you going to find Jason Bone?'

I shrugged, feeling mildly guilty.

Sian was up off her stool, gathering together the dishes and dumping them in the sink. Over the clatter, wrist-deep in hot Fairy foam as she gazed out across the sun-splashed yard, she said, 'How'd you two get on last night?'

'Left a trail of destruction in our wake, sank too much alcohol in a club as lively as a retirement home's rest hour, validated Tommy Mack's alibi and discovered that Jason Bone talks to a GP.'

She glanced over her shoulder. 'Waste of time?'

'Well, timing means we do know Tommy couldn't possibly have killed Jemima Laing.' She accepted that without comment, turned back and began stacking the dishes to drain and I said, 'What about Sam? We've all been there now, all had a chance to make judgements. What did you think of her?'

'I like her.'

'Having a tough time, working hard, looking to brother Tommy as the way forward?'

'He's not ideal. I mean, Lord knows what he does for a living, but he's certainly a rougher character than Sam.'

'Plays poker, for starters,' Calum said, getting up from the table. 'Serious business, according to Manny. That means high stakes.'

'And he does tell lies,' Sian said, and she stripped off yellow rubber gloves and came away from the sink.

'Yes. The alibi's watertight, but he still hasn't explained the blood on his T-shirt.'

Calum had drifted away through the living-room and I knew he'd be standing outside in the bright sunshine, lighting up a cigar. I followed Sian through. She went to the window. I hesitated, my mind half on the investigation of a host of interconnected crimes, half on the realization that Scots Greys were not getting painted and that, in the office, I had a paperwork mountain.

Then I went over to Sian, took her shoulders and turned her gently into my arms. Kissed her on soft moist lips and lost myself in the giddy scent of high mountain slopes and summer breezes caught in the wildness of her blonde hair. Took my face away to look deep into blue eyes like flecked, summertime lakes reflecting an infinity of cobalt skies.

'What's all this?' she said.

'A big thanks. You could have gone straight to bed at Meg's. Instead you made an effort to help me, went out into the scary darkness.' I smothered a grin. 'Did you ask Sam for a photograph of Jason?'

She brought a fist up to punch my shoulder. 'No. You phoned, and I went all dreamy.'

And then Calum was back. Sian and I stepped apart.

He cocked his head, black eyes catching the early afternoon light. 'So what was decided?'

'Didn't get that far,' Sian said. She'd shed her early morning mountain gear and was wearing a dark green T-shirt over faded jeans, bare feet light on the Indian rugs. I thought I detected a roguish wink flashed in his direction.

I said, 'It's true. As a private eye I haven't decided what to do; as a maker of toy soldiers I'm falling behind with the casting.'

'Last I heard,' Calum said, 'you wanted more American Civil War figures for Frank Hahn in Philadelphia. Give me the list, I'll spend a couple of hours in the workshop.'

I nodded my thanks. 'Sian?'

'I think I'll take a drive down to Alun Morgan's. Another half a day's passed. He might have something new.'

'Right ...'

'But?'

'No buts.' I looked at each of them in turn. 'An opportunity for us all. We'll be pretty well alone with our thoughts, so when the mood takes you – and if it doesn't, bloody well force it – see what you can come up with on suspects, who they are, where they're likely to be found, how to apprehend.'

'Erm, would that be suspects as in the Case of the Stolen Merc?' Calum said with deadly, saintlike innocence.

'Suspects,' I said, 'in the case of a Bewilderment of Crimes – but most particularly and especially murder.'

The muted sound of the centrifugal-casting machine coming through the open office window was like the intermittent whine of a circular saw being operated by a forestry worker in the nearby woods. So evocative was it that I was fooled into believing I could smell the resiny sawdust; yet in the same breath I was reminded of talcum powder and hot rubber and molten tin alloy and so transported to the stone workshop adjoining the house where Calum would be peering through safety goggles as he used an iron ladle to pour metal through the central hole into the spinning, vulcanized mould.

Of all the processes in the production of toy soldiers it was the one I enjoyed the least. Yet, conversely, the very first pouring into a freshly powdered mould made from new master figures was always an exciting event, for within three or four minutes that hot mould could be taken from the turntable and carefully prised open to reveal up to ten gleaming military miniatures attached to sprues radiating outwards like the spokes of a wheel.

The very first batch of the latest design to come off the Magna Carta production line.

Well, not so much a line....

I came back to reality with a start, and the realization that I was grinning like a fool and my pen had been poised over my chequebook as I drifted on a pleasant cloud of satisfaction and fulfilment. Well, why not? If work was a pleasure, even bill-paying could be tolerated. I filled in the amount, scribbled a signature and threw the cheque book into its drawer.

All done. A chat to the metal suppliers about the late delivery that had delayed the Gibraltar order; a new Men at Arms reference book ordered; a call made to Frank Hahn in Philadelphia about his Civil War figures.

And now...?

I eased away from the desk, walked to the window and looked across the yard to the workshop. Down-slope under the trees, not quite a Welsh long house but low-slung and slate-roofed, roomy and dry. In there a Calum Wick disguised by goggles and leather gloves would be casting soldiers on automatic pilot while he did what I'd asked him to do and racked his brains over who, in the short list of people we had met or heard about in the past few days, could have committed bloody murder.

Between making phone calls and paying bills my own mind had touched abstractedly on the subject, and even without going into it in greater depth my feeling was that bewilderment was the right word to describe my state of mind. We had nothing to go on. Very little idea of what a number of unidentified people were trying to do. And not the faintest idea of where or how to begin.

Was that being negative? I was still looking out across the yard and debating that gloomily when the phone rang.

I half-turned from the window, let the answering machine cut in.

It was Sam Bone.

I leaped to grab the receiver.

'Sam, I'm here.'

'Oh God!'

'What is it?'

'They found us. Sian had been gone ten minutes.'

'What!'

'Honest to God. I think they must have followed her—'

'No.'

'What, you mean she's too clever?' Her laugh was hollow, nervous. 'Well they fuckin' got here, didn't they. And now I've got an ultimatum.'

'Go on.'

'Twenty-four hours. Hand over that stereo and the fuckin' drugs, or that's it. Finish. For me an' Tommy.'

The silence was one of those that seems to buzz inside the brain like the onset of a stroke. I could hear both of us breathing harshly. The tension was so great I grabbed for the swivel-chair and sat down as my knees went weak.

'Sam, don't worry, we'll sort it.'

'How?'

'I don't know. But we'll be back in Liverpool very soon.' I hesitated, mind racing. 'We could move you again—'

'Only you can't because I'm back home and there's one of them sittin' in the other room, isn't there, an' if he knew I was talkin' to you – God, I'll have to go!'

The phone went down with a clatter.

As the connection was severed it was as if the room was flooded with fresh, cleansing air and crystal-clear light that showed me the way. Suddenly, I knew what to do. Violence was something I hated. But I thought of Ronnie Maguire, the only clear lead I had to the theft of the Mercedes, the man who could prove that Sam Bone was an innocent victim of circumstances – and I knew that the only way to get his co-operation was by threats, or intimidation.

'Sam didn't go to Tommy's house,' Sian said. 'He hasn't got one. I think he lives in a scruffy little bed-sit. I helped her move to a friend's house in Cuckoo Lane.'

It was pouring with rain and we were in the Quatro blasting along the M56 towards the Runcorn turn-off in three lanes of traffic with the windscreen wipers flapping madly.

After the phone call from Sam I'd crossed the yard to bring Calum up to date, called Sian on the mobile, then impatiently kicked my heels as Calum wrapped up the casting and locked the workshop. When the Shogun came bouncing and popping across the gravel to park behind the house we were packed up and standing alongside the Quatro with its nose pointing towards the bridge ready to go. It took Sian less than four minutes to grab her overnight bag from the bedroom and join us in the late afternoon sunshine, something like forty miles of concentrated driving before three people busy struggling to gather thoughts that circled and wheeled as elusively as sea-birds in a storm were ready to talk.

'It doesn't matter now,' I said. 'They found her anyway. You'd been gone ten minutes when the thugs moved in and took her back home. She thinks you were followed.'

'They could only have followed me,' Sian said, 'if they'd

been watching the house, saw us move out. I don't think they were.'

'So how did they find her? Nobody knew she was moving. It was spur of the moment, on Manny's advice.'

'Advice given to you in Night Owl, which you passed on by phone,' Calum said.

I glanced at him as I indicated and turned off the motorway.

'What's that mean?'

From the back seat Sian gave an unladylike snort. 'He means you were overheard.'

I frowned, thinking back. 'Who was listening?'

'Feller called Tobin. Who happens to be a mate of GP Vick Valentine. And a GP,' Calum said, 'is into drugs legally, treats addicts, so the temptation to stray is always there. As Manny pointed out.'

'A GP would be a kind of upmarket pusher,' Sian said from her cosy corner, 'and unlikely to do his own fetching and carrying.'

I looked at her in the mirror.

'So the Merc's not his car?'

'Too risky. He's the big chief of his band of pusheroos.'

'And now he's got his hands on an innocent woman,' Sian said.

'Someone has,' I said. 'We're guessing it's Valentine.'

'I'll give Manny a call later,' Calum said, 'pick his brains, see if the GP's reputation's blacker than black.'

'Do that,' I said, and glanced at the dashboard clock. Five. 'We've got nine hours to convince whoever's holding Sam that she knows nothing about that missing stereo.'

In the mirror Sian's face was tense. 'How the hell can we do that?'

'According to Tommy Mack, these people are minnows. They just need something to scare them rigid,' I said, 'so it's time to get a little help from some powerful enemies in Old Swan.'

★

Time passed quickly. We parked, piled into Calum's flat and Sian and I brewed black coffee and filled a plate with a mountain of ham sandwiches smeared with English mustard while the Scot phoned Manny. Result: a report from the Lime Street PI that in Vick Valentine we had the wrong man for a drugs baron, but a man not averse to dipping his toe into murky waters.

'Old Swan means Ronnie Maguire,' Calum said, 'so tell me about this cunning plan without scaring me to death.'

We'd retired to the living-room with the third mug of coffee. Calum was prowling around the Scots Greys. Satan had worn down Sian's token resistance and was curled up warmly in the cleft of her crossed ankles as she sprawled on the settee. I was standing at the window looking broodingly down on the parked Quatro, its sleek lines inevitably reminding me of its sojourn in Maguire's garage after the tyre-slashing incident and my ambitious plans for freeing Sam Bone.

'Maguire was behind the Mercedes carjacking, changed its identity, drove it to Dunbar Close,' I said, moving back into the room. 'Jason Bone must have gone to him to order that particular car in person, face to face; deals like that can't be done by phone or e-mail. What I'm hoping for is something on paper implicating Bone – maybe even a signature. Something Maguire can vouch for and Sam can identify.'

Calum frowned. 'If e-mails and phone calls are out, why would Bone risk signing his name?'

'Maguire puts himself at risk.' I thought for a moment. 'Written evidence – just a scrap of greasy paper – could be his guarantee that customers won't shop him. If he goes down, all those people driving his hot cars are going down with him.'

'Like lodging a sealed envelope with a lawyer,' Calum said. 'And they're sitting in their Mercs and BMWs knowing the evidence is there.'

I'd settled into my leather chair, but now I was up again and restless. Sian sensed my mood. Satan mewled, rolled

onto his back and aimed a drowsy left hook at her ankle as
she uncrossed her legs and sat up.

'They must have taken Sam home,' she said, tucking away
loose strands of fair hair, 'because if she's got the stereo, it'll
be hidden somewhere in or near her house.'

'They searched,' Calum said. 'Junked the place, found
nothing.'

'What does that prove? People are cunning. Bodies get
buried in back gardens. Anyway,' she said to me after a
pause, 'do you think Maguire will be at his garage now?'

'We'll try there. If no luck we'll track him to his lair.'

And so we began our preparations. Which meant, well,
nothing very much. Dark clothes were donned again. I
suggested heavy shoes with cleated soles so we had an even
chance of staying upright on the garage's oil-caked floors.
Calum went into his bedroom and emerged carrying two
rubber torches bright enough to guide in helicopters, heavy
enough to fell an ox. Or two.

'Calculating the odds, us against Maguire and Max,' I
said, 'I reckon two of us add up to one of them. Worth
going?'

'Lighter makes for fleeter of foot. We can run faster.'

'Unless we're trapped.'

Calum grinned. 'Then, laddie, it's down to fast talking.'

'No contest,' I said, and went over to kiss Sian.

The weather we had barrelled through on the M56 had
moved away, the dark clouds drifting westwards with the sun
to be snared by the soaring Welsh hills. In Liverpool the
roads were dry, all signals on green, and in something like
ten minutes we made it from Grassendale to Derby Road
and so into the side street where Maguire's timber and
corrugated-iron garage stood rotting on its patch of oil-
stained concrete.

I pulled in, took the Quatro in a slow, sweeping circle on
the greasy surface to finish up facing the right way for a hasty
departure. When we climbed out of the car toting heavy

torches and closed the doors with the merest whisper of sound it was to the deep-throated baying of several big dogs.

'Three German Shepherds, all loose,' I said.

'Loose as in well-placed to savage intruders who swarm over the fence,' Calum said. 'We're going in the front door – you first.'

Half six and still daylight. I took hold of the hasp, eased open the big door and we sidled through into the deserted workshop. Last time here I'd been alone, feeling my way like a first-day apprentice, and was caught cold by Maguire and big Max. This time I knew my way around and had backup, yet even that was of little consolation when my eyes were drawn to the door of Maguire's office under which I could see a sliver of white light beckoning with all the dazzling charm of a near-death experience.

'Someone's in there,' I said softly.

There was the sound of a phone being replaced, followed by silence. Somewhere beyond the workshop's rear door a hammer clanged on metal, then rang on concrete. If it was big Max out there, maybe he'd dropped his angle iron épée and we were in luck.

Somewhere uncomfortably close a door slammed. German Shepherds went wild, howling at the darkening skies. I shivered at the thought of big paws pattering across hard ground, a private eye showing the first signs of irrational terror.

Standing patiently watching and waiting in the gloom, Calum had an amused gleam in his eyes. 'What's the plan?' he said. 'Starve him out?'

'That's one option.'

'On the other hand—'

'We could walk in now, and to hell with the consequences.'

So we put the heavy torches on the nearest bench, and kicked open the door.

Ronnie Maguire's green eyes narrowed with shock then pinned me with slitted animosity as the heavy door crashed back against the wall. His belly was squashed behind the ex-

British Rail desk. One hand as black as a coal miner's lifted a can of Budweiser to lips from which a hand-rolled cigarette drooped. The door bounced back and hit my foot. Ronnie spat out the cigarette and half rose from his creaking swivel chair.

'Save your strength for serious thinking,' I said.

He glared and sank back. Calum followed me in and closed the door. It was my second visit, and already I felt at home. I dropped into my usual chair, my head nuzzling the overalls hanging from the iron hook. Calum squeezed past and stood against the wall.

'Who's the nerd?'

'Intelligence Corps,' I said. 'We're about to blow your cover.'

'From where you are, you'd have a hard time blowin' out a fuckin' candle.'

'So where are we?' Calum said.

'Deep in the shit,' Maguire said. His massive chest swelled as he sucked in a breath to yell for reinforcements.

'Don't even think about it,' I said. 'What happens now is Wick keeps you occupied while I use your phone to pass some interesting information to the police. About stolen cars in general, a black Mercedes in particular.'

One big, greasy hand reached out, picked up the phone and dropped it in a drawer.

I slipped a hand into my pocket, pulled out my mobile, waggled it under the dangling naked bulb so it caught the light.

'No signal. The roof's full of lead in case war breaks out,' Maguire said blandly.

'It just did,' Calum said.

'Like fuck. It's a stand-off. I can't get out, you can't phone, so why don't you piss off.'

'The balance will swing our way when you're immobilized,' Calum said.

'Fuck me gently.' Maguire shook his head. 'Max an' three starvin' guard dogs're thirty yards away an' you two dickheads think you can—'

The door banged open and Max lumbered in, leering and hefting his rusty chunk of angle iron.

I reached up, tore the greasy overalls from the iron hook. They dropped on Max's head, folded limply over his face. He clawed at them with one hand. Lazily, Calum swung a leg and kicked him hard in the balls. He doubled over, moaning and clutching his groin. The angle iron fell with a dull clang. Calum picked it up, chose his spot on the enveloping overalls and whacked the giant over the head.

As Max went down, Maguire started around the desk. Calum spun, lifted the angle iron and slammed it down like a sledge-hammer. A huge chunk of desk ripped off, leaving a long white scar. Maguire froze.

I freed my foot, dropped to one knee, dragged the overalls off Max's head. He was out cold. His face was an unhealthy white. I climbed to my feet, looked squarely at Maguire.

'I have a proposition. I want you to come with us, and give a certain man the name of the person who recently ordered a black Mercedes C200.'

'Why the fuck should I?'

I leaned over the desk, plucked the phone out of the drawer.

'Leave it,' Calum roared as Maguire reached down to rip the phone's lead from the wall socket.

'All it takes,' I said, 'is one 999 call.'

'Les is still out there.'

'But Les is not Max,' I said, 'and look at Max now.'

'All right, so I give you the name and you tell this feller, no need for me to be there.'

'I know the name. Jason Bone. But I need proof. Something in writing would help.'

Maguire snorted. 'What d'you take me for?'

'Twice as intelligent as your comatose friend,' Calum said, 'but still way short of genius. If your business is half as good as I think it is you'll need to record names and addresses.'

Maguire tapped his head.

'Memory's no good,' Calum said. 'If you're thinking house

numbers and confuse a six with a nine a high court judge could find himself the proud owner of a stolen Audi.'

Maguire's grin was knowing. 'That happens, believe me, without any fuckin' confusion.' He waited, still leaning against the wall where he'd backed away, his eyes blank as his mind wriggled for a way out. On the floor Max groaned, twitched, relapsed into stillness. Maguire shook his head.

'In there. Top shelf.'

He pointed to a steel locker.

I eased behind Calum, went around the side of the desk and opened the locker. On the shelf the expected rusty tin box with a peeling label. I took it down. The lid was loose. Inside, scraps of paper torn out of reporter's notebooks, held together with bulldog clips.

'Give it here.'

Maguire took it, flipped through, pulled out one of the clips and squeezed it to extract the top slip. He handed it to me, dropped the box on the desk.

I was holding a piece of paper that was oil-smeared, creased, faded and torn. It was dated. The printed name on the paper was JASON BONE. Then the address, and what looked like a stipulation, probably a reminder of part of what he and Maguire had been discussing: *it must be that Mercedes, no other*. And then a scrawled signature.

I had the proof. Now we had to convince Vick Valentine.

chapter eleven

I swung the Quatro past the ornamental conifers and into Sam Bone's gravel drive as dusk was falling, and this time the security lights over the garage detected us and pinned us in their dazzling glare. I took my time getting out, letting my eyes sweep over the gardens, garage and house as I shut the door. By the time I'd decided nothing – other than the curtains being closed over the front window – had obviously altered since our previous visits, Calum was out of the car and standing close to big Ronnie Maguire who had been sitting alongside me in the front. He was in dirty boots and filthy overalls. The inside of the car reeked of old oil. If Sian rode in the front, she'd slide off the seat.

Our arrival had been noted. The front door swung open as we climbed the steps.

Not Valentine. Billie Tobin.

In Night Owl, Tobin had looked like an old lag who'd learned to roll his cigarettes in a Walton gaol cell and took his first drink of supermarket cider every morning when he crawled out from under tangled blankets. But that had all changed. His bald head glistened as he stood under the basket of petunias, his clean-shaven face gleamed, his bony frame was clad in a 500 quid black-leather bomber jacket.

'She called you yesterday, didn't she?' Tobin said. 'I heard the phone go down, wondered then who she'd been talkin' to.'

'And now you know.'

The aviator shades were pushed up. Light glinted on the lenses as his head moved fractionally to look at me.

'Yeah, you were in Night Owl talkin' to Manny Yates. It was you told her to move. An' I've been askin' around. You've got a rep 'cos you killed a nutter with a single blow, Speedy-fuckin'-Mendoza, quickness of the hand an' all that shite.'

'So if you've finished polishing my ego,' I said, 'why don't we go inside and get this cleared up? Or should I call the police?'

Tobin was either unimpressed, or confident that I was bluffing.

'What's with the grease-monkey?'

'Ronnie Maguire,' I said, 'deals in … er … up-market used cars. He can provide information that suggests somebody else has the stolen stereo.'

'A stolen stereo,' Billie Tobin said, 'is not what this is about.'

'I know. I've been askin' around.' I grinned in his face. 'Where's Valentine?'

'The only Valentine I know is a useless quack,' Tobin said.

Scrutinizing me through narrowed eyes, he was obviously tossing a mental coin to decide if we there to help or gum up the works. Then he turned on his heel and went into the house. He left the door open.

We trooped in.

They were in the front room.

Sam was sitting on the settee, the throw draped over her knees, her fingers plucking nervously at its coarse, comfortable folds. A thickset man with a shaven head was sprawled in a chair with his feet on the mock-Indian coffee table and a half-full whisky glass and smouldering cigarette held in the same hand.

'You OK, Sam?'

She nodded, her eyes flicking from me to Calum and then to Ronnie Maguire as he crowded in behind us. Her sojourn with the baddies had worn down her natural sassiness, depleted her stores of optimism. I caught myself wondering what had happened to Tommy Mack. Her brother's presence would have given her strength, but Sian had made no mention of him other than to say Sam had not gone to his bed-sit. Perhaps, last night, he'd seen her safely to the house in Cuckoo Lane then gone home. But that had been some eighteen hours ago. I'd have expected him to check on Sam long before now.

So why had he stayed away?

Billie Tobin picked up a glass from the mantel over the electric fire, drained it, ran a thick-knuckled hand over his shining scalp. Wariness flickered in his pale eyes as he watched Maguire. The big man looked at the whisky glasses, noticed the absence of a bottle. He snorted nasally and wandered towards the kitchen in search of booze.

The man with his feet on the table swung them down with a thump. Gold glittered at his throat as he struggled to lift his bulk out of the chair. Tobin waved him back.

'So,' he said, 'what's all this about a stereo?'

'Valentine's Mercedes was stolen—'

'He never had a fuckin' Merc.'

'All right, but you were looking for *a* Merc, traced it to this house and found it sitting in Sam's garage minus audio equipment that had its value artificially inflated.'

'Yeah, an' guess who's plannin' on cashin' in?'

'Jason Bone.'

Tobin shook his head. 'Accordin' to her, he's been gone two weeks. The stereo was ripped out on Friday.'

'Stolen.' I nodded. 'It's gone.'

'Balls. She's got it.' He jerked his head at Sam. 'Her, or Tommy Mack—'

'Christ, no!' Sam yelled, 'how many times do I have to tell you—'

'Till you're blue in the fuckin' face, love, an' it'll still be a load of cobblers and that's when I get really pissed. An' turn you over to a real nasty feller called Carney, let him sort you out—'

'Carney?' She was frowning thoughtfully, mouth slightly parted, the tip of her tongue worrying her lower lip.

Tobin sneered at her. 'Yeah. A big step up the ladder, not the lad to play games—'

'The garage window's broken,' I cut in. 'That's a clear sign of a break-in.'

'They faked it.'

'So who killed Jemima Laing?'

'Some passin' scally her wacky husband jumped out on. Random killin', ask the cops.'

Maguire came back carrying two glasses and a bottle. Sam glared as his filthy boots scuffed across the nylon carpet. He wandered away towards the window, opened the curtain just enough to gaze out.

'We'd be delighted to talk to the polis,' Calum said, attracting Tobin's attention for the first time, 'but what we can offer is an alternative scenario that'll explain everything and save you from making a complete and utter tit of yourself.'

'Too late,' Sam said. 'He's spent the last twenty-four hours practisin'.'

Maguire let the curtains fall, turned away from the window and perched himself on the arm of the tattooed thug's chair. It was a small chair. For the thug it must have been like the onset of a total eclipse.

'Think about it,' I said when Tobin had dragged nervous eyes away from Maguire. 'Sam works nights at a garage, looks after her home, she couldn't possibly know how to arrange the theft of a Merc.'

'Tommy Mack—'

'Forget Mack, he's not here, Sam is and you're holding her for no damn reason.'

'The car was stolen an' this is where it ended up.'

'And you can take it,' Sam said, 'get it out of my sight.'

'Not unless what's missin' is put back—'

'Sam,' I said, again cutting in, 'have you got a photograph of Jason?'

'No.' The throw had been tossed aside, her face was flushed, her eyes blazing. 'I burnt every bloody one when he walked out an' I'm doin' my best to forget what the bastard looks like.'

'Doesn't matter.' I reached into my pocket and pulled out the fragile piece of paper that had acquired yet another couple of folds. 'This,' I said to Tobin, 'is dated a couple of weeks back. It was written by Jason Bone when asking for a particular car to be stolen for him.'

The words fell like stones.

I said, 'What Bone stipulated was: "... it must be that particular Mercedes, no other ...". He also wrote his address.' I held the paper up and waggled it. 'This address.'

I turned to Maguire. 'Ronnie, can you describe the man whose name's on this?'

The big garage man glowered. He was on his feet again. In his dirty overalls he looked as out of place as an unwashed elephant on a packed Easy Jet.

'Jason's tall an' dark haired,' Sam said, losing patience. 'Bit skinny, face lean an' hard. No distinguishing features you'd notice when he's got his clothes on.'

Maguire's eyes narrowed. 'Could be.'

I took a step towards the settee, held the slip of paper so Sam could see. 'Is that Jason's signature?'

She leaned across and took hold of the edge between thumb and finger. I'd never seen Jason Bone's signature. Sam recognized it at once, and nodded vigorously.

'Yes, that's his.'

Tobin shrugged. 'So?'

'So Sam described her husband,' I said, 'and Ronnie says that was the man who signed this paper.'

'No, what he said was it could be.'

I looked at Maguire.

'Yeah, we talked, he signed his name.'

'And now,' I said to Tobin, 'Sam has recognized her husband's signature.'

'So, OK,' Tobin said, 'it went like this. Bone got 'im to steal the Merc,' – he nodded at Maguire – 'then disappeared. When the Merc was delivered, he robbed it himself only made it look like the work of a scally.'

'Right. We all agree on that, so ...'

'So that's it, that's what's goin' on,' Tobin said. 'She's in it with 'im, Jason, and holdin' her is the only fuckin' way we can get that stereo—'

'No,' I said. 'Sam knows absolutely nothing about the Merc, or the stereo – but there are ways of getting it back that don't require a hostage.'

'Yeah, all right, go on.'

So I told him.

chapter twelve

Against the stands of dark green trees lining the west bank of Conwy harbour the yachts moored to buoys of red and yellow were like graceful white sea birds basking in the bright, early afternoon sunshine. A dinghy puttered away from the small quay and sliced through the flat water towards the marina at Deganway, pale-blue smoke from the two-stroke outboard lifting and hanging in the still air. Around us, late-summer tourists strolled and chattered.

I wondered, absently, which one of the yachts being photographed had recently been the scene of a bloody murder. Alun Morgan would be able to tell us, but he was already late. Or maybe not. Perhaps he'd searched and missed us, assumed we weren't coming and that was him out there in the now distant dinghy puttering smokily away to a belated midday pint in the Deganwy Castle Hotel.

Alongside me, looking nifty in three-quarter beige trousers by the Columbia Clothing Company of Oregon, off-white T-shirt from Hawkshead and a floppy flannel hat she'd picked up in Casemates Square, Gibraltar, Sian said, 'I cannot believe you agreed to consort with the enemy.'

'Wrong word.'

'What, consort?'

'No, agreed. It was my idea. Billie Tobin was stubborn, I finagled.'

She cocked her head, letting loose shiny fair hair brush a

shoulder. 'But we *are* here working for those crooks? Aren't we looking for the thief who's holding their stereo?'

'In a roundabout way. I told them that so they'd walk away from Sam. Now she's free we can indulge in the much juicier work of looking for the killer. Or killers. Which will naturally involve one or more links to the stereo, just as the Conwy murder's got Liverpool links – hence this trip to Wales and Alun Morgan.'

'While poor old Calum goes cross-eyed slapping paint on toy soldiers.'

'He's also spending some time seeing what he can dig up on Jemima and Silvester Laing' – I winked conspiratorially – 'while we are two undercover private eyes lazily soaking up the sun to avoid giving the impression of working our socks off.'

'An impression for the impressionable,' said dapper Welsh detective Alun Morgan, appearing from nowhere on shoes soled with rubber. 'For the discerning it's more a case of who do they think they're bloody fooling?'

'How are you, Alun?'

'All the better for seeing one of you, at least,' he said, stepping jauntily close to kiss a smiling Sian on the cheek. 'And probably thinking cynical thoughts similar to your own: there's all these people with cameras, and every one of them unknowingly snapping a yacht with a dark and bloody history.'

Sian was amazed. 'You mean it's still out there? Not impounded, compounded, confiscated – or whatever it is you police types do to them?'

'Jesus, Scott!' Alun said feelingly, 'and you talk about me extracting the urine. It's there, yes, that big yawl – and if you want to know what a yawl is, wait till we get out there.'

We were taken across by the harbour-master in a heavy carvel-built dinghy pushed by a powerful inboard Evinrude, the breeze ruffling our hair, the big boat that had been turned into a murder scene looming ever larger as we approached. We clambered aboard via steps hanging from the side – bear with me here, because wise to the lingo of the sea I definitely am not – and heard the dinghy purr away in a wide sweep and head back to the quay as Alun lead the way inside.

In no time at all we were in the panelled saloon seated on soft white leather and sipping tepid fruit juice courtesy of an absent owner whose generator had been shut down leaving double banks of flat batteries, Alun had explained something about a yawl having a mast stepped on the stern side of the rudder post whereas a ketch's would be stepped on the bow side and then, thankfully for my reeling head, it was down to business.

'The murder was committed in the bow cabin,' Alun said. 'Laing's prints were on the knife. But a murder solved has left a lot unexplained. Identifying the victim was no problem, because the lad's father's the yacht's skipper—'

'Lad?'

'Well, thirty or so but still a young executive and, unlike most who joke about it, he really was on his daddy's yacht. Daddy being Ed Carney, of Link Associates. But answer this, if you can: with his son a murder victim, why now is Ed Carney noticeable only for his bloody absence?'

'Ed Carney?' Sian cut in as I opened my mouth. 'That makes his son *Tony* Carney. Bloody hell, that's reminded me why I recognized Laing's name.'

The big yawl rocked gently as a seagoing cruiser slipped by, motoring towards the open sea. Alun Morgan leaned back against the leather, nursing his soft drink, waiting for Sian to elaborate. I watched her too, not with curiosity but with a sense of nervous expectancy. Somehow I knew exactly what was coming, but I didn't know whether to laugh or cry for my Soldier Blue.

'Remember me telling you, Jack?' she said. 'It was on my very last survival course, just before the start of the Gault case, and in the heather east of Cape Wrath I kept a weakening man alive in a force eight with standard survival technique: cuddle the victim.'

'That was Tony Carney?'

'Mm. And now he's dead.'

Her eyes were wide and misty but there were no tears and I knew her too well to believe she'd dwell on a tragedy it was beyond her power to prevent.

'What about Laing?' I said, gently pushing.

'Much older than Tony, but he was on the same survival course, and they knew each other.'

'They would do,' Alun said. 'Laing was a partner in Link Associates.'

'Tony and Laing, one the boss's son, the other … well, another boss.' Sian smiled at the delicious irony. 'Being on the same course would make for a strange business relationship, wouldn't it, but what they constantly argued about was something much more personal.'

'Like?'

'Apparently Laing, a vain, arrogant bastard, was knocking off a younger woman. Tony thought it was hilarious, wouldn't leave it alone.'

'What was this girl, a Link employee?'

'In accounts, probably. I heard Tony complaining to Laing that she'd messed up his previous month's figures – his expenses, I think, hotel stays, petrol costs, bar bills, plane tickets, Hertz rentals and so on – he was probably fiddling them, and his father was hounding him.'

Something had occurred to me, and now I put it to the Welsh detective.

'Laing knifed Tony Carney, then fled – right?'

'That's it. A quiet night – but that's the beauty of a knife, isn't it. Then Ed and his guests woke up to a misty morning, a dead boy and a cabin soaked in blood and no sign of Laing. And a short while after that the skipper was seen heading down the gangplank.

'So, on seeing what had happened to his son, and realizing Laing was missing, it's not hard to imagine what Ed Carney would be thinking.'

'Two things, actually,' Morgan said. 'Either Laing had also

been murdered, and was floating face down in the harbour – or he was the murderer.'

'On Friday night Laing was stabbed to death – and Ed Carney is still missing?'

'Yes.' A light flared in Morgan's grey eyes. 'But according to Merseyside police, Laing's death was a random killing.'

'They had to put a lot of trust in what they were told. Unfortunately, Jemima Laing was the only witness – and now *she*'s dead.'

Sian leaned forward, placed her empty glass on the table. 'I think I know why she was murdered – but I'd like to hear it from you.'

I pondered her question for a moment, then nodded slowly as it all began to come together.

'According to Jemima Laing, she saw a scally walk down the road carrying something with trailing wires, saw that person stab her husband when he ran out into the rain.' I looked at Alun Morgan. 'But suppose Jemima Laing made that up. Suppose the thief went merrily on his way, and some time after that Ed Carney appeared on the scene.'

'If he did,' Alun Morgan said, 'and he stabbed Laing, he would have had to entice him out of his nice warm house.'

'Before he went out there,' I said, 'one of the things Laing did was answer his mobile phone. I think he was talking to Carney.'

Morgan was frowning. 'It adds up, yes. Carney drawing Laing out, perhaps with a sly invitation to talk, only of course with a very different motive.'

He sprang from his seat, stretched, restlessly walked a few steps and swung around.

'You told anyone about this? Haggard, perhaps?'

I shook my head. 'He warned me off the case.'

'So with Tony's death avenged,' Sian said, still pressing, 'why was *Jemima* murdered?'

'She saw her husband stabbed by Carney, invited him to her house and tried to blackmail him. He belted her with the wine decanter.'

'Jesus!' Morgan paced again, walked far enough across the saloon to gaze across the sun-drenched harbour, again came back. His eyes were alight. 'If that's what happened, it explains why Carney took off.'

'From here?'

'Not here, no. He buggered off from here because he was after Laing. If he did kill Laing, then it explains why he's *still* missing.'

'No.' I shook my head as he glared in surprise. 'No, Alun, that's the one piece that doesn't fit. Carney had no reason to flit, every reason to stay in Liverpool and be visible. You said it yourself: on board the yacht it was a quiet night and they all woke up to a bloodbath. In Liverpool there was just the one witness to the latest killing, the person who saw Silvester Laing stabbed. Jemima Laing – and dead witnesses don't talk.'

'If Ed Carney did murder the Laings,' Sian said lazily, 'you realize a lot of your brilliant theories have been shot down in flames.'

Four o'clock and we were in Sian's big Shogun, the warm sun slanting through the rear window as I pushed along the A55 towards Queensferry and Liverpool.

The meeting on the yacht had quickly been wound up, and a phone call had brought the harbour master across to pick us up from the yawl. We'd left Alun Morgan in Castle Street, pressing on up the slope towards the car park while he slipped into the Castle Hotel. Minutes after bidding the Welsh detective farewell we'd negotiated Conwy's one-way circuit towards the castle but, instead of crossing the bridge towards the A55, we'd turned right and headed up the Conwy Valley and so to Bryn Aur. It had occurred to me that the car I was driving was flashy and conspicuous, and we both decided it was worth switching to the Shogun.

'All I realize,' I said at last, 'is that we went to Conwy believing Bone was guilty, and any sensible man would now bet on Carney. Trouble is, I'm not sensible – and anyway, in the end the murderer may be someone we haven't considered.'

That left us nowhere, but when I pulled up outside Calum's flat in Grassendale my subconscious had already thrown up the next act in the saga of the missing murderers. I'd been thinking of Haggard and Vine, and Haggard and Vine were not going away. Calum greeted us at the top of the stairs with the news that he and I were wanted down at the Admiral Street nick. Zapped supermarket dinners were put on hold. It seemed we were about to be force-fed much stronger fare, and the only place I could see that leading to was painful, mental indigestion.

Last time it was an interview room, this time it was again Haggard's office. Windows were open but the room was too warm, too smoky. Vine sat us down in hard chairs and sort of faded into the background. Haggard was behind his desk, in no mood for claptrap.

'Where were you Tuesday night?'

'Enjoying a drop of the Macallan with Manny Yates. In Night Owl. That's a—'

'Mucky little night club.' Haggard sneered around his king-sized cigarette.

'But you already knew I was going there, because I told you, didn't I?'

'Yeah, and you told me why. You had questions about a feller with blood on his T-shirt, so what happened?'

I looked across at Calum. 'Nothing. It was all a mistake. And after that we …'

'Motored in a leisurely way across the border,' Calum said.

Haggard was in shirt-sleeves, tie tugged down, collar unbuttoned, sweat glistening on his forehead. His face was flushed. Smoke curled from the cigarette in his fist. He fixed me with a brooding, ominous stare.

'What time'd you get to the Owl?'

'Must have been just before eleven.'

'Try again.' That was Willie Vine. He'd come to life, across the room by the window, leafing through the contents of a manila folder.

'I'd better pass.'

'Yeah, and we won't bother askin' Haggis,' Haggard said, 'because you both know it was more than an hour later than that.' He cocked an eyebrow, blew a stream of smoke, casually dropped a bombshell. 'You went there from Sound Bites.'

I waited long enough to suggest bewilderment, then frowned. 'You've lost me.'

Haggard glared. 'When you were last in here I mentioned Sound Bites, the Gay Gordon, and a drug connection. That set you thinkin', an' what you did is you went there to destroy evidence.'

'No, we didn't.' Which was strictly true: we'd gone there to *gather* evidence.

'You were seen.'

'Destroying evidence?'

He scowled. 'Breakin' in. A Park Road shopkeeper lives over the premises. He went for a pee, heard glass breakin' an' looked out across his back yard. Two fellers he could describe down to their underwear were climbin' into Sound Bites through a window.'

'And he rang the police?'

Vine shook his head. 'Not then. Sound Bites has a tough reputation. But he did come forward when a police unit raided Sound Bites and found the place an empty shell. Everything gone, furniture, computer, files—'

'Damn,' Calum said, 'all that effort and we needn't have bothered.'

There was a lengthy pause I was supposed to fill. Eventually, I sighed.

'We went there looking for something that might lead us to the owner of a stolen Mercedes.'

Haggard's dark eyes were gleaming. 'The only client you might have had is dead. So who for?'

I shook my head. 'Confidential.'

'That's a pity. Because we've got you for breakin' and enterin', obstructin' the police, pervertin' the cause of justice, perjury—'

'All right.' I spread my hands in surrender. 'Now's the time to reveal my hole card.'

Haggard grinned without humour, sat back and searched for a cigarette.

'The trip to Wales,' I said, 'gave us the killer of Jemima and Silvester Laing.'

That got everyone's attention, and especially Calum's because on the drive to Admiral Street there'd been a lot of fraught silence and no attempt to bring him up to date.

'Fantastic,' Haggard said with deadly sarcasm. 'So where is he?'

'He's ... er ... gone missing.'

'And what's this killer's name?'

'Ever heard of Ed Carney, of Link Associates?'

'When did he go missin'?'

'The guests and crew on his yacht awoke to a body, and then the skipper skipped. He's not been seen since. As you must know if Alun Morgan's doing his job.'

Haggard looked at Willie Vine.

Vine lifted the manila folder for my attention, and patted it.

'Carney is in there,' Haggard said. 'A comprehensive dossier compiled by Willie.'

'Willie doesn't know all the consequences of what happened one recent moonlit night on board that yacht moored in Conwy harbour.'

'But you do – and you're about to tell us.'

I did so, in great detail. What had seemed complicated became simplified in the telling, and I almost – but not quite – came to believe that Carney really was a better bet for double murder than Jason Bone. Revenge was a powerful motive, and my relating how Ed Carney had walked off his yacht carrying with him the haunting memory of his son's bloody body and then disappeared when the boy's killer had himself been murdered was powerful and dramatic.

I looked at Haggard and Vine, got no visible reaction and went on to tell them how Silvester Laing had taken a call on his mobile shortly before he ran out into the road, and I could see Haggard's mind drifting back to that wet night and picturing a scheming killer using modern technology to draw his victim into a trap.

Of Jason and Sam Bone I deliberately said nothing.

'Interestin',' Haggard said, as I stuttered to a halt, 'but what you don't know is that Carney didn't disappear. He's been here in Liverpool ever since his lad was murdered, an' he's been throwin' his weight around. And he's well able: Link's big chief has got friends in high places. That's why when all this started the late Mrs Laing got her own way and, at her behest, you trotted off to her place to listen to a load of nonsense.'

'Is that what her story was, nonsense?'

'Didn't look that way, at first. A scally stickin' a knife in Laing on a wet night looked possible, even feasible; Laing was dead, his wife the only witness. But then there's a killin' on a yacht moored in Conwy harbour, an' we get a finger-print match: the dying Laing clutched the knife stickin' out of his chest, those prints were found on the Conwy murder weapon which almost certainly proves Laing killed Tony Carney. Hours after that, Jemima Laing's dead, probably killed by someone she knew because there was no forced entry and it looked like she'd been sharin' a cosy drink.'

Calum had dug out his Schimmelpenniks and a match flared as he lit one of the thin cigars.

'If you'd progressed that far, knew so much,' I said, 'then Ed Carney was under suspicion long before I told you my story?'

Haggard's glare was contemptuous. 'Sure Ed Carney was a suspect. Laing killed his son, revenge is sweet. A lot of what's in that file came from the hours Carney's spent in interview rooms.'

'What about his alibi – presuming he had one.'

'They've always got an alibi, but that means bugger all.'

He sniffed. 'Problem is, not much of what you told us can be corroborated; just about everyone who said anything worth-while's dead....' He looked at his cigarette, then said, 'Maybe we can do something with Laing's mobile, get onto the phone company for a log of incoming calls.'

'If you can find it,' Calum said.

Haggard studied the end of his cigarette, then looked up at me. 'It's not just a phone we're lookin' for.'

'I was wondering what was going on. Alun Morgan said Carney hadn't been seen since leaving the yacht. Then you tell us he's been here.' I studied Haggard's impassive face. 'So which is it?'

'He was free to move around, although he was told not to leave Liverpool.' He shrugged. 'There's no sayin' he has – but he's not at home, not been seen in his old haunts.'

I said: 'I think we can help you.'

'By findin' Carney?' Haggard said.

'By giving you the killer.'

Willie Vine's face registered puzzlement. 'Isn't that what Mike just said?'

'Ed Carney's not the killer,' Calum said.

'Then what the fuck did bright-eyes mean,' Haggard said, 'by sayin' the trip to Wales had given him the Laings' killer?'

'I'll ask him afterwards, over a pint, when you've released us without charge.' Calum grinned.

'Don't piss about,' Vine said with uncharacteristic coarse-ness. 'Giving us a name might just save your bacon, which at the moment I have to say is beginning to look rancid.'

'A name came up during our visit to Night Owl,' I said. 'Vick Valentine ring a bell. A GP,' I said. 'Dodgy prescrip-tions were mentioned.'

'He hasn't signed any of those recently,' Haggard said. 'Vick Valentine hasn't been seen by family or friends since Sunday – which is the very day a certain PI hit town like the bubonic plague.'

chapter thirteen

It was gone eight o'clock when we were gathered around the table in Calum's kitchen with the lateness of the hour enabling us to eat cod and chips, fresh from the local Chinese takeaway and tipped from polystyrene onto warmed plates to steam merrily alongside cups of rich dark coffee.

During the partaking of the meal a certain emasculated black cat with one mangled ear and a nose frantically sniffing the air must have paced several hundred yards back and forth across the kitchen and wound itself many times, and with feline elegance, around three pairs of ankles as it did its best to persuade somebody, anybody, to leave scraps. With the cunning gained from long experience, Satan concentrated on Sian. When her chair scraped back he was a black shadow falling across his bowl. One soft paw batted her hand as she bent with plate and fork; a faint mewl and a glance from heavily lidded eyes were her thanks before he got stuck in.

And then, with everyone satisfied, it was down to business.

'We've got until Saturday to come up with the killer.'

Sian blinked. 'Who says?'

'Haggard. He knows we were at Sound Bites. It was agree to that time limit, or you'd now be looking at my handsome face through iron bars.'

I sipped coffee, cocked an eyebrow at Calum. 'When we were away, what did you find out about the Laings?'

'Silvester Laing was as Manny Yates described him: a money-lender with no scruples. He got rich, met Ed Carney and became a partner in Link Associates. Jemima married him for his money – Christ, what girl would marry a man like that for anything else – and so the likelihood is that when he was murdered she would immediately look for a replacement.'

Sian had been with me when I'd raised with Alun Morgan the possibility that Jemima had tried blackmailing Carney. I'd quickly given Calum details of that Conwy discussion on the way back from Admiral Street. All of us could now see how the killing of Tony Carney in Conwy led in neat, logical steps to the two Liverpool murders.

Yet, looking at my companions, I knew not one of us wanted to believe that was the way it had happened. Jason Bone was our man; we'd need more than a trail of circumstantial evidence to change our allegiance.

Leaping in at once to confirm those thoughts, Sian said, 'Why would we investigate Carney, if we still believe Jason Bone is guilty?'

'I don't think we will,' I said, and saw Calum shaking his head in disagreement. 'What, you think we should?'

'Everything from the carjacking of the Mercedes to what we believe Bone has done is about drugs. I think we've got to consider a possible link to Ed Carney.'

'Carney's gone missing. If we're going to investigate him, where do we start?'

'Billie Tobin, Vick Valentine,' Sian said.

'Valentine's been missing since Sunday.'

'All right, then Tobin.'

Calum was pouring more coffee, his face thoughtful.

'So whither now?'

'The other room.'

'Is that it? The sum total of your wisdom?'

'I'm not at my best on a hard chair in a kitchen reeking of fish and chips—'

'And cat-litter,' said Sian, with a poisonous glance at Calum.

'And cat-litter,' I said. 'So let us retire to more salubrious surroundings, carrying with us our cups of coffee.'

'Lead on, Macduff,' Calum said, and pushed back his chair. 'For in that other room, you will be pleased to know, the blessed Macallan awaits.'

The Anglepoise shone down on the column of gleaming Scots Greys on Calum's work-table, the table lamp added a comforting glow, our cups of freshly laced coffee from which vapour curled cast welcoming shadows on the occasional table. Sian was relaxed and elegant on the settee where Satan lay as still as death with slitted eyelids through which sightless eyes gleamed. Calum was – as always – stretched out in his chair with socks wrinkled around his crossed ankles.

From the depths of the leather chair I had made my own I took a deep breath, made an effort, and set the ball rolling.

'Let's start with Bone.'

'Aye,' Calum said, 'for me it has to begin with Jason Bone ordering a hot Mercedes from Ronnie Maguire. He did it: Sam recognized his signature on the dirty bit of paper, Maguire reckoned her description matched the man. Then – according to Sam – after ordering the car, Bone went missing.'

'That can easily be checked,' I said. 'I'll ask her for the address of the insurance firm he works for, go there, see what his boss has to say.'

'Assuming he confirms Bone was AWOL, we've then got a problem: he went missing and nothing happens for two whole weeks. Then – last Friday, was it?'

I nodded. 'The Merc was delivered to Sam's on Thursday. Things started happening the next day.'

'Right, so we believe that on Friday Bone broke into his own garage to steal the car's audio system, then stabbed Silvester Laing when he was unexpectedly confronted.'

'But why go to such extraordinary lengths?' Sian said. 'Why not go to Maguire, then stay at home and carry on as normal? Two weeks later the Merc arrives, he retrieves the drugs without any ridiculous breaking and entering, and walks off into the sunset.'

'What if Sam kicked him out,' I said. 'She was complaining to me that he'd walked out on her, but if her marriage was breaking up she was bound to portray him as the villain.'

'Yes,' Sian said, 'that could be it.' She looked at Calum. 'What happened next?'

'Bone had got the drugs he was after so he carried on with whatever plans he'd made. I cannot see how he can be connected to the Jemima Laing killing, and I don't think we should try to do that.'

'Which leaves us with just the one conclusion,' I said. 'We're looking for one killer for Silvester, another for Jemima.'

'And,' Calum said, 'we know them both by name.'

'Jason Bone, Ed Carney.' I nodded.

'And for Carney's story,' Sian said, 'we have to go back as far as my last course, in Cape Wrath. For your benefit, Cal, Tony Carney was having a go at Silvester Laing over a young woman the older man was knocking off. Most of the jibes had to do with age-difference. But Carney was also upset because the girl – a Link employee - had messed up his previous month's accounts. I've already said I think it was about expenses he'd submitted, something like that.'

'There's just the one solid fact,' I said, 'based on fingerprints found on two knives - and that is that Tony Carney was stabbed by Silvester Laing. Then there is conjecture – this time using motive, opportunity and, yes, that call to Laing's mobile phone Jemima Laing mentioned, to build a case against him: Ed Carney avenged his son's murder by stabbing his killer to death.'

'Which theory,' Calum said, 'effectively buggers up any case against Jason Bone.'

'Jason Bone,' I said, 'could still be guilty of ... well, of ordering a hot car and making off with the package of drugs it contained.'

'And if we accept him for those minor offences,' Sian said, 'it leaves us with the possibility of Carney as a double killer:

Carney also murdered Jemima Laing because she tried to blackmail him.'

I nodded. 'Which then rules out any link between Carney and Bone. And we're going round in circles.'

'So far,' Sian said, 'nobody's mentioned the possibility that Jemima Laing was right all along: a scally stole the stereo and murdered her husband. Streetwise, he'd soon have realized that left a widow alone in a big house, and so he came back and that visit ended in Jemima's murder.'

'If we accept that third possibility,' I said, 'we're left with fingerprints *proving* Laing murdering Tony Carney, Jason Bone's guilty of nothing worse than receiving a stolen car, and Ed Carney's innocent.'

'There is one little bit of information that, in the heat of several moments, I may have neglected to pass on,' Calum said. 'If you recall, I visited some of the Woolton hostelries playing hunt the stereo. It did sell, just as I told you, and I located the man who bought it. The stereo he bought was a cheapy. A 2004 Mercedes C200 would almost certainly have a Mercedes audio unit.'

I took a deep breath, let it go very slowly.

'So what's the verdict? Two stereos were up for sale in Woolton? Or one, but it wasn't the right one and it was sold in an effort to put certain people off the scent?'

'I'd plump for that,' Sian said.

'But who was doing the selling?' Again I looked at Calum.

'A tall fellow. Dark hair, skinny, looked tough …'

'Sam's description of Jason.' I relaxed enough to smile ruefully. 'Back to square one.'

'So what now?' Calum said.

'Line up the suspects,' I said, 'and pick them off one by one. Or do what we were suspected of doing in the Gault case: stand back and watch them all snuff it, and the one left on his feet's got to be guilty.'

Sian chuckled softly, which was never going to be enough to drown the thud of the downstairs door and the thump of heavy feet on the stairs. It was to our credit that not one of us believed that it was Haggard and Vine again paying us a visit, though whether we should be proud of the ability to recognize the tread of individual detectives was a moot point.

In the end, it mattered not a jot, for when Calum opened the door to a most refined knock it was to discover, with the onset of severe and collective trepidation, that the bogeyman had come a-calling.

chapter fourteen

Things were getting bloody serious. That was the inspired thought that hit me like an ice-cold shower when I was escorted down the stairs and out into the fresh breeze coming off the Mersey where Ronnie Maguire opened the door and manoeuvred me into Ed Carney's big Mercedes.

They'd been insistent. Ed Carney, immaculately dressed, grey hair as soft as a dove's breast, shoes as shiny as Fred Astaire's, had stood in front of big Ronnie, stared at us with empty eyes and stated that the felling of Max in Maguire's office had been the equivalent of a sucker punch and could never be repeated. Meaning don't make stupid moves.

So Calum and Sian had sat there with laced coffee and unreadable expressions and watched me go, and now I was in the back seat of an expensive car being leaned on by a man twice my size as Carney himself drove the big Merc with just a whisper of sound through the lighted streets that eventually saw us drifting up Woolton Road in the general direction of Sam Bone's house – which didn't do my stomach cramps much good – only to turn into Springwood Avenue and the dark and ill lit grassland of Clarke Gardens and park under the trees.

And I couldn't help remembering that the local crematorium was in the next field, Allerton Cemetery across the road.

Carney, well-dressed but with a voice straight off the Dock Road, fired up a fat cigar and half-turned in his seat to fix me with his pale, unreadable eyes and snap a command from the side of his mouth.

'Take a walk, Ron.'

The door snicked open and big Ronnie Maguire went for a stroll in the park.

'You realize,' I said, 'that you're now vulnerable and I could bop you on the head and make my escape across the grass.'

'In your dreams,' Carney said. 'If your present position's anythin' to go by, I'd say you were runnin' out of luck.'

'So what now?'

He eased down the electric window, puffed on his cigar, narrowed his eyes.

'The drugs scene in this city,' he said. 'It's a multi-layered operation. The way it works is most of the gravy's scooped up by those sittin' on the top of the heap.'

'And that's where you are?'

He shook his head. 'I get my share of the rich pickin's, but if you were talkin' to the man at the top you wouldn't be talkin' to 'im 'cause you'd be dead.'

'Right, I think I've got that – so, what's this about?'

'The bottom layers,' he said.

'Vick Valentine.'

'Vick's down there, but I'm talkin' about those workin' for him, the bottom of the pile, the scallies scratchin' and scrapin' for left-overs – an' what we thought was happenin', probably wasn't but still could be.'

'You're talking in riddles.'

'All you need to do,' he said, 'is listen.'

'I'm listening.'

'When Ronnie Maguire was asked to steal a particular black Merc,' Carney said, 'he knew whose it was, made a guess at what was goin' on, and told me. I was intrigued by what looked like an upstart's stupid audacity. I told Ronnie to go ahead, him and Max caught up with it in Park Road an' did the necessary.'

'Not Vick Valentine's Merc,' I said, 'because he didn't own one.'

'But his cocky young cousin did, and what me and Ron

reckoned then was young Danny Valentine was arrangin' the theft of his own Merc so he could split the meagre profits when the goods he was carryin' were sold.' There was a tiny moist kissing sound as Carney again sucked on his fat cigar.

'But then you looked more closely, people close to you started dying, and suddenly all was not what it seemed.'

'Don't let a man who talks in riddles fool you into thinking everything's complicated,' Carney said. 'Don't assume blood ties make everyone bosom pals. If I've got a son who pushes another guy too hard and pays for it, that's his fuckin' problem.'

'But something a man in your position would be obliged to avenge.'

He was looking into the distance. 'Position?'

'Not as boss of Link Associates. Most of the staff would be law-abiding. But when wearing your other hat there's a certain *machismo*, a code—'

'Yeah, but I didn't kill Silvester Laing. And three people dying didn't bother me because I was still left with the names of three different people who'd stepped out of line.'

'Two. Jason Bone was never part of the set-up – was he?'

'Jason Bone,' Ed Carney said, 'was a name that gave us a startin' point. But around about the time you came on the scene, so did Danny's Merc. At Bone's house. As we knew it would, because Ronnie stole it, worked on it, and delivered the fuckin' thing.'

'Complete with fake stereo,' I said, 'which you left *in situ.*'

Carney nodded. 'Bone,' he said, 'had to be a nobody. He couldn't afford to finance the theft of the Merc, so maybe it was his idea and he peddled it on the hush-hush at the Owl. Or maybe *he* was bein' used, an' was fed the idea bit by bit by someone with the cash to make it work. Either way, so what. He was going to tell us, because we had him – only then we didn't. We looked the other way, he went missin'. An' then when the Merc arrived, the stereo went the same fuckin' way.'

'You couldn't chase Vick Valentine, the dodgy doctor,

because he'd also gone missing.' I waited. 'What about the cousin?'

That got me a blank stare behind which the first signs of fury seethed.

'Missing?'

'Which brings us,' Carney said, 'to you. And Jason Bone.'

'Why me?'

And Ed Carney lifted his right hand and rubbed the ball of his thumb against the tip of his middle finger.

Friday

'Ed Carney will give us a thousand pounds apiece,' I said, 'if we give him Jason Bone's head on a plate.'

I was drinking the Macallan with ice. My safe return, in their eyes, had been a foregone conclusion. It was after midnight, Sian was as tired as Satan and wilting, Calum still bent over his work table with his tongue in the corner of his mouth as he put the finishing touches to the Scots Greys.

'There was no mention of Tobin. My feeling is that in the hierarchy he ranks somewhere below a private soldier and was harassing Sam under orders, and to save his own skin.'

'It's Sam I feel sorry for,' Sian said.

'I brought her name up after the money was mentioned. Carney accepts she's unlucky, caught in the middle of something she knows nothing about.'

Calum, squinting at a coat of arms, said, 'But if Tobin's of no use …'

'That's not what I said.'

'You mean,' Sian said, 'that if he's desperate to avoid the chop, he could still be a help?'

'The impression I got from Carney was that much of the skulduggery was hatched at Night Owl.'

'Deary me,' Calum said with feigned languor, 'does this mean yet another trip to that den of iniquity?'

'Yes,' I said. 'Grab your coat.'

He looked up, blinking through his smeared lenses. 'Now hold on a minute, the bloody time's creeping on and in any case how do we know—?'

'Mobiles have been invented. I phoned. Tobin's there. So's Manny, and he'll hold him for us.'

'Count me out,' Sian said. 'Although, on second thoughts, a slinky siren fluttering long eyelashes—'

'And flaunting this and that,' Calum said.

'Might just do the trick,' Sian said, 'if you see what I mean.'

I did. Behind Sian's offer to accompany us was her understanding that while women are often still considered little more than attractive wallpaper when seen in a male environment, for the woman of intelligence that brings an enormous advantage. Like the ability to watch and listen without being noticed.

I liked the idea, and it showed.

'No stone unturned....' Even as she yodelled the slogan Sian was bouncing off the settee, eyes bright as she gaily fixed her hair.

Calum, absently washing his brush in a jamjar of white spirit, said, 'If it's any help, I think Tobin's a waste of time.'

'Yes, and past midnight means it's already Friday, and the tempus set by Haggard is rapidly fugitting.' I pulled a face. 'We've still got a bewilderment of crooks, and at least one of them still living who insists he's not a murderer.' They were both watching me, and I nodded. 'That's right, Ed Carney didn't kill Silvester Laing – he says. Nevertheless, if Night Owl is where the skulduggery began, what better place to start the run for home? I say we give it a try.'

When we walked into Night Owl the same stale air hit us in the face like the clammy breath of a seriously ailing beast, in the gloomy sepia paintings the same gents carried the same swords and stared morosely across at the same bedraggled Highland cattle wallowing in the same murky waters.

If I'd been asked I'd have sworn blind the three men

studying their cards at the table where Vick Valentine's chair was still vacant were playing the same hand for the same meagre pot. Just when I was about to rub my eyes like a man awakening from a dream I caught sight of Manny Yates beckoning us to, yes, the same table against the same dadoed wall. And it was only when we had made our way there and dropped gratefully into the not too uncomfortable seats that I noticed Billie Tobin, with a fresh growth of designer stubble, hanging on to the antique timber bar.

'You managed to keep him here.'

'Keepin' Tobin here's not the problem,' Manny said. 'The problem is kickin' him out at closin' time.'

I looked across, caught the barman's eye and nodded at Tobin.

Manny left us to it, waddled over to the nearby table and sat down in Valentine's empty chair. Tobin came over carrying his refreshed glass of Theakston's bitter. Close up, he looked not drunk but tired and twitchy, the stubble accentuating hollow cheeks and the purple shadows beneath bloodshot eyes. He dragged up a chair from the next table, sat down, cleared his throat nervously.

'Is this bad news?'

'Not at all. I want you to go back over the past few days. Fill in the bits I don't know. Like, details of the search of Sam Bone's house.'

'I wasn't there.'

'So who was?'

'Vick Valentine. Ronnie Maguire.'

'Only now Valentine's missing. And so is his cousin, the young man who owned the Merc.'

Tobin nodded. He'd reached into a pocket and was tipping Old Holborn onto a cigarette paper.

I waited. He was deliberately absorbed in his task. 'What? You mean you *know* Valentine's missing?'

'They searched Bone's house, found nothin', and Ronnie pissed off. Valentine stayed behind. Maybe he was hopin' someone'd walk in an' he could grab their wrist an' give them the dreaded Chinese torture until they cracked.' He grinned to himself, licked the paper, rolled it, pinched the end, squinted across at me. 'But nothin' happened, so then Valentine went 'ome.'

'And went missing.'

'Yeah. Ronnie tried to reach him the next day. Only nobody knew where he was.'

'How do you know that?'

He shrugged. 'Word gets around.'

'If you were available,' Calum said, 'why would Valentine do his own searching?'

Tobin's thin lip curled. 'Because if I'd gone an' searched Bone's place an' come up with nothin' he'd've had to go anyway. So he saved time.' He spat a shred of tobacco. 'An' a fat lot of fuckin' good it did him.'

'Why?' I said. 'What d'you think's happened to him.'

He sneered. 'You're the fuckin' private dick, you work it out.'

Sian was shaking her head. Tobin lost interest. From the nearby table Manny Yates had turned towards us and was beckoning. Calum saw him, winked at me and ambled over to the bar. I touched Sian's hand, left her to her quiet observing and went across to the Lime Street PI. One of the card-players dragged over a chair, and I sat. Their playing-cards were face down. Coloured chips were heaped in the centre of the table.

'We got talkin' about this and that,' Manny said, 'and Bone's name cropped up. Remember, I told you he spent a lot of time with Valentine?'

'I do.'

'Right, so I asked the obvious question: what the hell did the two of them talk about? I mean, it sounds like the start of a joke, doesn' it? – have you heard the one about the GP an' the insurance salesman—'

'Class,' said a grey-haired card player with watery eyes, a retreating chin and a tone that was haughty, 'has no place in Night Owl.'

'Tell that,' Manny said, 'to the fuckin' marines.'

I grinned. 'So what was the reply?'

Grey Hair had elected himself spokesman for a lean colleague with the thick lenses of his Peter Fonda glasses magnifying an awful squint, and a sweating fat man who was down to his last two chips and looking for the door.

'Insurance,' Grey Hair said. 'And financial planning.'

'Is that all? I was hoping for a sniff of something ... iniquitous.'

The watery eyes didn't waver at the outrageous suggestion, but the tone definitely wobbled. 'Dear me, no. Bone works for a city firm. Valentine's a GP, and always facing the prospect of litigation.'

'But he has money to invest.'

'As is the way with all professional men of standing in our community.'

'In Night Owl,' I said, 'class has no place.' I heard Manny Yates chuckle as I said to the man with watery eyes, 'Do you know the name of this city firm?'

'Crass and Co. India buildings.'

'And, as a matter of interest, do you know where Bone has been for the past couple of weeks?'

'You'll have to ask Valentine.'

'I will, if I can find him.'

Manny came with me back to our table. He told me he'd gone over to the card players specifically to introduce Valentine into the conversation, but the table was home to an insular clique and they'd closed ranks.

'Not,' he said, 'that they'd know anything. Valentine hasn't been seen here since Sunday afternoon – end of story.'

'And mine just got tougher,' I said. 'Billie Tobin's gone.'

Manny snorted. 'Forgotten everything I taught you. I remember tellin' you once, in this game you need eyes in the back of your head. Willie pissed off when you were talkin' to Minnesota Slim over there an' your sidekick was at the bar.'

'The sidekick at the bar was as one with our trained observer,' Calum said, and winked at Sian. 'We both saw

Tobin leave, our eyes met across the room and the silent decision was made that he'd been milked dry and was free to go.'

'As are we.'

'At once, but without haste.'

'A disorderly retreat,' Manny said, grinning.

'A tactical withdrawal to regroup,' I said.

'Balls.'

'I have a name and address, courtesy of Minnesota Slim at the card table. I'm convinced Crass and Co will give me the whereabouts of Jason Bone.'

'Haggard'll be pleased.'

'Haggard won't know about it.'

'Haggard,' Manny said with a grin, 'has just walked in through the door.'

Two in the morning and behind the bar a thin bald man who might have been the Owl's owner had appeared out of the wings as if on cue and body language suggested he was already reaching reluctantly into his back pocket for a fat wallet to grease official palms itching to get hold of his licence.

Haggard's sharp black eyes had alighted on Calum Wick and the big detective was bulling his way across the room to Manny Yates's table. Willie Vine looked towards the bar and winked. The inscrutable bald man nodded, and I was hit with the sudden realization that it was amateur night at Night Owl and I was the star.

Chairs were dragged up. Vine sat with his back to the wall as Haggard fired up a king-sized, and I caught the usual whiff of Aramis and old sweat as the burly DI adopted an ungainly sprawl and let his coat fall open to expose a wrinkled white shirt. Drinks were brought to them by the barman, on a battered tin tray awash with spillage. Haggard glowered, then turned his dark gaze on me.

'We're makin' progress – right, Willie?'

Vine nodded. He was holding a half of Guinness. His urbanity was untouched by the lateness of the hour.

I said, 'You've found Laing's mobile?'

Vine shook his head. 'No trace of it.'

'We've been talkin' to certain unsavoury characters,' Haggard said, and watched me with knowing eyes as he took a sip of his favourite single malt and rolled it around his tongue. 'Ronnie Maguire in Old Swan. Billie Tobin.' Still watching me, he said. 'We tried talkin' to a young feller called Danny Valentine. Know who he is?'

'Vick Valentine's cousin.'

'Who owned a certain …?'

'Black Merc.'

'But?'

'He's missing.'

'An' you know that because?'

'I was told by Ed Carney.'

Haggard grinned at Vine. 'I'd make a fuckin' good dentist.'

'Specializing in extractions,' Vine said.

'I see him more as a sly bastard squeezing blood out of a stone or stealing coins from the offertory tray,' Calum Wick said. 'But when we're done discussing his disgusting personal habits, perhaps he'd get to the point and tell us why he's here.'

'It's his good nature,' Sian said. She'd just returned from inspecting the Owl's cloakroom facilities, and had missed the opening volleys. 'Jack's floundering, and Mike wants to help.'

'Young Vine,' Haggard said, rolling his eyes, 'is a dab hand at – what is it, psychiatry? Psychology? Or psychiatric psychology?'

'Watching and listening,' Willie Vine said, and he grinned at me. 'And something told me that Maguire and Tobin were holding back. Not telling the truth.'

'I suppose it depends,' I said, 'on what you asked.'

'A battery of questions,' Haggard said, 'usin' all the words that fit the case and their filthy habits. Like Mercedes, carjackin', drugs. Jack Scott, private eye.'

'They expressed injured astonishment,' Vine said.

'Open-mouthed disbelief,' said Haggard.

'Incredulity,' Vine said. 'But we know you were there at the garage, because big Max ended up in dock, didn't he?' He flicked a glance at Calum. 'And so we wondered if your in-depth investigations had borne fruit.'

'Or to put it more simply,' Haggard said with a leer, 'did you locate the fuckin' Merc?'

'Twenty-four hours,' I said, 'and all will be revealed.'

'Yes or no?'

'Yes. On Sunday.'

Haggard took a deep breath. 'Where?'

I shook my head.

'Confidential,' Willie Vine said softly.

'Are you suggesting,' I said, 'that the death of Laing and his wife is connected to drugs?'

'We've been following your trail,' Vine said. 'So far every-thing you've *touched* is connected to drugs.'

'Problem is,' Calum said, 'by the way you warned Jack off on Sunday I don't think you'd have bothered picking up his trail until after Jemima's death. If that's so, it leaves an annoying wee gap.'

'And in that gap,' Haggard said, 'you found that missin' Mercedes – and what else?'

Vine shook his head. 'Not *what* else. *Who* else?'

I looked at my watch.

Vine sighed. 'Yes. We know. Twenty-four hours.'

From Night Owl I'd dropped Sian off at Meg Morgan's. That meant she was absent from a later-than-usual morning parade in Calum's kitchen, and as the tall Scot and I munched and slurped we came to decisions that I knew she would appreciate. Calum had almost finished the Scots Greys. While he finished off the soldiers, I would take a taxi down to India Buildings and talk to someone at Crass & Co.

For a while when we'd finished eating we were both silent, me finishing my coffee, Calum getting rid of the dishes. That done we moved into the other room, Calum began work on the Scots Greys, I wandered to the window and looked out over the sun-splashed Mersey as it rolled sluggishly towards the Irish Sea.

Silence. In it the liquid sound of a paintbrush being rinsed. Gulls mournfully calling as they wheeled high above deep water. Sammy Quade banging about in the downstairs flat.

'I think we'd better keep well away from Sam Bone,' I said.

'Aye. The polis are on your tail, so we steer well clear.'

'But as they haven't yet got to her, she can move freely. I'll phone her, ask her to go to Meg Morgan's flat. Then I'll call Sian, tell her what's happening.'

'Nothing wrong with your thinking, but what's all this in aid of?'

'I want Sian, very gently, to pick Sam's brains. She's Jason's wife. He's walked out on her, but they had a life together. Surely she's got some idea where he could be.'

'And you're going to Crass and Co?'

'Definitely. I'll tell Sian to pass that on to Sam. If it does nothing else, it might jog her memory.' I thought for a moment and said, 'I also want Sian to reassure Sam we're still working for her. She's a good kid.'

I took a taxi down-town to avoid the bother of finding a parking-place, got out near the Adelphi when traffic backed up, and began walking briskly towards the Pier Head. The skies had clouded over, a cool breeze had sprung up and it was pouring with rain. By the time I reached the town hall and started down Water Street I was pretty well soaked.

I was so deep in my own damp misery that happenings all around me became blurred, the awareness that the rain had driven people under cover and passers by were fewer didn't fully register; the insistent, monotonous slap of footsteps that had been dogging me for too long to be happenstance raised no flicker of alarm....

Until, suddenly, I was snapped back to reality. The steady beat of those footsteps increased to a rapid drumming as the man following me broke into a run. I had time for a half-turn, a twist of the head; a brief glimpse of blank eyes, a white face glistening with rain, a dark shape bearing down on me.

Then I was bundled, faster than I could resist, into a narrow alley of dark, streaming walls and paving-stones awash with dirty water. Ten feet, twenty feet. A thick forearm slammed against my chest and drove me back against rough wet bricks. My attacker held me there with his left hip. His left fist grabbed a handful of shirt at my throat. I saw his right arm draw back, the glitter of a blade.

I was choking. I sucked a breath, clawed at his face, groped for his eyes. He ducked his head, cracked the bridge of my nose. The hand gripping my shirt clamped into a fist, twisted. Breath whistled in my throat. My shirt became a tightening noose. I couldn't breathe. Through streaming eyes I stared into a blank, contorted face. The man hissed through clenched teeth. He tensed for the killing thrust.

I grunted and let my knees go slack. My weight dragged me down. I was too heavy to hold. I could smell the stink of his sweat. My face scraped across his belt-buckle. I locked my knees, clamped my left hand on his knife wrist. Then I uncoiled. Still gripping his knife wrist I drove upwards, twisting to my left. My right forearm slammed high into his right armpit. His arm popped out of its shoulder socket with a sound of tearing. He screamed.

The knife hit the ground with a tinkle. He fell back against the opposite wall, his right arm hanging limp, his mouth wide and wet with pain.

From the mouth of the alley a voice yelled, 'Hey, what the hell's going on there!'

And as the man who had shouted stepped warily closer I listened again to the sound of running footsteps, this time as my attacker turned tail and lolloped away down the alley like an injured crab.

When I looked in the mirror in the visitors' toilets in India Building there was a faint red mark on the bridge of my nose,

I was still pale with shock, my eyes were a little too bright, and I roughly combed my hair with fingers that were not quite steady.

But I was alive, and recovering fast.

The visit to the gents was followed by a quick look at the business directory board and a run up three flights of stairs to the offices of Crass & Co, the insurance company where Jason Bone worked. The strenuous activity completed the restoration of my damp clothing to its normal state of stylishly rumpled untidiness, brought colour back to my cheeks and told me that there was no permanent damage to my throat.

And when I spoke to the blonde receptionist there was an unexpected bonus: she was so intrigued by the huskiness of a voice that was sexy but obviously painful to the speaker that she listened without question and summoned someone who could deal with my request.

His name was Phil Daley. He was an executive of obscure seniority.

'Yes,' he said, 'Bone works here. Has done for … oh, two years, I believe.'

'But he's not here now?'

'No.'

'Has been recently?'

'Why? What is it you want?'

I was expecting that.

'Not me, other than indirectly,' I said. 'Bone's wife hasn't seen him for a while. She's … distressed.'

We were in the sort of office insurance people use to interview unimportant clients. Phil Daley was frowning.

'I have heard rumours. But it's not our concern, is it, unless it affects his work. Which it hasn't, so far.' He raised an optimistic eyebrow. 'Perhaps that's why he took extended leave.'

'Ah.' My next question had been anticipated. 'So he's away legally – if that's not the wrong way to put it?'

He smiled. 'He had six weeks coming.'

'So he's not short of a few bob?'

'Without pay. He works on commission.'

'Christ!'

Daley looked miffed. 'Generous commission.'

'If the sales are made.' I nodded knowingly. 'I sold accident insurance for an American firm in Australia and left after two weeks to go hunting for food.'

His smile was weak. 'If that's all....'

'Almost. When did he start this long holiday?'

'Two weeks ago. Bit more, actually. Nearer three.'

'And he's due back when?'

'Work it out: six minus two. Or three.' This time his smile was patronizing. 'But you never know, perhaps he's like you,' he said, rising to see me to the door, 'out there in the wilderness, looking for a square meal.'

But that wasn't the end of Crass & Co.

I reached the swing doors leading out into the corridor, pushed through them and was followed by a dark-haired young woman. She touched my arm, and when I turned she was smiling hesitantly.

'Couldn't help overhearing,' she said. 'It's common knowledge in the office that Jason's marriage is shaky.'

'And that he's broke?'

'Well, insurance salesmen are usually very successful, or the reverse.'

'So he'd be staying in England—'

I broke off as the doors behind us whispered open, and a man in a suit breezed by and gave the girl a hard look.

'I really will have to go—'

'But you do know?'

She nodded, starting to turn away. 'One of the other girls told me he's been trying to raise a lump sum for some project. If he can sort that out, he's planning on going to Gibraltar.'

The doors closed behind her with butterfly softness, leaving me rejoicing while I cursed my own stupidity.

chapter fifteen

'Sam didn't mention Gib?'

'No. And I feel so sorry for her. I told her you'd gone to Crass and Co. She went pale with shock. I'm sure she wants to know where Jason is, but she's also scared stiff you'll find him and bring him back to her.'

Calum was testing the Scots Greys with the back of a finger, seeing if it was safe to pack them for the flight to Gibraltar. Sian had returned from Meg Morgan's minutes after I got back from town. I was still mentally kicking myself.

'I can't believe I saw that picture on her wall, a Mediterranean scene, and didn't twig. I was stationed in Gib, I know it so well. It's changed, but not that much.' I took a deep breath. 'And what's the matter with Sam? I *asked* her where he might have gone.'

'I told you,' Sian said, 'she doesn't know what she wants.'

'Mm. And she's probably got her brother telling her she's better off without her rogue husband; they've both told me to throw Jason to the wolves if we do find him – and I'm sure Sam can't believe she said that.'

'There's something else.' Sian was unhappy. 'Haggard's been to see her.'

I glanced at Calum, saw his surprise. 'What the hell did he want?'

'The present whereabouts of Jason Bone. Sam told him she doesn't know where he is, doesn't *want* to know. Haggard left it at that, asked her to get in touch if Jason turns up.'

'The police,' I said, 'are catching up with us, and fast.'

Calum had drifted away from his work-table. Sian was gazing moodily out at the rain drifting like banks of thin mist over the Mersey. She looked back at me expectantly.

'Did I tell you the man who dragged me into an alley wasn't Max, or Maguire?'

Calum nodded. 'Why should it be? They work for Carney. Carney wants you to find Bone.'

'*Who* attacked you is not important,' Sian said, coming away from the window. 'We need to know who arranged it. You were on your way to Crass and Co to ask questions about Jason Bone, so the conclusion is…?'

'Bone was behind the attack.'

Calum had plonked himself down in a chair and stretched his legs. I knew he was intrigued by what had happened in town.

'If it was Bone,' he said, 'it gives us a clearer picture of what's been going on. We had him ordering the Merc, lying low until it was delivered, then stealing the stereo. We assumed he then flitted; buggered off with the cash last Saturday.'

'But if he arranged the attack, he couldn't have done,' Sian said, 'because today he knew where Jack was going, or had him followed. No, Jason Bone was still here, in Liverpool. He was *forced* to hang around because, when he stole the stereo, all he had was a quantity of drugs, not cash.'

'Of course.' I'd briefed them on what I'd been told by the young woman at India Buildings, so they knew Bone had been trying to raise a lump sum. 'He had packets of white powder, and in that form it was of no earthly use to him.'

'He had to sell it,' Calum said.

'But he didn't know where or how,' Sian said. 'Stealing from the Merc was one thing, but after that he was in unknown territory. Getting rid of those drugs was taking time. And while he was sweating looking for a buyer, you came on the scene, Jack. So he watched you, or had you watched. Suddenly, today, you were getting too close.'

'But you said "was here", so you think he's gone?'

'I think so, yes. If you sell insurance you're used to talking to strangers – and you have loads of contacts.' She nodded to herself. 'Yes, it took time, but I think he could certainly find a buyer in seven days.'

'Flights to Gibraltar,' Calum said, 'are with Monarch or BA.'

I nodded. 'If he flew from Manchester, it's Monarch. I'll get on to Manny, ask him to get passenger information from those two airlines.'

'And us?' Calum said.

'If Haggard does follow the trail to Crass and Co,' I said, 'he'll find out about Bone's Gibraltar plans. I want to get to Bone while Haggard's still struggling. I'd like you to stay here, keep an eye on Sam. If you think it's worth it, go to see her, tell her to give nothing away to Haggard. And keep in touch with Manny, get help if you need it. Sian will come with me to Gib.'

Calum nodded. 'What happened to you this morning suggests things might get rough. Bone's not going to see you coming and roll over.'

'I'll let DS Luis Romero know we're arriving in Gibraltar.'

'He might have a nice empty cell you can share,' Calum said, grinning as he moved to the work-table to begin packing soldiers.

'The Rock Hotel for us,' I said, and now it was Sian's turn to smile. 'But at their prices, it *will* be a shared room.'

'Ah, but at this time of year,' Sian said, her smile turning sweet, 'it's still warm enough in Gib for you to sleep on the veranda.'

chapter sixteen

I confirmed our bookings by phone and we picked up the flight documents from the travel agent, drove to Manchester airport and put the Shogun in the long-stay car-park. The flight was uneventful, the landing on Gibraltar's short runway alongside Marina Bay as light as a heron touching down on a lake of glass.

At the Rock Hotel they gave us a key attached to a fluffy little Barbary ape which opened the door to a room on the first floor of the accommodation. We unpacked quickly, and spent the next ten minutes out on one of two verandas sipping excellent firewater from the complimentary decanters as we leaned on the rail and looked out over Gibraltar Bay. It was late dusk, the lights were twinkling in Gibraltar town, on the liners and smaller boats moored against the moles, in the border town of La Linea and across the bay in the town of Algeciras. But the skies were not yet dark, and in their immense arc there was that incredible Mediterranean luminosity that drew and held the eyes and caused the throat to ache with its beauty. And I had the weird yet wonderful feeling of being back home, for during three years of army service it was these skies and this view seen from the lofty eyrie of Buena Vista Barracks that had greeted me each reveille and bade me goodnight when the notes of the Last Post had faded into poignant silence.

Alongside me I sensed Sian thinking similar thoughts. When I looked at her there was a wistful smile on her face. I touched her hand, squeezed gently.

'Memories, how bitter-sweet …'

'Mm. But without them where would we be? I think we should go down and get something to eat.'

'What an excellent idea.'

We took the lift down and sat at one of the tables close to the windows in the casual dining-area at the front of the hotel on a sort of mezzanine floor overlooking reception. Below us the night-shift had taken over behind the desk. Dinner was still being served in the main dining-room, but from a waiter who came to us from the Barbary Bar we ordered coffee and huge fresh baguettes filled with juicy sliced beef and salad.

We had arrived in Gibraltar. And we had followed Jason Bone.

Not literally, because he had been some way ahead of us. But Sian had been right. Bone must have remained in Liverpool after stealing the stereo from his stolen Mercedes because he was finding it difficult to get rid of his haul of drugs. That seemed to be confirmed by the information we got from Manny Yates, who told us Jason Bone had taken a BA flight from Heathrow to Gibraltar early that morning. Bone had his cash lump sum – and he'd been in Gib for just twelve hours.

But where was he now?

I thought about a recent phone call and said, 'Luis Romero can't do much for us.'

'If you've been speaking to him, it must have been when I blinked.'

'No, you were on the veranda, partaking a little more slowly of the complimentary hard stuff.'

'In a ladylike manner,' Sian said. 'I drink with the refinement commensurate with my upbringing in Cardiff Bay – and don't you dare laugh. So. What did suave Luis have to say?'

'He'll help if there's trouble. But the Gibraltarian police can do nothing because I have no authority, and there have been no complaints.' I shrugged. 'So we look for him, with Luis Romero's best wishes.'

'A tall order.'

'But there are clues.'

She raised an eyebrow. 'There are?'

'According to Sam, her husband likes the sea.'

'In Gibraltar,' Sian said, 'we are surrounded by the stuff.'

'With some excellent developing marinas catering to the nautical set.'

'Ah. Is that where we start?'

'Tomorrow. Right now I want to phone my other Gibraltarian connection. Tony Macedo. We've got six boxes of Scots Greys he thinks are still in England. Or Wales. So I'm about to make his day.'

'You're an old softy,' Sian said, smiling. 'I'll pop up to the room, get our coats.'

She headed for the lift. I dug out my mobile, but before I could dial Tony's number it rang.

It was Calum Wick.

'Anything?'

I shook my head, said, 'Not yet. We start looking tomorrow, Queensway Quay Marina, then Marina Bay. What about you?'

'Bad news. Tommy Mack's gone missing.'

I frowned. 'Christ! Where d'you hear that?'

'I called on Sam, keeping a watchful eye and all that. She can't reach him by phone, he's not at his bed-sit, and she's going bananas.'

I got up from the table, began walking towards the lift.

'Your thoughts, Cal?'

'Two extremes: he got fed up, or he's dead.'

'Mm. And your money's on?'

'Well, Ed Carney said he'd leave them alone, but can we trust a bloody gangster?'

'I think he's willing to give me some time to deliver Bone. The trouble is, we're not convinced Bone murdered Jemima. If he didn't, there's another killer on the loose.'

'Amend that: we weren't convinced Bone murdered Jemima. After what we've discovered, I'm bloody convinced he did.'

I frowned. 'Go on.'

'We assumed he left town as soon as he'd got the drugs. But then you were attacked on the way to India Building, and Bone was the only person with a reason to keep you away from Crass and Co. So, we decided he'd stayed behind after all – and that's been confirmed by Manny Yates.'

'Yes,' I said. 'But why kill Jemima?'

'He stabbed Laing when the naked wee feller came bounding out of his garden. The lights were on in the house. Jemima was watching from the bedroom window. If Bone saw her – and, Christ, he must have done – he'd know her evidence would send him to prison for life.'

I found myself nodding. 'Haggard said there was no sign of a break-in, and that fits.'

'Yes, because Bone lives across the road and she'd know him, if only by sight.'

'That's what she said. And she told me she thought the killing was the work of a scally so—'

'She wouldn't suspect Bone, and he'd get into the house with a toothy grin and a plausible story for wanting to see her.'

'So what's happened to Tommy Mack?'

'Despite your faith, it's got to be Ed Carney … and that's bad because with Mack gone, Sam's on her own.'

'Not quite.'

'Your faith,' Calum said, 'is touching.'

'I know you'll do your best.'

'Indeed. I'll requisition a driver and vehicle for hi-tech mobile patrols.'

As I shifted my feet and turned, my eye was drawn to a man and a young woman. They were below, walking away from the reception desk towards the glass doors, probably heading down town.

Watching them idly, but with a strange feeling I couldn't quite pin down, I said, 'Hi-tech and mobile would be Stan Jones, his clapped-out van, and a couple of Nokias?'

'No woman has ever been safer.'

Away to my right the lift hissed. The door slid open. Sian came towards me, carrying my jacket and the room key attached to the fluffy little Barbary ape. On the lower floor the hotel's glass doors opened for the young couple. The man cast one swift glance behind him. Then they were gone. A taxi's interior lights blinked on as the driver opened the doors.

And then it hit me.

'Calum, I've got to go, talk to you later—'

I switched off, slipped the phone into my pocket. Sian was handing me my coat, frowning at my obvious agitation.

I said: 'I've just seen Tommy Mack leaving the hotel.'

'Mack's in England.'

'I've been talking to Calum. Mack's missing.'

Sian shook her head. 'I think you're seeing things, but one way to find out is to ask at the desk.'

On the way to reception I watched the taxi pulling away to swoop down the steep slope of the hotel's drive which would take it onto Europa Road and down the hill towards Trafalgar Cemetery and so on to Main Street.

The pretty receptionist smiled at Sian as she placed the little Barbary ape on the counter, then looked at me enquiringly.

I spread my hands helplessly. 'We were supposed to go with him,' I said, putting a lot of chagrin in my voice.

'I'm sorry?'

'Mr Mack,' I said, smiling ruefully. 'We're dining with him, he was keeping the restaurant a secret, and he just left in that taxi.'

'Mr Bone.'

'No, Mr Mack—'

'Yes, of course, I understand what you are saying,' she said, 'but that was not Mr Mack, that was Mr Bone.'

'Really?' I looked wide-eyed at Sian, the genuine amazement on my face drawing a little giggle from the receptionist. 'But we know him too, and I can't believe I didn't recognize him. Is he staying here?'

She shook her head. 'He came to collect Marianne.' She smiled. 'You must have recognized her, too, she was on duty when you arrived.'

'Jack,' Sian said, 'gets jet lag on short-haul flights and wouldn't recognize his own mother.' She let the girl give another little chuckle at that, then sprang the question. 'Where's Jason dining?'

'Bianca's. I think.' She shrugged, and hid her confusion by sweeping the ape and its tinkling key off the counter.

'If we order a taxi,' I said, 'how long will it take?'

'Five or ten minutes.'

'Could you do that for me?'

She smiled, nodded, and picked up the phone. We wandered outside to wait. It was a balmy evening, the moon a thin crescent, the air in the driveway warm, perfumed by the drifting scents from the Wisteria Terrace. The hotel's foyer lights shone through the glass doors. Sian's fair hair was touched with gold. Her eyes were alight with excitement.

'Serendipity,' she said. 'I can't believe we found him so quickly.'

'We could lose him even faster. As he went out, he glanced back.'

'And he knows you by sight.'

'If it was his man who attacked me near India Building, then he must do.'

'And that taxi can just as easily head for the border.'

'Yes. But we'll try Bianca's first. I'd hate to go racing into La Linea when he's sitting in Gib stuffing himself with paella and chips.'

I took her arm as a taxi roared up the road, passed the hotel then did a sharp U-turn into the uphill end of the drive and cruised up the slope to brake to a halt alongside us.

Bianca's, I learned from the driver, was a restaurant on the edge of Marina Bay. At that time of night it took us under five minutes to get there at a cost of less than five Euros. We climbed out with the floodlit cliffs of North Front at our backs and before us the marina's jetty was a smooth strip of concrete jutting out into the placid waters flanked by luxury yachts and cruisers rocking gently at their moorings.

I paid the driver. The taxi headed off to join the tail-end of the ranks alongside Casemates Square and I escorted Sian into a restaurant where noise was a whisper but not yet a hum, the couple we were seeking at once spotted in a table at the far end of the room.

Breathing much more easily, I went to the bar and ordered drinks: Jameson's with ice for me, gin and tonic with ice and lemon for Sian, and, 'The same again for the couple over there – didn't they just come in?'

The barman nodded, busy pouring.

'Mr Bone, isn't it?'

He shrugged. 'Sure. Jason.'

'A regular?'

'His friend has a boat here....'

I was given a tray and carried it across the room, threading my way between mostly empty tables with commendable skill. Perhaps it convinced Bone I was a waiter, for he gave me not a glance as I approached. When I placed the tray on his table he looked up with surprise but not, I thought, with recognition.

Not good. One theory gone to pot?

'We didn't order those drinks.'

'No,' I said as Sian pulled out a chair and sat down, 'and I'm not a waiter.'

'So ...?'

'You're Jason Bone?'

'Ah.' He sat back looking disgusted, gave the girl sitting on his left a quick glance. 'And I saw you at the hotel, I know you're fresh off the plane from the UK, so this is about Sam.'

'Is it?'

'Well, didn't she send you looking for me?'

'Actually, it's about a Mercedes.'

That was Sian. As Bone's attention shifted, I sat down. The girl who was his companion was watching me. I smiled mysteriously.

'What Mercedes?'

'The one you had stolen,' I said, 'because you need money.'

'Don't talk bloody nonsense.'

'But you do need money?'

'Never mind what I need, what I *don't* need is a stranger barging in to ask stupid questions and make preposterous accusations—'

'It's also about murder,' I said, and that stopped him dead.

After a moment he said, 'Whose murder?' Then, 'Are you the police?'

'Let's deal with money first, because that's how it started.'

He rolled his eyes. 'This is getting farcical. How what started?'

'Why do you need money?'

The jump disconcerted him and he said quickly, 'I don't, not now.'

'Because?'

He was still sitting back. The girl had reached out, and below the table they were holding hands.

'That's none of your business, is it? But I suppose if I play along maybe you'll get to the point. And then leave us to enjoy our meal.' He took a breath. 'I have a friend who has sufficient funds.'

'Did he pay for the Mercedes scam?'

'We're going into business together.'

'And that's why, for some time, you've been seeking a big lump sum.'

That got to him. Memory kicked in, and I saw him recalling talking too freely to people he worked with. He blinked, frowned.

'You arranged for the Mercedes to be stolen,' I said. 'Then you sold the drugs hidden in the audio system, skipped town and left your wife and her brother to take the rap.'

And suddenly he oozed confidence.

'Now I know for sure you're talking utter bloody nonsense.'

'Prove it to us, Mr Bone,' Sian said quietly. 'Prove to our satisfaction that we're talking nonsense, and I promise you we'll go away.'

He looked at me, a challenge in his eyes. 'My wife hasn't got a brother.'

Inside me, something froze. 'She introduced me to him.'

'No, she introduced you to someone she said was her brother.'

'Tommy Mack.'

He looked genuinely stunned.

'You're kidding!'

And even as he spoke my mind was racing because it was obvious that if I'd mistaken the man walking out of the Rock Hotel for Tommy Mack, then the mistake could be made in reverse.

Ronnie Maguire had admitted that Sam's description fitted the man who had walked into his garage and asked for a particular Mercedes to be stolen. Sam had recognized the signature on a dirty scrap of paper. But a spoken description is always going to be unreliable, and even the same person's signature will vary from day to day.

I remembered, too, that I had phoned Sam to warn her we were bringing Maguire to her house. When we arrived, Mack was not there. That wasn't coincidence; he had deliberately stayed away to avoid recognition.

'Why do you think I'm kidding?' I said, casting a glance at Sian and recognizing in her blue eyes the dawning of doubt, that same awful recognition of the likelihood that we'd flown a thousand miles in pursuit of an innocent man.

'Because I know my wife, and I know Tommy Mack from a club called Night Owl,' Bone said. 'He's done time in Walton prison. Been out no more than six months, lives in a two-roomed flat no better than a squat. How he got to Sam, I don't know. Maybe he used the garage where she works, chatted her up. Who cares? I certainly don't. But Sam is an only child. No sisters, no brothers.'

Sian, recovering fast, said, 'Yes, but even if we believe you, nothing has changed. What label Sam pins on Tommy Mack is her business, and irrelevant. What matters is that a car was stolen, a man and a woman died violently, and all the evidence points your way.'

'I asked you before: who died?'

'The Laings.'

'Jesus! They live in the close, they're my neighbours – and you think I killed them?'

'In cases such as this,' the young woman said quietly, 'don't the police look at alibis?'

It was the first time she'd spoken; I recalled the hotel receptionist telling us her name was Marianne. She had a soft round face framed by thick hair as glossy and black as warm wet tar, a husky accented voice fashioned and mellowed in hot sunshine somewhere across the border, lustrous dark eyes that gazed at me with intelligence.

'He was not in Liverpool,' Marianne said. '*We* were not there, and we can prove it easily.' The smile she gave Jason Bone was a rich outpouring of relief.

He looked at me. 'When did all this happen?'

'A stolen Mercedes was delivered to your house a week last Thursday, it was broken into Friday. Laing was murdered that same night, his wife on the Monday.'

Bone smiled. 'By that Friday, I'd been gone two weeks.'

'So your wife said. But we see that as part of the plan. You broke into your own garage to make it look like the act of a stranger. But when you ran, you were seen by Silvester Laing. He tried to stop you. You stuck a knife in his chest ...'

While I was talking he'd taken out his wallet and was poking about in an inner pocket. I stopped. My words hung in the air like the echoes of a hollow, wasted valediction. I waited with a terrible dread. Bone opened a slip of paper, turned it round and placed it face up on the table in front of me.

'The Hotel Élan, Paris. My itemized bill for a stay of three weeks.'

I didn't bother looking, knowing it was genuine. Instead I looked into his eyes, saw in them not hate nor even resentment, but genuine puzzlement: he couldn't understand why I'd come to Gibraltar to accuse him of such terrible crimes.

'Eurostar,' Sian said valiantly, 'has made a fast return trip to England something of a doddle. A stay in Paris is no longer a safe alibi for crimes committed within such easy travelling distance.'

'You're right, of course,' Jason Bone said, 'but both of you must realize by now that you're talking to the wrong man.'

I sighed, leaned back, took the first, belated taste of Jameson's. Rolled the whiskey around my tongue. Lifted my glass to Jason Bone in acknowledgement of my defeat.

'Have you two ordered?'

He shook his head.

'Let's do that. Sian and I will, too. We'll eat with relish. I know I'm starving. And after that, if you're agreeable, we'll do some more talking and get this thing sorted out.'

We had eaten. Marianne had tactfully wandered away to talk to friends seated near the bar. Sian and Jason Bone were looking with expectation in my direction.

'Tommy Mack,' I said, 'has a lot to explain. Trouble is, he's disappeared.'

'Jumped ship, or been jumped on?'

An intelligent man, Jason Bone.

'I got the news before we caught up with you, and my first thought was he'd been got at by the baddies. Now I'm leaning towards Mack as the guilty man – and going in that direction throws up some very unsavoury possibilities.'

'No.' Sian had been listening hard, and now she shook her head. 'No, I *know* Sam's not involved.' And she looked at Jason with the appeal for confirmation naked in her blue eyes.

He shook his head. 'She couldn't do it.'

'Why? She's involved with Mack, we've seen him there in your house, she's already lied about him.'

'Spur of the moment to explain a stranger's presence. That's like her. Impulsive. Sometimes recklessly so.'

Sian thought for a moment. 'Jack, suppose it went like this.

Tommy Mack got wind of the big Merc's movements from something Valentine let slip in Night Owl. To get his hands on those drugs he worked out a complicated scam. But a vital part of the scam was having somewhere to hide a stolen car – and we know Mack had no garage because he lived in a scruffy little bed-sit.'

'But then,' I said, swept along with the possibilities, 'he remembered someone called Jason Bone he'd seen in Night Owl. And if he knew Jason had left home—'

'Common knowledge,' Jason said.

'Right, then all he had to do was come up with the right tale of woe to relate to a sensitive young woman.'

'Who was also impulsive, sometimes recklessly so,' Sian said looking at Jason.

'Possible,' he said.

'Probable,' I said, 'if he offered a sweetener, a share of the proceeds.'

'No.' Again Jason was shaking his head. 'I can see her taking him in, but she would never do that if she thought the man was involved in something illegal.'

'All right, I'll go along with that,' I said. 'Because we're forgetting something, aren't we? Tommy Mack looks like you, and he signed your name and gave your address to Maguire. He schemed well, chose Sam for more reasons than a handy garage. He was going up against the bad guys, he wanted to cover his tracks and by operating from your house he was already pointing the finger. Sam was convenient, you were the fall guy.'

'So where is he,' Sian said. 'Where's he gone?'

'It's the same situation, but a different perp,' I said. 'He's been trying for seven days, but now he's sold the drugs and he's gone. We were asking that question about Jason: where? Now we're asking it about Tommy Mack, but we've got to go back a thousand miles just to start looking.'

We left Jason and Marianne to finish their evening – he was opening a boat charter business with his mate and they had a late meeting on board the luxury motor cruiser that would make their fortunes – and by the cool light of the crescent moon I stood with Sian on the edge of the quay and phoned Calum to give him the latest news.

Instead, he took the wind out of my sails and turned Sian's bright blue eyes into dark pools of sadness.

'Before you say anything,' he said, 'I requisitioned that vehicle and Stan drove me to Sam's. A final check of the night. Lights were out, as expected, I imagined her all tucked up in her bed – yet there was something I sensed and so we pulled in, parked with those bloody security lights blazing down on us.'

'And?'

'She's gone, Jack. Missing, presumed ... well, I'll let you finish that and at the same time hope to hell we're both wrong.'

'Jesus Christ, Cal!'

'We rang the bell, knocked, tried doors back and front. Nothing. Phoned. Still nothing. There was no way into the garage other than through that broken window. I didn't bother. Those security lights had made night vision a joke, but through the window I could make out the shape of the Merc, beyond that ... I'm pretty certain the Clio's still there.'

Sian had her hand on my shoulder as she stood with her head close to mine to listen. When she looked at me, I could feel her moist warm breath on my cheek. Her eyes were haunted.

I said into the phone, 'Cal, we found Jason Bone. He's not our man. We've spent the evening talking, worked our way around to Tommy Mack using Bone's name, his wife and his house, with Sam the innocent victim. If we're right, Mack's a thief, and a murderer. If Sam's car's there but she's missing ...'

'I'll keep looking.'

The phone bleeped. I put it away.

Neither of us had mentioned the police.

I saw Sian watching me, knew she was thinking of Haggard – couldn't bring myself to make the call.

'Calum's wasting his time,' I said, and Sian stepped away and put her fingers to her lips and closed her eyes. 'Tommy Mack has put the finishing touches to a complicated scam. He's signed off with another murder.'

chapter seventeen

We went back to our room at the Rock Hotel and retired to a huge, shared double bed at the time of night that is always the start of a new day, but a telephone call had left us bereft of feelings or emotion and we might as well have slept outside beneath the waning moon.

Thin moonlight from across the straits filtered through the gap in the curtains, glinting on mirrors and coffee table and crystal decanters from which the last of the whisky and wine had been drained. I was conscious of the warmth of Sian's body as she lay on her back alongside me, staring at the ceiling; reached out once to touch her hand and found her fingers as smooth and cold as those of a marble statue. In that wan light we were physically almost as close as we had ever been, but our thoughts were bleak and lonely: there cannot be a worse time for solitary, brooding reflection than those silent hours after midnight. Sian, I knew, would be thinking about Sam Bone, and I could tell by her breathing that the emotion deadened by Calum's shocking news had returned like an unseen assassin to grab her by the throat. We had chased the wrong man to the shores of the Mediterranean. Our mistake had put a helpless woman in danger.

For me, the image I could not get out of my mind was of that young woman wrapped in the warm folds of a bright, lemon-yellow kimono. Sam had been wearing it when I returned with Calum Wick on the night her home had been searched and vandalized by Vick Valentine and Ronnie Maguire, had been wearing it again on the night Jemima Laing was murdered. On that first occasion it had, perhaps, been an unusually intimate garment to slip into in a room where thugs had recently trampled without respect and furniture had been tossed about as if by a freak storm. But assailed from all sides by the evidence of a sinister violation of her home, the thing Sam Bone most craved was normality, and for a tired young woman returning home from night work that meant slipping into a cosy housecoat and relaxing with a nightcap. Preferably something stiff enough to soften the sharp edges of perception. Prepared for her by her brother.

Only Tommy Mack was not her brother.

We rose early, opened curtains and veranda doors wide to let in brilliant morning sunshine, the smell of the sea and the growl of motorists heading for work up and down Europa Road; showered, rode the lift down to the dining-room for an early buffet breakfast eaten to the refined clatter of plates and cutlery but, as to conversation, mostly in silence.

Later, I booked two seats on that day's Monarch flight to Manchester. It was due to leave at eight that night. More precious hours wasted.

Although not entirely, of course; Sian went shopping on Main Street. I phoned Eleanor, my mother, and got diplomatic Reg's suave tones on the answering machine. Out. Could be anywhere, from the Copacabana on Main Street to the bazaars of Tangier. And I had a parcel to deliver.

The warmth of Tony Macedo's welcome when I knocked on the door of his flat in Ironside House on the Glacis estate lifted the last traces of the cold gloom that Gibraltar's hot sunshine had already begun to evaporate. Tissue paper flew as he unpacked the six red boxes. Then he lined up the Scots Greys in the shaft of sunlight slanting across his dining-table and couldn't stop gazing at them with a delighted grin on his face as he talked animatedly into the phone to invite over the other collectors who had placed an order and, like Tony, waited with patience. I left before they arrived. I don't know if he thought I'd made a special trip to deliver the goods, and I offered no explanation. My arrival sent my reputation sky-high. Amongst the members of the Gibraltar Model Soldier Society I now had several satisfied customers, and could look forward to more orders.

Back at the Rock Hotel, Sian returned from Main Street empty-handed but with the sparkle back in her blue eyes. Morning coffee in the shaded lounge was followed by lunch in the heat and perfume of the Wisteria Terrace. The hot afternoon crawled lazily, blurred by newspapers read from front to back, paperbacks from the Saga cupboard flicked through then returned, and several catnaps. Dinner was skipped; with yawning approval we listened to forties' favourites played by the resident pianist and drifting to us from the dining-room. Darkness fell. Sian and I left the old-world luxury of the Rock Hotel, took a taxi to the airport, moved quickly through customs, drank coffee more slowly in the departure lounge as time dragged. Eventually boarded the plane. Drank more coffee, a miniature bottle of wine with our meal. Dozed.

And then it was Manchester, a dash across the road to collect the Shogun from the car park, and home.

Sunday

'So where do we start?'

I was at the window in Calum Wick's living-room. It was gone midnight, lights from across the water reflecting in the sluggish river, my head still buzzing from the flight and the fast drive down the M56.

When I swung to face the room they were all looking at me: Calum his usual stretched-out lanky self, Sian curled up with a black cat so contentedly limp it appeared dead; white-bearded Jones the Van sipping whisky from a tall tumbler and blinking bloodshot eyes as he tried to stay upright on Calum's straight-backed work-chair.

'Sam's house to make sure,' Calum said, answering my question. 'With luck, she'll be tucked up in bed as if nothing's happened and we can all get some sleep.'

I looked at the gently teetering Jones. 'Stan?'

'Fuck knows,' Jones said, and waved a vague hand trailing thin smoke from his roll-up. 'I can drive, like, but I'm not guaranteein' I won't bounce off a few fuckin' lamposts an' suchlike—'

'Stay here,' Calum said. 'Get your head down and leave my bloody firewater alone.'

'Fairy nuff,' Stan said, and grinned. 'Only remember, if you get bogged down in stuff goin' over your head, I'm a mine of information on all kinds of low life.'

'Metaphors were never so mixed,' I said.

'Yeah, well, my imagination's awful good,' he said, 'for an oxymoron,' and he puffed mightily on his fag and winked at Calum.

'Sian,' I said, smothering a grin, 'will you drive the battle-wagon?'

'Wow, what brings this on?'

'In the event of a combat situation involving gangsters, I need both hands free to protect my true love.'

'It's my considered opinion,' Calum said, 'that if the man we're after *is* Tommy Mack, we're up against a solo artiste, a one-man band.'

'The point being?'

'Stop arguing about who's drivin' the friggin' car,' Stan Jones said.

'And for Christ's sake,' Calum said, 'get a bloody move on.'

So we did just that.

It was a short drive and a fast one, and it seemed that Sian was setting out to prove that if any car was inconspicuous, it certainly wasn't her beloved Shogun. When she pulled into Sam Bone's drive and braked hard to send a shower of gravel rattling against the garage doors as the security lights clicked on to dazzle us with a blaze of light, she was looking at me with a glint in her eye.

'And now it's time,' she said, 'to draw lots to decide who climbs in through the broken window.'

'House first,' Calum said, and headed for the steps.

The bell tinkled distantly and without result. Hammering on the door brought no response. The front-room curtains were closed. Sian dug her big Maglight out of the Shogun and handed it to me and I walked round to the back of the house where the yellow gleam of sodium streetlights was blocked by shrubs, sheds and a pseudo-Victorian conservatory, and shadows were long and inky. The torch was still switched off. I stumbled and sent a tin bucket clattering against the wheelie-bin. Stood still, praying not that the almighty clangour had gone unnoticed but that someone inside had been scared witless and would come to investigate. I moved to the back door. Listened to my own pulse hissing, the distant crunch of gravel, the faint murmur of Sian's voice. But from the house there was nothing, no sign of life or death, and when I shone the Maglight's white beam in through the kitchen windows there was nothing in that familiar room that gave me a hint either way. It was neat and tidy, no meal half-eaten on the table, no half-full cups of coffee; not the glimmer of a suggestion that, like the crew of the Mary Celeste, the sole occupant of this house had for some reason walked out of a perfectly normal day and disappeared.

Which left the garage.

When I returned to the front of the house, Sian and Calum had already moved away from the steps and across the drive and were waiting for me by the Shogun. I think all of us were experiencing disturbing forebodings. Something was terribly wrong, and my skin was prickling with tension.

We exchanged glances. The fierce security lights beating down on us drained our faces of colour. Our eyes were lost in dark hollows like the eye sockets of three naked skulls.

'I'll go in,' I said, 'and open the door.'

We trooped round the side of the garage to the broken window. Five days ago, Calum and I had stood inside this same garage and looked at this same window, examined a stolen car, taken flash-photographs. Yesterday Calum had returned with Jones the Van, had looked through the window into darkness and had seen the shadowy outline of the black Mercedes and beyond that the Clio – he thought.

What would I find?

I handed the Maglight to Sian and said, 'I won't need that,' and saw the understanding in her eyes. I would climb in. I would open the doors. But I was born squeamish, and without a heroic bone in my body. Whatever was in there, we would look at together.

The window was quite low, and the thief had done a good job of smashing the glass. I reached inside, found the catches.

It opened inwards. I swung a leg over the sill, sat on one haunch, lifted a hand to the wall overhead then brought the other leg over and dropped inside. Glass crunched underfoot. I stood there with my jaw painfully clenched, listening to silence ruined by my own ragged breathing.

Heard footsteps as Sian and Calum returned to the front of the garage to wait for me to open the door.

Something stunk.

And that didn't make any sense.

Where I live, in the rugged valley beneath the high peaks of the Glyders, I have become used to carrion lying in fields and hedges; I am familiar with the sweet stench of rotting flesh.

If Sam Bone was dead, she had been dead for thirty-six hours at the most. But something here, in this garage, had been a long time dead.

On the back of my neck, the short hairs bristled.

My eyes were adjusting to the gloom, but too slowly. I moved away from the window, again tripped, this time on a pile of tyres; stumbled hard against the Merc's shiny body. The big car rocked. Suspension squeaked.

I leaped away, walked quickly down the length of the car and reached out two hands to feel with the flat of my palms the wide sweep of the garage's cold door. The catch, I guessed, was at the bottom. I crouched, fumbled, found it, turned the handle and pushed the door away from me. I came to my feet, pushing it forward and up as it juddered on stiff pivots. Yellow light flooded in, casting two long shadows that fell across me. The door reached the horizontal and stopped with a hard, vibrating thump.

'Jesus!' Sian said, and put a hand to her nose.

Whoever was dead had been lying here, rotting, since Sunday. Or longer. I knew it, Calum knew it, and I could see him backtracking in his mind and wondering if there was anything he had heard, or sensed; anything we could have done then to save a life.

'When I was taking photographs,' he said quietly, 'we really should have looked in the boot.'

I nodded. But first, there was a girl to find.

Yet even with the apparently simple line of reasoning that had progressed in logical steps from the guilt and then innocence of Jason Bone to the disappearance of Tommy Mack and the girl, with all the obvious and glaring implications, we had again arrived at the wrong conclusions.

The sleek shape of the Mercedes had been revealed by the lifting of the garage door, and in the glint of sodium street-lighting that was now misting as a fine cool rain began to drift we could see at once, even from the rear, that a killer had turned it into a makeshift hearse.

It seemed that, with us, bad news always came with the rain.

The driver's electric window was half-open. Tommy Mack was sitting in the driving-seat. He was slumped sideways, his back against the tan leather. His head was canted towards his right shoulder. From the tiny bullet hole in his right temple, blood had trickled to congeal and blacken.

Sian made a small, soft sound and turned away. She was still outside standing on the now glistening gravel. Her blonde hair was beaded with drops of fine rain.

'Get in the Shogun, Soldier Blue,' I said. 'I don't think it'll be pleasant when we open the boot.'

As I turned away I heard her crunch away across the drive, the thump as the big 4 x 4's door slammed shut. Calum gave me a cold grin.

'Your treat.'

I nodded; worked the catch; lifted the boot and concentrated on breathing through my mouth as I peered in through narrowed eyes. But it was like that foolish habit we have of ducking our heads when we hear a bang, or run out into the pouring rain: it did no bloody good at all.

The man wearing the crumpled dove-grey suit didn't mind the smell. In the roomy boot he was folded like a roll of cheap carpet, but he'd been dead long enough for rigor to come and go and his body had bloated and the cravat Manny Yates said he always wore was embedded in the swollen flesh of his neck and the once-elegant vandyke beard looked like nothing more than a mess of grey bristles.

'Vick Valentine,' I said. 'When did Haggard say he was last seen?'

'Sunday.'

'Yes, that's right, the day I hit town like the plague.' I grimaced wryly. 'And we found the Merc the same day, because Sam called us when her house had been broken into and searched.'

'According to Billie Tobin,' Calum said, 'that search was done by Ronnie Maguire and Valentine. They found nothing. Valentine stayed behind when big Ron left in disgust. Then, after a while, he went home.'

'But Tobin couldn't know that, could he, because he wasn't here.'

Calum took a last look at the grisly remains of Vick Valentine, then slammed the boot and turned away.

'Tobin would lie for the sake of it,' he said. 'It was a way of life.'

'For Valentine,' I said wearily, 'his search of this house turned out to be a way of death – but what I'd really like to know is where the hell all this leaves us?'

Yet even as I asked the question, I knew it was the wrong

one. Alongside the Mercedes, just as Calum had predicted, there was a blue Clio – Sam's car. So the question I should have asked, the one we *had* to answer, was where did all this leave Sam Bone?

chapter eighteen

The two constables drove into Sam's drive and slid to a fierce halt less than five minutes after I'd dialled 999. One stayed outside in rain that was slackening to a thin damp mist and took brief details of what we'd found in the Merc. The second went into the garage, flashed a torch around like a kid with a new toy, came out again quicker than he'd gone in and began talking rapidly into his radio while casting guarded but what I interpreted as suspicious glances in our direction.

I would, wouldn't I? I had a guilty conscience, because I knew what was coming.

What was coming with all the speed and clatter of a decrepit Green Goddess to a dying bonfire was Willie Vine's battered Mondeo, which bounced and creaked in off the road in what seemed like no time at all because I spent it talking to Sian with my elbow on the Shogun's open window. Haggard and Vine climbed out, spoke briefly to the uniformed officers, then Vine went into the garage with one of them and Haggard came over to the Shogun with his jacket flapping open and his eyes dark with fury.

'I'm calling SOCOs, the doc and the meat-wagon,' he said, 'an' when they're all finished you're going to tell me exactly what you an' the Gay Gordon have been pissin' about at for the past week. Get in the car with her, and wait.' He looked around. 'Where is he?'

'He didn't come with us.'

'That's not an answer.'

'I don't know.'

'An' that's a lie – the last one you'll tell tonight or you'll be listenin' to a lot of silence in a very empty room and wonderin' what the fuck happened to your shoelaces.' He glared in at Sian, said: 'Pardon my fuckin' French,' and swung away to join Vine.

'As a matter of interest,' Sian said, 'where *has* Cal gone?'

'He took off without a word when I was phoning the police.'

'So what's your best guess?'

'The investigation's ground to a very messy halt. If he's got any sense he's in hiding somewhere looking up the number of Australia House.'

'You think Carney's got her?'

'I don't know what to think. The way it looks, Tommy Mack was the man behind the Mercedes scam and his luck ran out. What worries me is if Carney caught up with him, but couldn't find the drugs.'

I walked around the front of the 4 x 4 and climbed into the warmth. We sat in an uncomfortable silence, neither of us willing to answer the question I'd posed because the possibilities it led to were too horrific to contemplate. Lost in our own private torment we stared numbly as vehicles came and went and men in white coveralls crawled like grotesque maggots over the Mercedes and its gruesome contents. Flashguns lit up the interior of the garage like summer lightning. Haggard and Vine hovered. Crime-scene tape flapped.

'You think he's looking for her?'

I met her troubled gaze.

'Calum? Where would he start?'

'If she works at a twenty-four hour petrol station and *if* she's changed her shift....'

'That's a thought. It would explain why she wasn't here when Calum came around; perhaps explain how Carney was able to murder Tommy Mack and dump him in the Merc.'

Sian was thoughtful. 'I did see Calum take off, you know. He came across the drive, and it looked as if he was going behind the house. But he never came back.'

I grunted. 'He was sensible. Like me, he knew what was coming, but there was no need for both of us to be here.'

And suddenly she smiled. 'He's a bugger, isn't he? A wee bugger, as he'd put it. But I tell you what, I bet he didn't flit around the back of this place just so he could make his escape over the fence. He was after something.'

'And you know what it is, don't you?'

'I've an inkling,' she said, and chuckled. 'A funny word that, our literary luvvie Willie Vine would go to town on it. As in duckling, you see? It sounds like an ink's chick, doesn't it – but what's an ink?'

'We may never know,' I said, 'because here comes trouble.'

The last time I'd been quizzed inside Willie Vine's ugly green Mondeo we'd been parked on the edge of Sefton Park with the woods of the Fairy Glen dark and sinister and the many facets of the Palm House's glass dome glinting in cold moonlight. Calum and me. Brooding over a case that had been falling apart. Like this one.

But now I was slumped resentfully in the back seat alongside Sian, and I was apprehensive. The death of Tommy Mack had rocked the boat and, looking back over a week spent deliberately perverting the cause of justice, the only answers I could see myself plucking out of thin air to all those questions as yet unasked were certain to be incriminating.

'All right,' Haggard said with weariness and scorn fighting for supremacy in his hard voice, 'let's have it.'

'We're wasting time,' I said. 'There's a young woman missing.' I let him think hard on what might be happening to Sam and said: 'Mack was the man behind all this, by the way.'

'Behind what?'

That was Haggard, clipping his words, knowing much but giving nothing away.

'He was using Sam Bone's house and her husband's name to work a scam involving a stolen Mercedes and its unusual in-car audio system. His corpse suggests Ed Carney, with his involvement in drugs, had serious objections. Hence my concern for Sam Bone.'

'You think this is Carney's work?'

'Tommy Mack's death, yes. But I'm pretty sure Mack murdered Valentine. Valentine searched the Bones's house, then waited behind to confront Sam.' I hesitated. 'Maybe I should go back to the beginning. It gets a bit complicated.'

'If you go slowly,' Willie Vine said, deadpan, 'I'm sure Mike will take it in.'

'As opposed to bein' taken in,' Haggard said, and the growl in his voice could have been a warning to me or to Vine.

'Jason Bone had left his wife,' I said. 'Tommy Mack is of similar appearance, and he used his charm on Sam to work his way into her good books and her house. Then, using Bone's name, he turned up at Ronnie Maguire's garage to arrange the theft of a Merc carrying drugs in its in-car audio system. Carney heard about it, because he knows Maguire. And Maguire delivered the Merc, so he knew it was in Bone's garage.

'Carney thought the Valentines were behind everything, working a clever double-cross: he had Vick and his cousin – who owned the Merc – using Bone as a way of robbing themselves. When the drugs were sold they'd split the proceeds but look like victims, not villains.'

Haggard looked at Vine. 'So now we know what happened to Danny Valentine.'

'Yes,' I said, 'I talked to Carney in Clarke Gardens, asked him about Danny. Missing, he said – so draw your own conclusions. Vick Valentine did, so he was desperate to recover the drugs. He knew Bone had the stolen Merc, but found nothing when he searched the house. Fear forced him to stay behind to get at the truth. But instead of Bone, in walked Tommy Mack.'

'And Valentine died,' Vine said.

I nodded. 'Sam told us Mack was her brother. I think she did it because, you know, husband gone two weeks, new man in place …' Haggard snorted. 'So we've been sort of sniffing around on the periphery of a complicated scam, working for Sam Bone and her supposed brother. Chasing Jason Bone, because everything pointed his way. We found him, in Gibraltar, and if everything had gone according to plan we would have given you your killer. Only—'

'Only, as per fuckin' usual,' Haggard cut in, 'you'd got things arse about face.'

'Yes. We'd got the scam worked out—'

'Remind me,' Haggard said. 'Tell me what happened the night Laing died.'

'Tommy Mack broke into the Bone garage so it would look as if the stolen drugs had been stolen again, by a scally. If they'd gone from Bone's house, Mack was in the clear and the hunt led by Ed Carney would have moved on. It worked, because after that everybody was chasing Bone; everybody thought Bone had broken into his own garage for the same reason: to muddy the waters.' I shook my head. 'But it was Mack, and things had already started going pear shaped. He stole the stereo, and Silvester Laing saw him. He ran out to stop a thief, and in the struggle Mack stabbed him.'

'Who killed Jemima Laing?'

'Mack.'

'Why?' Haggard pulled a face. 'He had the drugs – but he'd made it look like he didn't have them. You said it yourself, he'd shifted possession of the drugs on to an unknown scally. So why another killing?'

'One obvious reason. He saw the lights on in the Laings' bedroom, saw Jemima watching him murder her husband. It was possible she'd recognized him. So he talked his way in under some pretext …'

'So you had it all worked out,' Willie Vine said.

I pursed my lips ruefully. 'Yeah, but I was hunting the wrong man. From the start it was Tommy Mack who had worked hard to cover his tracks. He used subterfuge to point the finger at Bone, Sam helped unwittingly by saying Mack was her brother, and we were fooled.'

'Clever,' Haggard said. Then he looked at me. 'So where are the drugs?'

'If this is Carney's work, then either he's got them, or he didn't find them.' I shook my head, feeling genuinely helpless. 'Maybe their whereabouts died with Tommy Mack. But in any case, so what? Do a body count. Laing stabbed Tony Carney on the yacht. Mack stabbed Laing, beat Jemima to death, murdered Ed Valentine.'

I felt Sian touch my arm, and I reached for her fingers. 'Then Ed Carney caught up with Mack,' I said, 'and – angry because the drugs were still missing, or chuffed because he'd got his hands on them and Mack had led him a dance – he killed him stone-dead with a shot in the temple.'

'But we don't know what's happened to Sam,' Sian said quietly, 'and we really would like to be allowed to look for her.'

'When I hear ex-sergeant Sian Laidlaw goin' all soft and gooey,' Haggard said, 'I get the nasty feeling something's goin' on.' He flicked the cigarette out of the window, and again turned to look at her. 'Why should I do that – why should I let you two go at all – when all you've been doin' for the past week is obstructin' the law?'

'How?'

He glared at me. 'Withholdin' information.'

'Come on! Hell, you're Merseyside Police, you must have heard something, known about Carney and his crew, had Mack down as a dodgy character – whereas I had it from Sam that he was her brother and from what I could see he was giving her valuable support. The rest are drug dealers, pushers and car thieves, and if you don't already know all about them you're in the wrong job.'

'Pots and kettles?' Haggard said in mock amazement, and Vine shrugged.

'We're still wasting time,' I said. 'Remember, Ed Carney on the loose, Sam missing?'

'Already taken care of,' Vine said.

I was stunned. 'What, he's being pulled in?'

'Not *being* pulled,' Haggard said, 'has *been* pulled. Bein' questioned as we speak. And he knows nothing about Mack, or the girl.'

Sian gave a little exclamation of disbelief. I shook my head.

'No, Mike. You can't possibly know that.'

Haggard tapped his temple with a forefinger. 'It's all in there,' he said. 'Police experience. Of course I don't know, because he's down the nick an' I'm sittin' in here with you an' her. But if I was a betting man ...'

'I'm telling you, he's got Sam.'

'Then believe me, we'll know about it.'

'Bear with us,' Willie Vine said. 'You got almost everything right. In fact, you did very well. But what if there's doubt over who murdered Jemima Laing?'

I felt baffled. 'What's the reasoning behind this?'

'If you're right, and Jemima saw Mack kill her husband,' Vine said, 'she'd turn him in, not invite him into her house.'

'Willie's right,' Sian said, and shook her head as she looked at me. 'From a distance Jemima might have thought it was Jason Bone – but not when he reached her door. So that rules Mack out, doesn't it?'

I felt deflated, looked at Haggard. 'You think there's someone else out there, don't you? Someone we've never considered – perhaps because we've never met him. Is that it?'

Haggard shrugged. 'You'll get no more from me. I'm not holding you, so what you do next is your business, not mine. And I mean that. Stay a country mile away from my official investigations, and we can both be reasonably happy.'

It was Willie Vine who threw in the parting shot that left both Sian and me thinking hard.

'Last time you got tangled up in nasty business, Jack, it was the fair-haired lady sitting next to you that suffered. But think about this: just as there are more ways than one of skinning a cat, so there's more than one way a person can get hurt.'

★

Sian drove home with heavy tyres swishing over the wet streets to emphasize the silence as we stared through the windscreen with our minds on the consequences of murder and the possibility of an unseen killer who had passed our way like a wraith. I remembered leaving Conwy with Sian, and saying that the killer could be someone we hadn't considered. That chance remark had come back to haunt me.

We both looked at our watches at the same time. Exchanged glances. It was one of those nights when talk was unnecessary because minds were in tune, and it was another of those nights when it was too late to wake DS Meg Morgan. The unspoken decision was made. Meg was left to slumber in peace. Sian raced along Booker Avenue without a glance to the side and so on down to Aigburth Road and Grassendale.

When we parked on the edge of the Mersey and climbed out to the dank smell of the estuary it was to find Calum's flat in darkness. Perhaps we both thought of calling his mobile. Neither of us made the attempt. Instead we climbed the stairs and I used my key and after draping damp coats over the backs of kitchen chairs we heated coffee – that night, that late, nothing would keep us awake – and then we retired to bed.

It was after 2 a.m. We had starring roles in the same old movie, but this time, probably because we had shared a bed in the Rock Hotel and come to no lasting harm, the decision to occupy separate rooms – single bed or settee, a coin tossed to decide – seemed like an act of stubborness, stupidity, or a lot of both.

So we didn't.

We slipped like nervous burglars into the dark spare room, undressed quickly and snuggled up in the single bed; and that, unsurprisingly, was more than enough to send us off to sleep glowing warmly. Too tired for gymnastics, we nuzzled and kissed, murmured goodnight, and slept like spoons.

Yet even as I dozed off the words of Willie Vine lingered, an ominous harbinger of something I knew would become clear on the morrow.

There are, he had said, *more ways than one for a person to get hurt.*

As it turned out, the literary DS – perhaps unintentionally – had coined a painfully apt aphorism.

chapter nineteen

The discovery of bodies in a Mercedes in Dunbar Close was hot news on Radio Merseyside as Sian and I peered blearily at each other over our toast and coffee and strove to make sense of what had occurred in the dark wet night.

Our clever theories had been exposed as flimsy pipe dreams. I had come down from the Welsh hills and blundered around like a lost sheep looking for a gap in the hedge – when I couldn't even find the hedge. It didn't help when the newsreader informed us that Merseyside police were trying to identify an intruder who had slipped in and out of the Bones's garage through the broken window when the crime scene was sealed and uniformed police were on duty.

'Calum,' I said around a mouthful of toast. 'He surfaced, demonstrated his remarkable talents to the police – but where had he been, and what was he doing in the garage?'

'There were two cars there,' Sian said 'Perhaps he thought Sam was in the Clio's boot.'

'Mm.' I shook my head. 'Both cars would have been searched.'

'Maybe, maybe not – but he was after something.'

'Yes, and he had to be quick because one or both cars will certainly be moved today.'

'We've all got to be quick,' Sian said, 'if gut feeling is right and Carney's got Sam.'

I finished the toast, drained the coffee, ran a hand across my chin and pushed back from the table.

'I'll shave, wash, be ready in five minutes. Can any woman match that?'

'I was up before you, abluted before you opened your eyes.'

'Abluted?'

'I minted a new word. A hybrid of ablution. It means washed.'

'Coined, not minted. A mutation, not a hybrid.' I grinned as light-hearted banter had its usual effect and the clouds of gloom and doubt were whisked away like Dysoned dust. 'I'll go and ablute.'

The petrol station where Sam Bone did shift-work was on Higher Road in Halewood. I drove the Shogun in and began filling the tank. Just the one van had pulled in after us. I nodded to the driver, let the trigger go at twenty quid and Sian and I walked across the forecourt and into the shop.

Two people were on duty, one young woman at the cash desk, another placing red plastic bottles of motor oil on the shelves. Sian mouthed, 'I'll pay,' and while she went to the desk I approached the other young woman.

'Hi,' I said. 'I was hoping to see Sam Bone, is she in today?'

'No, she's not,' she said. 'She hasn't been in for more than two weeks.'

'On this shift, you mean?'

'Not on any shift. She's been off.'

I frowned, thinking back. 'Not a couple of Sundays ago. I spoke to her that night, she'd just come in from work.'

'Not here.' She frowned, bent to the cardboard box, pulled out two more bottles of oil and placed them on the shelf. Then her face cleared. She wiped her hands on her jeans, and shook her head. 'No, I'm positive about that. I was in that day. Sam'd been off a week then, an' she never came in while I was here.'

The doors swung open as the van-driver came in, smelling of diesel, boots squeaking. He went to the cash desk, scooping up a couple of big Yorkie bars on the way. Sian had paid for my petrol and moved away, and was pretending to be interested in the rack of tabloid newspapers.

I said to the girl, 'Did Sam say why she was off? Was she ill, or what?'

'She was always off. Always with big ideas, like, you know, Del Boy, "This time next year we'll be millionaires", " this time next month I'll be on me dad's yacht".' She grimaced. 'Yeah, always big ideas, but always lookin' for someone to lend her a fiver, that's how well off she was.'

'Maybe she had a sugar-daddy,' I said, spur of the moment – and got rocked back on my heels by the reply.

'Oh, absolutely, she did. An' she was cheeky enough to waltz in 'ere with him once.'

'What was he like?' This time a desperate stab in the dark, but I left myself exposed for the cruel riposte.

'I was off that day. So was Mal.' She nodded at the girl on the cash desk. 'One of the other girls told us, said he was all right....' She shrugged.

I thanked her and moved away. Sian had been watching progress, and she left the newspaper-stand and timed it so that she reached the door in time for me to hold it open for her.

'Anything?' I said.

'Let's get in the car and find somewhere quiet.'

I pulled out of the petrol station and crossed the road to head back towards Hunts Cross, turned right at the shopping-park traffic lights and fifty yards later I was cruising down Springwood Avenue. Another quarter-mile and I swung off the road by the streetlight where big Ronnie Maguire had lingered menacingly while I talked to Ed Carney, parked beneath the same trees in Clarke Gardens, and settled back in the quietly ticking Shogun alongside a woman who was bright-eyed and pink-cheeked with excitement.

'You learned something,' I said.

'Mm. So did you. Any definites?'

'Two, and one wild theory.'

'That beats me. I'm floundering with one possible – or maybe a probable – so off you go.'

'Sam's been lying,' I said. 'She hasn't been into work for two weeks.'

'Is that bad?'

'Well … I don't suppose so. If times were normal. We know Tommy Mack wasn't her brother, so work might have gone way down the list of priorities. And with him on hand to rub her back – I should have twigged, you know, when I first saw them together – she certainly had a compelling reason to stay at home. However …'

'Yes. She lied about Tommy Mack. Now we know she lied about work. So what else has she been telling us that's a load of rubbish?'

The sun had come out and was bathing us in dappled brilliance. I lowered my window all the way, opened Sian's to a thin slit and let the warming scent of rain-soaked grass and trees waft in.

'She also lied by omission,' I said. 'She's got a sugar daddy.'

'Oh my God!' Sian said. 'My possible that was pushing hard for a probable has just become a certainty. And you've been using the wrong tense.'

I thought for a moment, then nodded. 'Right. Sam hasn't got a sugar daddy,' I said. 'She *had* one.' I raised an eyebrow. 'What put *you* on to it?'

'You were questioning the girl in the petrol station. That van-driver came in while I was loitering. He signed for his fuel.'

'So?'

'If he signed, he had an account. Remember when I was at Cape Wrath I heard Tony Carney and Laing arguing? Carney was complaining that the young woman Laing was seeing had messed up his accounts. And I made that one, unforgivable error: I assumed.'

'Of course!' I was nodding, suddenly seeing it all too

clearly. 'You assumed she worked in the accounts department at Link Associates. She didn't. She worked in the petrol station at Halewood, where Tony Carney had been signing for his fuel.'

'All the time, the woman they were arguing about was Sam Bone,' Sian said. 'Silvester Laing was her sugar daddy.'

Mixed emotions was the best way to describe our feelings as I pulled out of Clarke Gardens, pointed the Shogun towards the river and set off to cover the remaining mile or so to Grassendale. And I was again kicking myself as I recalled something Sam Bone had said when I first met her and realizing, from the drastically altered perspective the new information put on things, that I had misunderstood her.

'She was angry,' I said as I reached Aigburth Road and pulled out into the traffic. 'We'd been talking about Laing, the way he ran out into the road. She said something like "Why the hell did he do it? What in God's name possessed the bloody man". I thought she meant Laing, and I told her that's the way some people are made. But I was wrong, wasn't I?'

'You think she meant Tommy Mack?'

'Of course. She must have been in the scam with Mack from the beginning – and she couldn't believe Mack had walked down the road and murdered her boyfriend.'

'It looks that way, doesn't it,' Sian said. 'But if a rich man like Laing was her boyfriend, what the hell was she doing involved in a scam with a man like Tommy Laing?'

'I don't know,' I said. 'I really do not know because that's the part of it that doesn't make any sense. That,' I said, 'and the other murders.'

And with those ghastly thoughts to keep us occupied that was the way it remained for the time it took us to reach Grassendale, climb the stairs to Calum's flat and find the lanky Scot stretched out with a mug of coffee and more bad news.

★

'Carney's been released,' he said. 'Haggard won his bet: he knows nothing, and can prove he was nowhere near the scene of any crime.' He paused for effect. 'And the polis are anxious to talk to a Mrs Sam Bone in connection with recent murders. Like us, they can't find the wee lass.'

'That's where you've been, isn't it? Looking for her?'

'If I'd come across her it would have been a bonus. But, no, that's not what I was doing.'

'But you did break into her garage?'

'Oh aye. And wandered about the garden. In and out both times, polis all around, me playing the elusive bloody pimple.'

'Why the garden?'

Sian had dumped her coat, kicked off her shoes and disappeared into the kitchen. Now she reappeared carrying two steaming mugs, handed one to me, and sat down.

'Looking for the stereo,' she said, 'that's why. And I know where it was, because my mind, too, works wonderfully well with hindsight.'

'Oh, God!' I groaned. 'You mean everything's been crystal clear to all of us, if only we could have seen it?'

'Sadly – yes. I even remember when I said this. It was Wednesday, we got around to the whereabouts of the stereo – and what did I say?'

'A clue,' I said gloomily, 'would be helpful.'

'Never mind, we're wasting time again and I can remember it almost word for word. I said: "I know I could put something where nobody would find it. People are cunning. Bodies get buried in back gardens".' She looked at Calum. 'Right?'

'Oh aye, he said, 'that's where it was, all right.'

'But not still there, surely? You found the hole,' I said, 'but not the stereo.'

'I found the hole, and then I found the stereo. There was a wheelie-bin close by, the lid flung back because when the stereo was dumped in there it was dumped in a hurry.'

'So how did you read it?'

'I didn't. Guesswork's not my forte, so I toddled off with what I had and presented it to a mate of mine who can work wonders with shiny bits of plastic.'

'Manny Yates. And that's where you spent the night.'

'In his office. He's got an ex-army camp bed. You'd love it.'

Sian was sipping coffee and looking at me ruefully. The canny Scot had got there before us, because there was only one possible reason for Calum taking a hunk of shiny plastic to Manny Yates, then returning to break into Sam Bone's garage.

'You and Manny compared the fingerprints on the stereo you recovered from the bin with those you lifted from Sam's Renault Clio,' I said.

'Aye. A perfect match. Sam had hold of it all right. But when? Did she help Mack remove it from the Merc? Or was she the one who dug it up when he was murdered?'

His meaning was clear. As soon as Sian and I walked in I'd told him what had happened at the Halewood petrol station, and everything we'd discussed in Clarke Gardens. So now he was stating the obvious by asking a question he could – perhaps should – have phrased in a slightly different way.

So I did it for him.

'What you mean,' I said, 'is was she the one who dug it up after she'd murdered Tommy Mack?'

Sian nodded. 'There's more than one way a person can get hurt,' she said, and I realized she was quoting Willie Vine. 'I trusted that girl, thought she was badly done to, thought she was battling on against the odds.'

'Don't give up on her yet,' I said. 'Remember, I posed one question neither of us could answer: why would a young woman seeing a rich man like Laing get involved in a risky scam stealing a measly stash of drugs from Mickey Mouse dealers?'

'That's one question we couldn't answer,' Sian said. 'Now here's one I didn't ask. When we were talking in Clarke Gardens, you said you had two definites and one wild theory. The definites gelled with my possible that became a certainty; what about the wild theory?'

'That,' I said, 'is almost certainly going to lead us to Sam Bone's hiding place.'

Lunch had come and gone.

Sian had slipped away into Calum's spare room to catch up on her sleep.

The lanky Scot was sitting slumped at his work-table toying absently with a paintbrush as light from the Anglepoise shone down on the empty, paint-stained board and reflected into a grey-bearded face and distant, brooding eyes. I was hunched over the coffee table, playing a game of Demon patience.

Suddenly I was aware of Wick's baleful glare.

'If she's on the yacht,' he said, 'pick up the phone and tell Haggard now and we can slip gently off the bloody hook and go about our business.'

'I will,' I said. 'When I've given it some thought. Perhaps.' And I swept the cards together, piled them in a crude and ragged stack and flung myself back in my chair.

'And if you don't intend to bubble her, go to Wales now and bring the bloody woman in.'

I knew he was right. I was again seeing Sam Bone in her bright lemon-yellow kimono. She'd been wearing it when I saw her for the second time, and now I was certain she had changed because the clothes she was wearing had been badly stained with blood: Vick Valentine had remained behind after his search, and Sam had helped in his murder.

Tommy Mack had dumped her clothes in the washing-machine, then covered the smaller bloodstain on his own T-shirt by zipping up his leather jacket. It had still been there the next day, and so the spur-of-the-moment tale of an altercation in Night Owl.

Sam had again been wearing the kimono when I called in to see her on the night Jemima Laing had been murdered, and my mind now threw up a nightmare vision of a young woman wielding a heavy wine decanter with frenzy. Sam, her clothes once again bloodstained.

I was quite sure Sam Bone was guilty of murder. But there were questions lying unanswered, and if I gave her up to the police that was the way they would remain. I needed answers. Custody could wait. Intuitively, I sensed Sam was going nowhere.

I straightened in my chair, took a deep breath, looked up. Calum was watching me. Reading my mind. He nodded. Agreement? Approval?

The talking had woken Sian. She wandered in, cuddling the black neutered moggy.

I said, 'We know Carney's been released. So what will he do now? Will he go after Sam?'

'Carney wants his drugs back,' Calum said, 'so it really depends on who's got them.' He shrugged enigmatically. 'Or should I say, who he *believes* has got them.'

'Mm.' I nodded. 'In one short week we've become acquainted with several very nasty characters. But I think the person who's at last going to give us a straight answer is a young woman, and right now she's being lulled into a false sense of security by the gentle rocking of a very expensive yacht.'

But once again, I'd got it wrong.

To make it more difficult for Haggard or Ed Carney to pick up our trail we left the journey into Wales until well after dark. Just to make absolutely sure we weren't followed – belt, braces and a wee length of knotted string in Calum's words – we ruled out motorways and the A55 and opted for the Mersey tunnel, Queensferry and the old coast road, with Sian burbling us along in the Shogun at a sedate fifty or so while we kept our eyes constantly peeled.

The fine rain had returned, then drifted away to the east like a grey curtain trailing its hem, leaving in its wake slick roads in which headlights and a late-summer moon picked out bright, dancing highlights. Some miles ahead of us a luxury yacht moored in Conwy harbour was swinging gently to the tide. On board, a murderer. Straightforward enough, grist to the mill for any fast-thinking PI blessed with the deadly reflexes of a striking rattlesnake. The only problem I could foresee lay with the identity of the killer.

Over the past week or so our efforts had come to naught as the mantle of guilt had passed from Jason Bone to Tommy Mack and was then left floating on the night breeze like a dirty black bin-bag unsure which shrubs to desecrate.

I was finding it almost impossible to believe that it had finally settled on the softly rounded shoulders of Sam Bone.

Every one of her lies could have been the fruit of innocence. Her fingerprints could have been plastered all over the stereo, not because she dug it up, but because she found it tossed as worthless scrap into her wheelie-bin. And just as all the lies she told could be excuses for what she considered her immoral behaviour, so Ed Carney's statements to the police could mask ulterior motives, and be all lies.

Pet theories are not easily dumped. Likeable characters are not readily branded villains – even if I knew from Tommy Mack that young Sam was in possession of a neat little pistol, and Tommy had been shot to death by a small-calibre weapon.

Impasse. Like banging one's head against a brick wall. And so it went on for mile after mile, Calum snoring like clogged bagpipes in the back seat, Sian humming softly under her breath as she drove like somebody out for a Sunday afternoon spin and me alongside her staring at the unwinding ribbon of road and becoming ever more confused.

Once or twice she glanced across at me, eventually saying, with a flash of insight, 'I don't like it either, Jack, love – but surely all we can do is wait until we get there, and see what transpires.'

She was right, of course, but I would have needed much more than comforting thoughts to prepare me for what lay ahead.

chapter twenty

Clouds had again floated across the moon when we drove across the bridge into Conwy, negotiated the roundabout under the ancient castle's stone walls and followed the circuit down to the quay. Lights from Deganway's marinas twinkled on the water. Yachts were pale white ghosts floating on a sea of calm. We climbed out, shivering a little after the enclosed warmth. For Calum's benefit I pointed to where Carney's boat was moored.

'There's a bloke over there on the shingle, messing about in something that looks like a coracle,' I said. 'I'll get him to take me across. You two wait here.'

'All this way,' Sian said, 'and we're sidelined.'

I shook my head. 'That's not it. I can't see his Merc, so I don't think Carney's here yet. I need you to hold him if he does arrive.'

'I can't see Sam's Clio,' Calum said, 'because it's still in her bloody garage – but still you think she's on that boat.'

'Yes, think – but I'm not sure. If she's not, I'll be straight back.'

Sian had broken away from the huddle to walk to the quay's edge and gaze out across the harbour. Calum was watching me with sardonic speculation in his black eyes.

'She has a pistol, my friend. Going across there believing Sam Bone's an innocent wee girl could be very dangerous.'

I sighed. 'Yeah, I know. But the pendulum could still swing either way, and I'd be a happy man if I could prove someone like Ed Carney's behind the killings.'

'You'd be a safer man with me watching your back.'

'No. Gut feeling tells me Carney's going to turn up. So I want you here. Stop him. Look after Sian.'

He spread his hands in acceptance, then wandered away to talk to the man messing about with the dinghy. Sian came back to me. She came very close, grabbed hold of my shirt-front with both hands and shook gently.

'Half an hour,' she said. 'Jack, if you're not back here in half an hour, I'm bringing in the police.'

'Time it from when you see me climb aboard,' I said, bending to kiss her lips. 'I've got an idea the bloke Calum's persuading to launch that thing is going to scull me gently across.'

He did.

But working from the stern of the scruffy little fibreglass shell he literally whisked me across to Ed Carney's motor cruiser, throwing in a couple of tacks to show off his skill and bumping us up against the big boat's hull with scarcely a jolt or a whisper of sound.

I reached out, found the boarding-ladder's rail with one hand and pulled myself across open water. It wasn't until I'd stepped on deck and he was moving away that he called up, with a musical Welsh lilt, 'Tell you what, if I'd known they were 'avin' a party up there I'd've made bloody sure I 'ad the outboard tanked up.'

He scared the life out of me. I felt the skin on my back crawl. A party meant more than one. I had expected Sam Bone. I had anticipated the arrival of Ed Carney – but not yet. If he was here – if *they* were here – where were the lights? Why were they waiting in darkness?

Despite the boatman's skill, had they felt the nudge as he brought the dinghy in? Had the heavy hull vibrated very slightly at that light touch, warning them of my approach? Warning *him* that I had arrived – for, surely, if Ed Carney was here then Sam Bone was dead.

I sucked in a deep, shuddering breath. Then, with a jaunty wave of the hand that I hoped was visible to Sian, I made my way cautiously across the deck towards the saloon.

Clouds still covered the moon. Although the glassy waters of the harbour were strangely luminous, clearly visible, light seemed to die before reaching the deck. Softly, my shoes whispering across expensive marine timber, I made it to the saloon's closed doors. They were mostly glass, but curtains had been pulled across. Behind me the night skies would be paler than the interior of the saloon. The occupants would be looking out, accustomed to the gloom. The curtains were thin. My shadow had fallen across them. There was nothing I could do to hide my approach.

My mouth was dry, my pulse hammering. I had no weapon. Yes, I'd seen off the man who attacked me in a Liverpool alley, but there I'd been threatened with a knife. This time I was expecting the single deadly crack of a pistol.

I reached down, twisted the handle, pulled the door open. Waited without breathing. Listening hard for the faintest of sounds – that did not come.

So I stepped inside that dark saloon and pulled the door closed behind me. And waited.

'Anyone there?'

Nerves had me by the throat and my voice had cracked. I almost giggled.

'I know someone's in here. The boatman told me.'

Bloody hell. That was playground talk, my brother's Mike Tyson, I couldn't believe what I was saying. Carney was probably biting his fist, choking back laughter. I knew he was there, in the darkness. Something warns you, doesn't it. Sixth sense. Or is it second sight? My thoughts were wildly out of control, my eardrums aching with the strain of listening, but as the boat moved lazily at its moorings all I could hear was a faint and eerie creaking like the dry rustling of my own fear.

Nothing ventured … One giant step and all that codswallop….

'All right,' I said into the muffled acoustics of a saloon panelled and furnished to a bent man's luxurious tastes, 'if you won't make a move then I will.'

I took a deep, silent breath, and stepped away from the door. To the side, away from the door's pale windows and into deeper shadows.

The sudden move was meant to shock him. My silhouette would be there – then gone. I wanted to hit him with the first taste of uncertainty, to jolt him into action, to make him do *anything* rather than sit there in the darkness and listen to me lamely twittering. Instead, the step intended to provoke turned out to be a rash move. It brought me to my knees.

I hit something solid with my foot, solid and immovable but at the same time soft and giving. A thrill of pure terror raced like an electric shock down my spine. My hair tried to stand on end. I cracked hard panelling with flailing knuckles as I flung an arm wide and tried to lift my foot from under that soft weight. Grunting with effort, gritting my teeth in fright, I felt my nails scrape across the back of a seat. But it was too late. I let my knees go slack, dropped heavily and with a sickening crack on what felt like a bony ribcage. Under my weight the prone person emitted an audible wheeze of exhaled breath. Then I had kicked free. My hands hit thick carpet. I rolled, my nostrils twitching.

In the sudden thick silence one thought hammered for attention: I'd blown it. My viewpoint had changed, my attention had been grabbed and now, in that plush saloon that was suddenly less dark, all I could see were the lights of Conwy filtering through curtained windows onto hard, bright metal glinting wickedly.

The pistol was pointing at my chest.

When I didn't want to see, I could see everything. Maybe it's down to focus. I'd walked into a saloon where the threat was all around me and seen nothing but blackness. In the glittering shape of a pistol the threat was crystallized. It drew my eyes, and all was revealed. They say that whatever you set out to do the waiting is always worse than the reality. So it was now. My fear left me. I'd come face to face with my demons and discovered they had feet of clay.

I climbed to hands and knees and said, 'I know you think

it's necessary, but if I promise not to move will you point your gun somewhere else?'

Silence. What did I expect, a round of ironic applause?

Then movement. A subtle shifting of light on shiny metal. The pistol wavered without altering its deadly aim; its owner wasn't about to give away the advantage. But it did move: in the deep leather seat that was a cavern of impenetrable shadow in a room where shadows gnawed at the soul, the person pinning me like a beetle to a card with that deadly little weapon slid sideways to be revealed by a shaft of wan light.

It was Sam Bone.

I was kneeling by Ed Carney.

My knees had slammed into his chest and driven stale breath from his body, but he had felt nothing. His eyes had a blank wet shine. A trickle of black blood ran from the hole in the centre of his forehead. It was like a thin leech slithering across the bridge of his nose.

Sam's face, in that feeble light, held the blued whiteness of a corpse. Her eyes were dark pools of torment. Dressed carelessly in a loose rust sweater over jeans and dirty trainers she had lost all her charm, and the black muzzle of the tiny pistol aimed at my head told me that all my hopes for her innocence had come to naught.

'Sam,' I said, and into my voice I put the hollow echo of bitter disappointment. 'What the hell have you done now?'

'Lost again,' she said, 'but isn't that the story of my life?'

'It needn't have been.'

'Oh, God,' she said, 'how could you possibly know?'

'From the very beginning I've gone by what you told me,' I said, 'but it seems it was all lies.'

'Necessity's the mother of invention, right?'

'So where did it begin? What made all this ...' I waved a vague hand at the body of Ed Carney, and beyond '... what made all this necessary?'

'This?' Her laugh was brittle, dangerous. 'Jason walkin' out, maybe. Me gettin' totally pissed off. Silver promisin' me the world....'

Silver. That would be Laing. The little gun wobbled as his name passed her lips. I stirred, my knees cracking as I climbed to my feet. She hissed softly and settled back, a deadly snake.

'So it was him, really,' she said. 'He came into my life and wanted to take me away because both of us were pissed off an' he'd had it up to here with that elegant tart he married. An' he was going to steal this yacht from Carney an' I wanted to go with him, my God, did I! But not on his terms. Because if he could walk out on her he could do the same to me when the shine wore off, an' I wasn't havin' it. So I needed money. And Tommy knew all about that.'

'And you used him from the start.'

'Yeah. I was hidin'. Little me, two steps removed an' deep in the shadows.'

'Clever,' I said. 'When the drugs went missing Jason's name was stamped all over it, and he was miles away. And when they did discover their mistake they'd go for Tommy, not you.'

There was a half-smile twitching her lips; an ugly smirk of conceit as she relived the scam.

'It was clever,' I said again, 'but you were too clever for your own good because you overcomplicated.' I saw the smile slip into a soundless snarl that showed the gleam of white teeth. 'Stealing the Merc under your husband's name. Then making it look as if a scally had stolen the audio system – again diverting attention, shifting the blame, when all you had to do was take the money and run.'

'It worked.'

'I suppose it did, to a point. But then it all went wrong.' I let her think about that. Let it eat away at her until, eventually, it would hold all her attention.

'When you had the drugs in your hand,' I said, 'why did you wait, why didn't you sell them.'

'Because Tommy fucked it up,' she said, so softly I had to strain to hear. 'Silver would've done the sellin' for me. I mean, he was Carney's partner so he had contacts.' She paused, her eyes distant. 'Only Silver was dead.'

'That's something else I don't get. There's this clever scam to steal drugs and sail off into the sunset – yet Laing runs out to tackle the man who's deeply involved.'

'Yeah, but Silver didn't know about Tommy,' Sam said, and I knew then that I'd been right: she'd woven such a tangled web of intrigue that she'd mislaid some of the strands and kept others a secret.

'I phoned him,' she said. 'I phoned his fuckin' mobile. I told him someone was stealin' the stereo, but that's all right, it was OK. If he saw this feller runnin' down the road, it was OK, do nothing – an' he switched off.' She was furious at the memory, her eyes blazing, just as they'd blazed on that Sunday night when we met for the first time – and so my most recent conclusions had again been wrong, because it *was* Laing, not Max, who had caused her fury: Max had wielded the knife, but by hastily switching off his mobile phone Laing had caused his own death.

'He didn't listen,' she said. 'He heard me tellin' him about a thief – an' he dumped the mobile before I'd finished an' that was it. He dumps the mobile an' runs out into the rain like fuckin' superman an' the whole scam went down the plug hole.'

'You were left holding stolen drugs you couldn't get rid of. The pack was closing in.' I paused. 'Then I landed on your doorstep.'

'Yeah, my knight in shinin' armour, someone to wave Excalibur, keep the wolves at bay, buy me some fuckin' time.'

Her tone was scathing and she climbed angrily to her feet. As she did so I stole a glance at my watch. It was too dark to see. I estimated I'd been on board fifteen minutes. When it reached thirty, Sian would blow the whistle.

Sam Bone had moved away from the leather seat. She seemed incapable of thought, at a loss what to do. The rust sweater was rising and falling with her tense breathing. The pistol had steadied; the whitest thing in the room was the knuckle of her trigger finger.

'What happened to Jemima?'

She glared contemptuously.

'What do you think? If Silver was my drugs contact, his wife was the next best thing. I went to see her. She wouldn't help, pretended she knew nothing about drugs – picked up the phone to call the police.' She shrugged, her face twisted with hate.

'And Tommy?'

'He was always just someone I used.'

'What about Carney?' I let her eyes drift to the dead man behind me, saw her face freeze.

'I was stuck with the drugs, Carney was being pressured by the barons. So I helped him out. Phoned, told him to meet me here an' I'd sell them back to him at a discount.'

'And he tried to cross you.' I shook my head in disbelief. 'Didn't you have enough people baying after your blood?'

'Yeah, but he's there an' I'm here,' she said,

And my mobile rang.

I looked at her, pointed to my pocket, said, 'May I?'

She nodded.

I took out the phone. It was Sian. Her voice was strained. 'Who's there with you?'

'Sam. And Carney. But he's out of it.'

Her breathing was a faint whisper against my ear.

'We've been talking to the boatman,' she said. 'He told us he rowed three people across.'

'That's right. Me, Sam, Carney.'

'Not counting you. Three went across before we arrived.'

I felt my scalp constrict. Unbidden, my eyes narrowed, darted anxiously around the room.

Sam was watching me. She licked her lips. 'Who's that?'

'The police,' I said. 'They want to talk to you.'

And I tossed the mobile to her, to one side, just out of her reach.

I thought she'd be distracted, snatch at it; for a single moment take her eyes off me. Without pause, I followed the phone, but the low table was in the way and I should have dived across it and instead I tried to go round and cracked my shins and I was stranded, getting nowhere, and she hadn't even looked at the phone as it bounced on soft leather.

I was still a yard away and floundering when the little pistol snapped. It was as if barbed wire had ripped across my arm. My fingers went numb. There was the instant wet feel of hot blood. I grabbed my upper arm, felt my lips pull back from my teeth, saw the pistol come up ...

Across the room an inner door exploded.

It tore off its hinges with a fierce ripping of marine ply. Billie Tobin came charging out. He was plunging from one dark room into another and he had on his wraparound aviator shades and on his wrists there was the glitter of gold as he ran at Sam Bone and I suppose he thought he was the bee's knees and untouchable.

She shot him in the chest.

He jerked, took two stumbling steps backwards, hit the wall and slid to the floor. His shades slipped from his nose, landed in his lap. His eyes were wide with shock.

'Sam, no!' I roared, and I took the final stride and grabbed her from behind and wrapped my bloody arm around her throat and with the other hand went after the pistol. I got it. My fingers clamped around her wrist. But I was too late to stop the second shot. The bullet hit Billie Tobin in the throat. He gagged, and died.

The police chose that moment to arrive.

Someone bellowed into a megaphone. Something – the police launch? – ran up against the yacht with a mighty thump. A searchlight raked across the saloon's windows and through those thin curtains the brightness was as if a hissing phosphorous flare had been lobbed into the dark room and for a long moment I was blind.

In that moment, Sam Bone fired the third shot. I'd dragged her hand back against her breasts as she'd shot Tobin. It made it easy for her. All she had to do was tilt her wrist backwards and her head forward and put the pistol's muzzle in her mouth. I heard it rattle against her teeth, heard the muffled shot and felt her jerk and stiffen. Then she went limp and I was holding a dead weight.

When, seconds later, the police burst into the saloon with their usual bellowed orders, I was still upright holding tight to the warm, flaccid body of Sam Bone. My legs were shaking too much to lower her to floor, but I couldn't bear the thought of letting her fall. My face was in her hair, inhaling its scent, my arm darkly glistening against her rust jumper. From her open mouth her hot blood was dripping onto my hand.

She was a killer, and now she was dead, yet all I could think of as I hugged her to me and closed my eyes in grief was a young woman standing on her doorstep under a basket of trailing geraniums. In my memory she had on a bright, lemon-yellow kimono – the way I would always, always remember her – and she was saying, in a perfect, deadpan riposte: 'The bandits're long gone.'

Well, they were now.

And it took some gentle words and the soft touch and understanding of Sian Laidlaw before I could be persuaded to let her go.

chapter twenty-one

'I think Sam shot Ed Carney as soon as he walked in the door,' I said. 'Then she forced Tobin at gunpoint into that locker, or whatever it was, and sat back to wait for me.'

It was the next day. Bright sunshine was slanting through Bryn Aur's kitchen windows. We were sitting around the kitchen-table drinking coffee. I had my arm resting on the table, all stitched and wrapped at A & E. My bandages were a brilliant white, and I was inordinately proud.

'How could she know *we'd* come?' Sian said.

'I'll rephrase that: she waited for someone. She had to. There was nowhere she could go.'

Calum had broken his rule and was smoking a Schimmelpennick in my kitchen. It was that kind of day, a day for rule breaking. He blew a plume of smoke, watched it drift towards the ceiling with the slanting sunlight transforming it into an errant patch of high mountain mist.

'Who attacked you in the alley by India Building? Did she know?'

'It wasn't discussed. If it wasn't Carney my guess is Mack arranged it, probably without telling Sam.' I shrugged.

'And they didn't take any cash out to the yacht, did they,' he said. 'No intention of buying what she had, and Carney took Tobin with him to scare her to death. They thought all they had to do was walk in, growl at her and show some fangs and she'd cave in.'

'Us wee girls,' Sian said, 'are made of stern stuff.'

'One wee girl,' I said, 'jumped the gun.'

'Lucky for you.' She was looking smug. 'You said half an hour, but it would've taken the police that time to get from wherever they were to where they were needed.'

'And then you heard everything. When I threw the mobile to Sam it was still switched on.'

'Alun Morgan swept me into the launch. I had my mobile pressed to my ear all the way across the harbour. But can you imagine what I was thinking? All I heard was something splintering followed by the crack of a shot, you shouting "No" at the top of your voice and then another shot.'

'Aye, well, we were all a touch bewildered throughout,' Calum said, 'but in the end we survived.'

'Some of us,' I said, 'less easily than others.'

'So if you can't stand the heat, stick to your toy soldiers.'

'And toil away over a melting-pot filled with molten metal?' I chuckled. 'You're right, though – and perhaps I will. Hahn is waiting in Philadelphia for those American Civil War figures you were casting. And I'm expecting a call from Gib to tell me the Scots Greys were best in show—'

The phone rang.

I grinned at Sian, wet a forefinger and made my triumphant mark in thin air, then hurried through to the office.

It was a man's voice, deep, but not steady, and thick with emotion.

'Hello,' he said, 'is that Jack Scott, the private investigator?'

I hesitated, wondering how to answer, then looked up at the ceiling and took the call that put me on a roller-coaster ride to … well, let's say it had nothing to do with toy soldiers and, as I listened and reached for a pencil to take notes, Sian crept up behind me and two warm hands encircled my neck with deadly intent.